Copyright by Petronella Devaney, 2012

first edition

The Vineyard Press, Ltd.
106 Vineyard Place
Port Jefferson, NY 11777

ISBN: 1-93006-96-8

CHAPTER ONE

High up in the Serra, at the north-western corner of the largest and most spectacular of the islands in the Balearic archipelago, lies the hill town of Santa Marta. For many decades, centuries even, it was the lure of artists and wanderers, of seekers after the unknown, the unspoilt, the unordinary; outsiders, who found themselves drawn along the old sea road that winds upwards through the olive groves and terraces of orange and lemon trees, up into the light-shrouded mountains of the high Tramuntana, to a place of sanctuary where they could live and work and love, free from the conventions and restraints of the everyday world.

Santa Marta's cluster of golden-stoned houses and narrow cobbled streets lay at the heart of what in mythic days was a tiny pagan realm, the bower, according to a certain poet who made his home there and knew about such things, of a jealous muse who caused mischief for the naive and the unwary, and exacted a costly tribute even from those she chose to bless. To survive in Santa Marta, he claimed, it was necessary to surrender to her wildish spirit or, at the very least, to acknowledge the underlying mystical nature of the place.

The most dangerous time was the summer, when the sun made people lazy and forgetful and the muse laid traps for intruders, playing tricks on the weak and the unsuspecting. Those who strayed into her sacred groves by chance, looking only for a pleasant spot to spend a holiday, seemed to sense this and promptly removed themselves, leaving Santa Marta to the few who truly belonged there, which they did by virtue of their willingness to cease to belong anywhere else.

Each year the numbers of this small enclave were swelled by a flock of visitors who alighted during the glorious summer months. Many of them owned or rented houses in or around the village, but spent the greater part of the year making money, or trying to, in the big cities of Europe or the Americas. They arrived a bit hyped up, a bit apprehensive maybe (though careful not to let it show), often a little heart-sore from the harshness of the city winter but, above all, smug at having escaped to their own private paradise.

The permanent residents greeted the summer season with ambivalence. Winter in the mountains could be bitterly damp and cold, and the first warm days were like heaven. But then there was the madness that came in their wake: the unsettling, freakish vibe that was disturbing to live with and impossible to escape.

And each summer seemed to have its own defining character. That year, it was the excessive heat, *el calor*: heavy, inescapable, relentless. The weather seemed to have turned on Santa Marta, and by mid-June temperatures were soaring to over a hundred. It had never been so hot in living memory, and there were those who saw it as a bad omen, their misgivings reinforced by newspaper stories of death by heat stroke and fears of widespread drought. There was no let up. By high summer, the sirocco had come twice, forcing the hot desert wind inland from across the sea. It arrived with a sinister slamming of doors and shutters, sending everyone scurrying to secure anything likely to be damaged in the dry ferocity of the gusts, reducing the whole of Santa Marta to a ghost town, tense and silent.

*

It was late one sultry afternoon that August that Georgia first noticed the strange scent. She and Peter were out on the terrace with Tamsin, who had dropped by after a late lunch at the *cantina*, the rough-and-ready fishermen's café down at the cala.

The cala, a rocky bay overhung by volcanic cliffs, was renowned, justifiably so, as one of the most idyllic beaches on that stretch of coast. But in August, it started to fill up from mid-morning with many of the same people who had crowded into the village bar the night before, so that the pebbled beach was strewn with bodies, and you had to search for a place to lay your towel.

Georgia preferred to take her swim in a hidden cove below the house. It was where she and Peter had spent long hours alone together in their early days, when he had first brought her to the island. There, beneath the pine trees, broad sun-bleached rocks slanted downwards to the edge of the sea, and the only sounds were the lapping of the waves and the distant call of seabirds. It was Georgia's favourite place.

Tamsin, unlike Georgia, enjoyed socialising at the cala, and swam there most days. She took her baby with her, a pink and gold bundle, at that moment fast asleep in a Moses basket swathed in muslin to protect its tiny occupant from the sun.

Leaning back in his chair, Peter was sorting through a pile of post he had just collected from the *correos*, occasionally stopping to read something that caught his interest, dropping the empty envelopes into a wicker basket at his feet.

Stretched out, bikini-clad, Georgia and Tamsin were lazing on old cane loungers like lizards on a rock, longing for sundown and the relative cool of evening. With a languid movement of her arm, Georgia reached for her glass, which Peter had just refilled, and suddenly, there it was: a thick, heady aroma that seemed to fill the air.

'Can you smell that?' she asked.

'Is it something *rotting*?' replied Tamsin, sniffing, her eyes squinting in the sunshine. 'Wouldn't be surprised, in this heat. It's like being in the tropics. It's like India or something.'

'India isn't actually the tropics,' said Peter, vaguely, not looking up from his letters.

'Oh, you know what I mean,' responded Tamsin, equally vague, her eyes squinting against the sun.

Peter was holding an envelope in his hand. With a deepening frown, he scanned the hand-writing. He did not open it but, with a quick glance in Georgia's direction, slipped it into his trouser pocket. He pushed the rest of the pile of unopened mail away from him, and eyed Tamsin with undisguised contempt.

'Look,' he explained, as if to a rather slow-witted child 'it's *Spain*. It's *summer*, it's *meant* to be hot.' Cleaning the lens of his glasses on his shirt-tail, he went on, 'It's a bit warmer than usual, but it's not equatorial fucking *Africa*. If you can't take it, you should go back to grey little England and spend your summer watching Wimbledon in the rain.'

He delivered his tirade slowly, pedantically, and without raising his voice.

'Mmm, sounds *divine*! Except I'd miss *you* so much, Peter, darling,' replied Tamsin, equally measured.

'Yeah, and we'd miss you too, Tamsin *dahling*. But don't let that stop you. Run away, if it's all getting a bit too much. We'd understand - lots of people can't handle it.'

Tamsin looked at him with narrowed eyes.

'And you'd *know* about running away, wouldn't you, Peter?' she said. 'Santa Marta's your little hidey-hole where you can be the big film producer without actually ever producing anything. Shame it doesn't work quite like that in the real world.'

'Bull shit!' Peter snapped back.

Georgia, deliberately ignoring their barbed exchange,

propped herself up on her elbows and looked around.

'It's like a perfume, a rich, exotic perfume,' she said dreamily, her head thrown back, trying to locate the direction of the scent. 'Peter, do you know what it is?' she asked.

'Some sort of plant?' he replied, not very interested. He had turned his attention back to his mail, and he was now poring over a letter from his agent in London. Tamsin had hit a nerve. He liked to take a break between films, but this time the gap had been too long. Three years, and now he felt as though this current project was make or break. There was a lot riding on this one, particularly since it was his own script, which made him even more edgy and guarded than usual. He had barely dared mention it to anyone other than Georgia. His agent's letter indicated that there was interest from a major studio. Peter read it over, trying hard not to let his feelings show.

'But it's so strange,' said Georgia, feigning not to notice the effect the letter was having on her husband. 'It wasn't there before. Where can it be coming from?' Not anywhere immediately visible, she thought. Jasmine climbed the walls of the old house, and there were a few roses, full-blown and dishevelled from the heat wave. The pink and yellow honeysuckle growing around the high arched doorway exuded a delicious sweetness. But this was different. She looked round to see if anything new had appeared, while the scent continued to suffuse the air, getting stronger every moment.

Georgia pulled her hair back and fastened it in place with an elastic band: the heat! Tamsin, noticing, automatically pushed her own unruly copper-coloured locks back from her forehead.

'You look about sixteen with your hair like that,' she remarked.

'Oh good,' said Georgia. 'Tell my husband.'

Peter leaned into his chair so that it balanced on its back legs, and scrutinised his wife.

'That's the reason she's lasted so long,' he said. 'I always used to say twenty-five was the outside limit.'

Georgia and Tamsin groaned in unison. They were the same age, their birthdays just a month apart.

Peter gave a twisted grin. His eyes were teasing. 'Anyway, what are you now? Have you crept past the danger mark without me noticing?'

'Work it out for yourself,' Tamsin told him. 'Almost exactly twenty years younger than you – not a *difficult* calculation. Unless you've forgotten your own age, as well? Which, incidentally, you look every inch of...' she added spitefully.

Peter put his hand to his throat. 'Aaagh! Straight for the jugular!' he groaned.

Tamsin irritated and amused him in almost equal measure. Running his fingers through his hair, he said, 'But, seriously, if it wasn't for all the grey... What if I got a dye job? Lots of guys in California are doing it. What do you think, Georgia?'

'Ask someone else,' she replied. 'You know I don't share your obsession with age and death.'

Peter choked out a harsh, bitter laugh. 'No, of course, I wouldn't expect *you* to understand. You're too young. But it's like Cavafy says: *Old age is a wound from a terrible knife...*'

'Peter, you're *forty-six* for God's sake!' Tamsin replied with exasperation. 'What are you going to be like when you're sixty?'

'Dead, with any luck! Unless they've found the elixir of eternal youth. Otherwise I'll down a bottle of Jack Daniels and drive myself off a cliff.'

'It amazes me how anyone can be so clever and so stupid at the same time. I don't know how Georgia puts up with you.'

'She doesn't,' Peter replied. 'She switches off. Just look.'

Georgia took a sip from her glass. 'I haven't switched

off. I'm trying to work out where that scent's coming from.'

'Oh, yes you have,' Peter argued. 'You're on another planet.'

'Don't start, Peter. Leave her alone,' said Tamsin, sitting up and glancing into the Moses basket.

'No - go on, Georgia, tell us what goes on in your little world. Or maybe we could take a guess ...'

'*Peter*!' Tamsin pleaded.

But Georgia just lay back and closed her eyes, and Peter, after glaring at her for a moment, went back to his letters. Tamsin let out a heavy sigh.

'Take it easy, Tamsin,' said Peter. 'Only joshing.'

They went on drinking their wine in silence until the baby showed signs of waking. Tamsin got up and pulled a pair of shorts and a crocheted vest over her bikini. At the table, Peter tidied his stack of mail, and rising to his feet, announced that he had promised to meet young Luc for a game of chess down in the bar.

'Are you coming, Georgia?' he asked, tentatively.

'No, I don't think so,' she replied, getting to her feet. 'I'm supposed to be meeting up with Tom Malek later.'

'Are you? Definitely not in that case.'

For a moment it looked as though he might try to persuade her, but then he seemed to change his mind. 'Right, then. I'll see you later,' he called over his shoulder.

Tamsin was gathering up her things. 'Georgia, I have to toodle off, too,' she said, putting on her sandals. 'See you tomorrow? Hang on a sec, Peter - you can give me a lift!'

*

The sun was going down and setting the sky ablaze with colour. Georgia watched the immense red disk sink fast below the horizon. The sky turned from fiery pink to pearly mauve, and in the twilight the mysterious fragrance wafted towards her even more potently than before.

As she stood there, a man emerged from the lower terrace. He stood by the house, leaning on the long wooden handle of a scythe. Georgia sensed his presence before she saw him, and her immediate instinct was to disappear inside. She went back to the lounger, snatched up the sarong she had left lying there, and quickly tied the swathe of filmy printed cotton round herself. She could feel him slyly watching her.

'Oh it's you, Randall,' she said, as if she'd just noticed him.

Randall turned his head towards her.

'Randall, there's something I wanted to ask you,' she said, glancing around to avoid making eye contact. 'Do you know what this amazing smell is?'

He strolled towards her, slim and wiry in his faded cut-offs and *espadrillos*. Various tools hung from a broad leather belt slung low around his hips. His naked shoulders and firm, sun-tanned arms were moist with sweat, and a silver talisman at his neck glinted as he moved. He inhaled deeply, his straight, sun-streaked hair falling back from his face. 'Yeah,' he said, with a lop-sided smile that didn't quite reach his eyes. 'Come. I'll show you.'

Georgia wished she had kept quiet. Reluctantly, she followed him to the side of the house but then, there they were, right in front of her: long, waxy-white, trumpet-shaped flowers, growing on the twisted branches of a shoulder-high shrub, the source of the extraordinary scent.

'Oh!' Georgia exclaimed. There was something shocking and unreal about them. 'I'm sure they weren't there before, were they?'

'Well, kind of. I mean, not exactly *there*...' replied Randal in his soft Mid-West accent.

'How *enigmatic* you are, Randall,' said Georgia.

Randall had become a regular feature since Peter started hiring him to do odd jobs at the house. As he helped clear terraces and tend fruit trees, Peter had noticed his natural talent for gardening, and so they came to a regular arrangement.

Georgia had been against the idea. 'I don't want him here,' she had told Peter. 'He gives me the creeps.' To make matters worse, he seemed to have developed a crush on her. 'Which is all I need: a drug-addled, lovesick hippy to contend with. Thanks, Peter,' she thought.

Randall, though, was unaffected by her dislike, and now he squirmed with pleasure at having unexpectedly gained her attention, at having her to himself. He moved closer to her, so close she could smell the earth and the open air and the salty mixture of sweat and sea on his skin. Looking out towards the horizon, he spoke in a hushed voice. 'That was a pretty incredible sunset back there, wasn't it, Georgia? That whole wild sky show up there?'

He always sounds like someone just learning to speak, Georgia was thinking to herself, as if he's not quite sure what order the words should go in. It made you pay attention, listen more carefully, as if he had something important to say, which, in Georgia's experience, had yet to happen. But he's only twenty, twenty-one at the most, she thought. And with what he had been through, it wasn't surprising he was a bit messed up.

'Yes,' she replied, gazing along his line of vision. 'It was...'

Randall's eyes widened. 'The sun's *insane*!' he said. 'Do you know about the sun, Georgia? Do you know about the sunspots and the solar winds? The sun is *awesome*! Do you know the sun makes up *ninety-nine point nine per cent* of the mass of the solar system? Think about it, Georgia!'

Georgia just kept her eyes on the horizon.

'But you know one thing about the sun, the sun is *predictable* – it's all male-type energy – the wild, colossal heat and solar storms and all. Up it rises and down it sets, starts and ends each day, right? Makes its presence felt. That's the *sun*. The moon, now - the moon's *totally* different.'

'Randall...'

But Randall was unstoppable. 'See the moon, Georgia, the moon's a *lady*. She's graceful, serene, mysterious. You can't count on the *moon* the way you can the sun. Sometimes, she should be up there, but no – she hides herself behind some wisp of cloud and you can't even get a glimpse. And when she's new, that's also when she's darkest, and the whole sky just kind of waits in anticipation, until suddenly there she is, just the tiniest, silver sliver of herself and all you can do is look and wonder and imagine. *La Doña Luna*,' he intoned. '*La Lady Luna!*' He laughed softly at the sound and rhythm of the words.

'And from way up there,' he droned, 'without doing nothing 'cept orbit round the old earth, she controls the tides, the weather ... she even gets inside our heads and plays with our minds. It's where you get the word *lunatic* - did you know that, Georgia?'

'Yes, Randall, of course I did. But, listen...' Georgia replied, desperate to get him off the subject, 'you were telling me about this strange tree you put here...'

Randall stared at her for a moment, wild-eyed, as if he had no idea what she was talking about. Georgia wondered whether to leave him in his trance and pretend she hadn't asked when, with a sudden, unnerving shake of his head, he came back to consciousness.

'Oh, sure. *Shrub* – not tree. Well, it used to be down there on the lower terrace – the one I'm clearing? But it seemed like it was being crowded out by all the other stuff, so I thought I'd bring it up here. Give it some space.' He leaned back to admire his handiwork. 'Yeah, looks like it's doing pretty good. And now you get the whole scent thing...'

Oh God, he's high, thought Georgia. She was standing quite still, trying to decide how best to make her departure without offending him.

Night had fallen and overhead the sky was thickly jewelled with stars. A shower of comets shot silently across the glittering darkness.

'It's so weird,' said Georgia, 'those great big flowers, wide open, in the night! They look like enormous lilies, don't they?'

'Not lilies,' said Randall. 'They're Mexican moon-flowers. They flower for the waxing moon, they say. She'll be up there tonight, working her crazy magic.'

He was right. Later that night, as Georgia lay alone in her bed, the moon's brilliance flooded through the louvered shutters, throwing stripy shadows across the whitewashed walls. And it seemed important, somehow, the heat, the night, the moon and the troubling scent.

'I must remember this,' she thought as she drifted off to sleep. 'It doesn't matter if I forget all the rest, but I must remember this.'

CHAPTER TWO

Casa Dura was a large, rambling, slightly forbidding house, which had risen out of the ruins of a twelfth century monastery. In the late 1750's, the land and the property had been bought by a certain Count Razvan, an exiled Romanian aristocrat who had chosen the location, it was said, for its remoteness and inaccessibility, but who must surely have been influenced by its stupendous beauty. No matter where you stood, or in which direction you looked, the view was breath-taking. Ancient, gnarled olive trees covered the mountainside that dropped seaward in steep terraces and, far below, the points and bays of the coastline gleamed stark and mysterious, the sea reflecting the mood and hue of the vast Mediterranean sky.

The house itself stood three full stories high, with a tower to one side. The outer walls were of richly toned, square-cut sandstone, studded with deep-set windows enclosed by sombre green shutters and framed in borders of yellowed stucco. At the top of the tower was a room that occupied the entire upper floor. Here, Peter had chosen to make his study. A heavy, leather-topped desk was covered in film scripts and correspondence and work-plans, all systematically laid out. Peter was very methodical, he could not bear mess. The room was lined with books and paintings and blown-up photographs of Peter and Georgia. One entire wall was hung with a Navajo weaving that Peter had brought back from America, and its potent combination of bold geometric patterns and vibrant colour dominated the room. Peter loved it, as he loved the house itself and all the things he had filled it with.

Count Razvan never took up residence at Casa Dura. Instead, he had used it to house his favourite mistress, a young local girl called Rosina, when she was stricken by the mysterious illness that caused her to go gradually blind and mad. The local people, believing her to have fallen victim to the plague, and disliking her immoral liaison with the foreign Count, shunned Casa Dura, leaving Rosina to die alone in terrible agony, not of the plague, but syphilis.

*

When Peter found it, the house had lain empty for many decades. It had long been the subject of local superstition, but for Peter it was pretty much love at first sight. He had bought it for a song, a tiny fraction of what its renovation would eventually cost in both time and money, but Peter did not mind. He was determined to afford it, even if it had to remain a work in progress for many years to come. This was the bolt-hole he had been searching for; the safe haven that he could escape to when the pressures of work - or lack of it - and city living became too much.

He was never daunted by the size of the task, or his utter lack of knowledge or practical experience in such matters, or even by the fact that he could barely make himself understood in Spanish. He simply put it all in the hands of Carl Frankel, an American sculptor with an architectural instinct for the restoration of interesting ruins located in dramatic settings. Carl and his team of stonemasons and carpenters rebuilt, slowly and lovingly, old houses that had fallen into disuse and been more or less abandoned. And, thanks to his fluency in the local dialect, and his familiarity with the region and its customs, he knew exactly how to negotiate a favourable purchase with owners who might feign reluctance but, more often than not, were actually only too willing to be rid of properties which, to them, were no more than encumbrances. The Mallorcan hinterland was, in those days, fairly littered with them.

As they drove around the island searching for architectural rarities to use in the renovation - beams, flagstones, window frames and shutters, bas-reliefs rescued from the walls of crumbling churches - Peter and Carl liked to reminisce about the old times in Santa Marta, back in the early sixties, when they had first met there. Carl, some ten years older than Peter, had stumbled upon the place during a period when, thanks to the G.I. Bill of Rights, he was living in Paris, studying art. He was one of a number of American ex-service men who had not been able to settle into the old life back home after the war, and so returned to Europe, seeking an escape from conventional expectations and their old identity. In Santa Marta they found what they were looking for, and for the best part of thirty years, it had been as good as perfect.

Peter, for his part, had been brought to the island by his friend, Gavin Johnston, a journalist who had worked with him at the BBC when they were both starting out, young men straight from Oxbridge, but toughened up by a couple of years in the army prior to university. Theirs was one of the last intakes before National Service was scrapped, but no concessions had been given, and as eighteen year old second lieutenants in their respective regiments, they had led their platoons out to potentially hostile post-war zones: Gavin to the Malaysian jungle, Peter to desert postings in Egypt and Libya. Both men had been marked by the experience, and when they met, there was a recognition, an immediate bond between them.

Years later, as foreign correspondent for an important

broadsheet, Gavin had come upon Santa Marta while in Spain on an assignment. It had been a *coup de foudre* from which he had never recovered and never wanted to. 'I came, I saw, I was conquered,' was how he liked to tell it.

It was always the men who fell for Santa Marta. Women came for the sake of husbands or lovers; Santa Marta was a macho kind of paradise.

*

Back in those early days, as he enjoyed recollecting, Carl had been able to buy what he called a *serious* house for the equivalent of a couple of hundred dollars. But by the early nineteen-seventies, the picture was gradually starting to change. With Franco old and sick, his power waning, the whole of Spain was opening up. Already a new breed was starting to trickle into that part of the island. Rich German businessmen, London 'A' list celebrities – film actors, rock-stars, fashion people and socialites - all came to look and enjoy and occasionally even to buy.

Santa Marta was experiencing the first tremors of this transition. There was a lot of uncertainty about, a fear that Santa Marta was in danger of becoming the next St Tropez. Sometimes people talked about leaving, exploring the potential of other possibilities they had glimpsed in Cuernavaca, Kerala, the Greek islands. But in the end, there was nowhere that could match Santa Marta; no other place they really wanted to be.

Georgia, Peter noticed, refused to show any interest in the subject. She claimed that she did not notice any change. This irritated Peter, who put it down to perversity. Although, in all honesty, he had to admit that she had become increasingly detached and introverted. Sometimes she seemed to hate Santa Marta. And Peter felt she resented him for continuing to like it, especially the social life, which he considered totally unreasonable on her part. Was he supposed not to see his friends? To hole up in Casa

Dura like some kind of recluse? Is that what she wanted? The people were a big part of Santa Marta.

Since Tamsin had moved into the village, she and the baby had become a focus for Georgia. Peter wasn't happy about this. He could not see it as a genuine friendship. Georgia was using it to distance herself from him and he did not know how to talk to her about it, how to close the gap. It was complicated.

Georgia was aware of how Peter felt, although they had not discussed it. She knew it bugged him, but she still went to see Tamsin most days. Frequently, she would set off early, before the air became muffled and dry with heat, sometimes taking with her a basket of fruit that she had picked from the trees that grew around the house: a few ripe apricots, oranges or clementines, some big yellow plums.

She loved the early morning. It was her time, private and alone, while the rest of the village slept. Patience was not one of Peter's virtues. He wanted everything to happen quickly, now! But Georgia preferred a slower pace. The early morning in Santa Marta was quiet and tranquil and, sitting out on the terrace, she would lose herself in her surroundings, listening to the sound of sheep-bells, the cocks crowing, and farmers calling their early morning greetings to one another across the terraces in low rumbling voices: *Buenas! Holá, Buenas!*

It was the one time, out there on her own, undisturbed, that she allowed the emptiness and yearning that gnawed at her, usually so carefully concealed, to surface. Then the colours and the drama of the landscape would render their bleaker aspect, matching her hidden sadness, her grief. She did not look for solutions; that belonged to later in the day, the reasoning hours. Now was the time for simply feeling and being - that was all that mattered.

Provided she was able to have this bit of space, Georgia could manage. She wasn't really lazy or incompetent, although she imagined Peter saw her as both. But the days when Peter woke early, even in one of his better moods, he dominated the proceedings to such an extent that, without meaning to, he drove her out into an area of nervous resistance. Then everything became a struggle, and the simplest of tasks defeated her. Those were her bad days.

As far as Tamsin was concerned, early rising had never exactly been her thing. Now, though, with the arrival of the baby, it was just a fact of life. And, rather to her surprise, she quite enjoyed sitting out on her little terrace with Georgia, eating their breakfast of freshly warmed *ensaimadas* and coffee while above them the sun sent streaks of colour flying across the pale, cloudless sky. In those empty hours they could be just girls again, careless and frank and funny, their fractured hopes restored, capable of pretty well anything.

CHAPTER THREE

Tamsin's baby was six months old. Her deep blue eyes were round and bright, her soft pink mouth pouted and smiled. Her skin was creamy and gold from the sun, and light brown hair sprouted from her scalp in silky tufts. Laid on her back on a rug beneath a lemon tree, the baby looked up at Georgia and waved her tiny starfish hands. Her name was Poppy. From a branch above her head her mother had hung a mobile of fluttering yellow and white paper butterflies. Georgia, sitting on the ground beside her, blew on the butterflies and Poppy watched excitedly as they danced up and down. Tamsin came out of the house carrying two earthenware cups of fragrant, steaming coffee and walked over to join them. 'I'm absolutely *dead*,' she announced, her voice husky with tiredness and cigarettes. A wave of tawny-coloured hair fell across her face as she leaned down and scooped Poppy up into her arms. The baby started to cry. 'Oh no!' she wailed. 'Lighten up, Poppy! Be happy!' She kissed the baby gently and held her against her shoulder. Standing up, she rocked rhythmically as she rubbed Poppy's back.

'Third night in a row she's kept me up. I'm shattered!'

'Poor you...' Georgia's response was purely automatic. Inwardly she was she wracking her brains for a half-decent excuse to make a quick departure. The breakfast with Tamsin routine had suddenly lost its appeal and she wanted to go, to be on her own somewhere. Anywhere.

'Ssh, don't cry Poppy, everything's all right ... there, there, now,' Tamsin cajoled in an attempt to quiet the baby's continuous but now less angry whine. At last Poppy's whimpering ceased, and Tamsin took the opportunity to place her back on the rug. She gave her a rattle to hold and watched as the baby waved it tentatively. 'Peace at last,' she said with relief and turned her attention to Georgia. 'So, how's things?' she asked.

'Oh, you know,' Georgia replied.

Tamsin gave her a searching look, but Georgia pretended not to notice. Today made six months – though she knew that, really, she couldn't seriously expect Tamsin to remember. Except, unreasonably, she did expect it, or at least she wished *someone* else might have remembered. Six months since she lost the baby she had been expecting. It had happened so suddenly, right at the end of the third month, when she should have been quite safe. And no proper reason. The doctors said it was just one of those random things. She was in good health and the pregnancy had been perfectly normal. Next time would probably be fine. Think of it as a trial run, they said. But it wasn't a trial run! It was her *baby*, and if it hadn't been for the miscarriage she would be holding him in her arms today. She felt her eyes begin to fill. She didn't want Tamsin to see. No-one had seemed to understand how terribly she felt the loss. So now she guarded it. It was hers alone, a private grief.

Quickly, she looked down, and dipping into her basket she pulled out a copy of a glossy English magazine. 'Look,' she said, and still intent on hiding the teariness, she made a show of blowing her nose.

Tamsin flicked through the pages eagerly. 'Here it is. Nice pics, Georgia!' she exclaimed. 'This one of you in your Thea Porter - very glam.'

'Do you think so?' said Georgia, glancing down at the

magazine.

'Definitely. And the house, all lit up at night, *lovely*. When was this done?' she asked.

'April – don't you remember? It completely took us over! Not a process I'd choose to repeat...'

'Of course – I arrived in the middle of it. But was it really so awful? I'd have thought it'd be quite fun...'

'Fun? It was *horrendous*!'

Stop, she told herself. This is all wrong. But somehow, having started, she felt compelled to go blustering on.

'I detested it – awful media types traipsing about the place, constantly asking questions, snapping away with their cameras. And Cristiane, of course, stage managing it all. I felt ... invaded. It wasn't my idea, having the house plastered all over their stupid magazine. And us like a pair of idiotic socialites.'

'But, Georgia, *Vogue*! I mean, it's not like some tatty old rag...'

'I know, I know – but, Tamsin, you have no idea what it was like. It was hateful. How could Peter *do* it? Well, actually, the answer to that is *Cristiane* – she's the one who set it all up.'

'Is she that bad?'

'You *know* what she's like!' Georgia replied, and then added, less confidently, 'Of course, Peter doesn't think so.'

'I expect he got a nice little *fee* for the spread?'

'I suppose so.'

'Ah. There you are, then...'

'No,' said Georgia, thinking about it. 'I don't think that was it. There's something else, I'm just not sure what.'

'He does like to play his cards close to his chest,' Tamsin replied. 'He's known for it in the business. Makes him a lethal negotiator.' She continued poring over the magazine and Georgia moved over to look with her.

'Honestly,' she moaned. '"Film producer, Peter Gael, and his lovely wife, Georgia". And there we are, grinning away. They've turned us into a pair of clichés.' With a slightly mystified look, she added, 'The weird thing is we look so happy. How did they manage that?'

'It's their job. It's what they do.'

Georgia, still upset, had the feeling that Tamsin wasn't with her on this. She snatched the magazine away bad-temperedly and started to put it into her basket.

'*Georgia*!' Tamsin scolded. 'Give it back!'

'No!'

Tamsin laughed and, somewhat sheepishly, Georgia handed the magazine to her. 'Oh, here,' she said. 'You can keep it.'

'Are you sure?'

Georgia nodded. 'We've got masses of them.'

'Of course - you must have,' said Tamsin with a conciliatory smile.

But Georgia was still not happy.

'I'm not saying they're not good pictures,' she ventured. 'It's just that it's all such a misrepresentation of who we really are.' Georgia was annoyed with herself for complaining. Tamsin must think she was being gauche; that, in fact, having your picture in the occasional gossip column or magazine was totally in keeping with who they were. Peter, after all, was a well-known figure in the movie world and he had always attracted a certain amount of publicity; notoriety, even. He was the sort of film-maker who was always pushing the boundaries, always sticking his neck out. But that was the whole point: Peter and his work might be public property to a certain extent. What Georgia objected to was having *her* home and *her* life splashed about. She wasn't a public figure, she didn't court fame. But there she was in the pictures, the glamorous wife of a famous man, dressed in her designer clothes, living in a great mansion. Peter knew how much she hated that kind of thing, and yet he'd gone ahead with the article anyway.

Her mind went back to an unseasonably cold day in late spring, sitting on a felled tree in the wilds of the Welsh border country, the sky overhead thick with cloud. Wrapped in scarves and old woollen sweaters, eating their picnic of sausage rolls and drinking stewed tea from a flask, she recalled Peter quoting a line from T.S. Eliot: *A condition of complete simplicity/ costing not less than everything.*

For her, simplicity would certainly be worth any price. Her life had been fraught with complexity since her parents had broken up when she was still small. Nothing had ever been simple, in her experience, and she loved the very sound of the word: simplicity. At that moment, it seemed as if Peter could see inside her, as if he knew her through and through. Everything he said seemed to resonate in her own heart.

Nineteen, she was then, and how little she had known. But Peter, she thought, could teach her, and being with him was all she had cared about. They were married, just a few weeks later.

Now he had become a stranger to her. She felt alienated from him, from the house, from everything. It's hopeless, she thought, and there was no-one to turn to. Seven years ago she had made a vow to love and honour him, and that meant that certain things had to stay forever within the bounds of the marriage. These things she could not share: not with Tamsin, not with anyone.

They sat in silence for a while. It was a drowsy morning, very still, apart from a soft breeze that kept the yellow and white butterflies in gentle motion. Georgia had another try. 'It's not only Peter and the house. It's everything, really. I feel as if I'm in the wrong life. The reason the article upset me so much is because it's not me, not the real me. Sometimes I'm not even sure who the real me is anymore. I always have to act a part in Santa Marta. It feels like I've been acting for so long.'

'Well *stop*! It's your big mistake, if you ask me. If you stopped acting, you'd feel much better and people would like you more.'

Georgia looked horrified. 'No they wouldn't! They'd crush me like an ant! It's how I protect myself. Whatever they say about me, it's not the *real* me they know, so it can't hurt.'

Tamsin closed her eyes against the glare and thought about this. 'You probably need something of your own to do,' she said. 'It's difficult to know who you are if your only purpose in life is to be at someone else's beck and call.'

'I do know who I am.'

'You just said you didn't.'

Georgia opened her mouth to reply, but then changed her mind. She wasn't in the mood to defend herself. Instead, she lay back in the sun. Eventually she said, 'It's so pretty here.'

'Mmm,' Tamsin, stretched out on the ground beside Poppy, agreed.

Georgia had found the casita when Tamsin wrote to say that she needed a place to stay following the birth of the baby and her separation from its father; the two events had occurred with an unhappy synchrony. *Casita*, Georgia reflected, was really a bit of a misnomer for what had become, with the gradual addition of rooms and a whole upper floor, quite a spacious little house. It was tucked away on a path up above Santa Marta's main drag, hidden behind a high wall covered in morning glory. A solid wooden gate led to a paved terrace where an old vine trailed over a long rusty trellis. Already, in August, bunches of semi-ripened, dark-skinned grapes nestled among the fan-shaped leaves. French windows at the back of the house opened onto a tangled garden of hibiscus and lemon trees, all of it surrounded by the horseshoe of mountains that loomed majestically over Santa Marta.

Inside, the ceilings were supported by gnarled and weathered beams. The main living room had an old style chimney-place, and the bedrooms were furnished with typical Mallorcan four posters, cane rocking chairs and rosewood wardrobes. Built into a corner of the entrada was a closet with a mesh covered door that enclosed the *cisterna*, the well that held the house's water supply. The floors were tiled in stone, and the roughly plastered walls were freshly whitewashed. Tamsin had approved, and moved in with a truckload of crates and packing cases containing pictures, music, books, soft furnishings, a vast amount of her own clothes and all of Poppy's baby paraphernalia: Tamsin's version of travelling light. Although it was never meant to be home in a long-term sense; just for the present, it was a port in a storm.

Santa Marta was one of the few places where she felt it might be possible to outwardly live down what she jokingly referred to as her Great American Disaster, and privately recover from the wounds inflicted by the distinctly unfunny collapse of her brief marriage. Her part of the deal was to keep silent. In return for an ample settlement, she was to keep quiet about the reason for the break-up, lest it harm her husband's star-rating with the puritanical American public. His agent had spelt it out to her.

'Go back to Europe and be a nice English girl again,' he had said. 'Forget all this. Find some clean, decent place to raise your kid far away from this shit-hole. This place degrades people. You're lucky, you can leave now and make a new start.'

You make it sound so easy, she remembered thinking to herself. She turned her attention back to Georgia. 'Did you tell Peter you were coming here?' she asked.

'No, he was still asleep when I left. God knows what time he got back last night.' She paused for a minute. 'He'd been out with Tom Malek.'

'Oh, dear.'

'Malek's the least of it at the moment. Cristiane's my main problem - she's just *there* all the time, advising, 'helping', arranging...'

'She's probably just trying to be nice. In that completely over the top way of hers.'

'Cristiane isn't nice. It's not her thing. And that doesn't bother me. What drives me round the bend is the way the moment she's through the door, she takes over.' Georgia caught the look on Tamsin's face. 'This is why I say I'm in the wrong life. I know what you're thinking – that I'm being un-cool. But I can't help it - it's how I feel. To me – the Cristiane situation - it's wrung me out. She's always there, always has been. Casa Dura was her home long before it was mine. She was involved in the whole renovation, right from the start. That's why she's so proprietorial about it. I often think my marriage was blighted from the word go.'

Tamsin began to say something, but changed her mind. Better to let Georgia get it off her chest, she thought.

'Then there's Luc,' Georgia went on. 'It's so intense, his relationship with Peter. It's like, they're this little family group, and me, Peter's actual wife, I'm the one on the sidelines, the interloper.'

'No, Georgia...'

'*Yes*. Peter says it's my fault, that I'm unfriendly, distant. And it's true – I can't find it in me to be nice to them. I have tried with Luc. I mean, he's only seventeen. He's still at school. And it's not his fault. But he must know I can't stand Cristiane. And even Luc, there's something not right. I sense him watching me sometimes, not in a nice way. But if I talk to him, he just becomes terribly polite and reserved. Maybe he's always wanted Peter and Cristiane to be together again. It wouldn't be so un-natural. Maybe it's what she wants too, deep down.'

'Stop torturing yourself, Georgia, it's all in your head - Cristiane's not interested in Peter. She's set her cap at Anton - no question. You should have seen them together at the cala the other day – all over each other!'

Tamsin had her own reasons for trying to divert Georgia from this line of thinking, although she understood what lay at the bottom of it. Un-cool it may be, but in love, jealousy came with the territory. That boring old green-eyed monster, she thought. How well I know it. Just a few months into her own marriage, it had been, when she discovered that Ben was making out with other women as if he was still single. She had tried to look the other way, tried to understand when he told her she must, being an actor herself. That freedom, he said; he *needed* it to create. If you love someone, set them free, baby. So she had tried to accept. And even when it hurt like hell, and she wanted to cry out, '*but I love you! I'm pregnant, I'm carrying your child*!' she said nothing. And she went on saying nothing, until the day she came home and found him in bed – *their* bed! - with a couple of girls he'd picked up on the set, the three of them off their heads on Bourbon and dope and he, Ben, oblivious to the blow he had dealt her, until she fell to her knees, weeping helplessly.

'Hey, baby!' he told her, angrily. 'Take it easy, don't spoil the party! For fuck's sake, Tamsin, go cry somewhere else...'

Tamsin laid an arm across her face, as if to shield her eyes from the brutish glare.

'Anyway,' she went on, 'never mind *her* - what about Peter?'

'Oh, Peter wants everything. I mean, I don't think he wants Cristiane in a romantic sense. He just hates letting anything go.' She pondered this for a moment. 'Cristiane, Luc, me,' she said. 'He wants it all. Except -' she stopped and left the sentence hanging in the air, unfinished.

'Except what?' Tamsin asked.

'Nothing.'

'Go on,' Tamsin insisted. 'Except what?'

'Except more children.' Georgia felt defeated. She had betrayed herself. She had not meant to say any of this.

'What do you mean - *more*? He hasn't got any children.'

'Well, Luc.'

'Luc's not his.'

'But that's just the point. When Peter and Cristiane were together, Peter became Luc's surrogate dad. There's a lot of history...'

Tamsin drank the last of her coffee. 'Exactly,' she said. 'History. It's all past tense. You're Peter's wife now. You should have your own family.'

'It's not that simple,' Georgia replied. 'You know what happened with Luc's father -'

'The suicide, you mean? That was an aeon ago, Georgia.'

'It's not an aeon to Luc.'

'Don't be so soft. He has to deal with it. Think of all the kids who've lost their fathers - in wars, for instance. There were four children in my mother's family, and they were all under ten when their father's plane was shot down. They and my grandmother - they just had to pull together. I'm not saying it's not a dreadful thing to happen, but there comes a point when you have to decide: what's it about, life or death?'

Georgia was still not convinced. 'Peter considered formally adopting Luc,' she told Tamsin. 'Even after he and Cristiane had split up. You don't just trample over something like that.'

'Even if the alternative is to be trampled over yourself?' Tamsin replied. She picked up the empty cups.

Georgia looked at her, surprised. She had sounded quite angry. Tamsin, noticing Georgia's puzzled expression, turned away towards the house.

'More coffee?' She asked.

'No, thanks.'

'Look, I'm sorry,' Tamsin said, turning back to Georgia. 'I know it's tough.'

'Oh, let's just drop it,' said Georgia, now sick of the subject, and guessing that Tamsin felt the same way.

'Gladly,' said Tamsin. And then, by way of making amends, she added, 'Like me to do a reading for you?'

'Aren't you too tired?' Georgia replied with a small flicker of enthusiasm.

Tamsin smiled wanly. 'Hang on,' she said. 'I'll be right back.' She returned a few minutes later, carrying a pack of

Tarot cards wrapped in a piece of purple chiffon. She sat down at a cane table. Georgia joined her, and sat opposite.

'Come on then,' she said. 'Think of your question.'

Georgia laughed dryly. 'I hardly ever think of anything else,' she said.

Imperceptibly, the mood had changed. Tamsin sat across from Georgia, shuffling the cards slowly. When at last she spoke, her voice was quieter, more measured.

'Ready?' she asked.

Georgia nodded.

Tamsin laid the pack down on the table between them. 'Cut the cards then, to your left, with your left hand.'

Georgia cut the cards in the middle.

'Three times,' Tamsin prompted.

Georgia cut twice more. Tamsin picked up the pack and began to lay the cards out in a spread. 'Let's have a look,' she said, turning the central card face up. 'Ah, the Tower. Lightning strikes. Be prepared for a shock!'

'Oh no, no shocks!' Georgia exclaimed with dismay. 'Let's start again!'

But Tamsin shook her head. 'Shocks can be good,' she said, and carried on. One by one, she turned over each card in turn, all the time keeping up a running commentary.

'Three of swords, beneath. The end of something. A bit of heartache? Still, three's one of the good numbers, it may be the end, but it also holds the seeds of a new beginning. Oh, look, the King of Wands there, in the past. Could that be Peter? Would you actually dump him?'

'I have been thinking about leaving. Separating…' Georgia was shocked to hear herself say the word out loud. But it was the truth. 'Really thinking about it,' she added.

'So, not just thinking about thinking about it?'

They laughed, a bit uneasily.

'Who knows,' said Tamsin, 'it might be for the best. Look, Nine of Cups in the future. Happiness - without Peter? Is that what it could be saying? And who's this? Knight of Cups at the top? A new suitor, perhaps – any idea?'

'A suitor? Not a clue. As long as it's not Randall. My weirdo admirer.'

'God, no! What a thought. But it's someone, and he's on his way. Sure there's not anyone on the horizon?'

Georgia shook her head. 'I wouldn't want anyone I already know. I mean,' reddening, she corrected herself: 'I'm not looking for anyone - full stop.'

'Is that so?' Tamsin asked archly as she started to turn the final four cards over one by one. 'Ten of Wands,' she said. 'Poor old you, struggling away under the weight of your terrible burden. You do have the option of putting it down, Georgia.'

Georgia suddenly felt defensive. 'Tamsin!' she said. 'It's my marriage! Yes, we're having a bad time, and it's horrible, but it's not something I can just dump, as you put it. I don't think you understand at all! For me, Peter and I, we were perfect. I thought it was forever and we'd grow old together. That we'd have a houseful of children, and grandchildren, and memories. And now look at us. And it's not only Cristiane. You know what it's like when Peter flies into one of his rages? Well, it's become a daily event, and over nothing. Like, we're out of marmalade for breakfast, and there are ructions. Half the time it's open warfare, the other half I'm walking on eggshells. My nerves are shot to hell.' She paused for a moment, swallowing hard. 'It probably will come to a separation,' she said, her voice quiet with resignation. 'I suppose that's what I'm trying to come to terms with.'

Tamsin reached a hand out to her.

'But, Georgia,' she said, 'look around you - marriages break up all the time. I mean - look at *me*, I'm surviving, aren't I? And Ben and I -' Tamsin gave up without even beginning to try to put into words how she had felt walking out of her own marriage. She turned her attention firmly back to Georgia's plight. 'I mean, it happens,' she said. 'Is it *so* impossible to imagine splitting up with Peter?'

'No,' Georgia replied. 'I *can* imagine it. But it's like imagining the end of the world.'

Tamsin stared at her, speechless. She went back to the cards, and turned another one over.

'The Queen of Swords...' Tamsin's eyes were fixed to the card. She appeared completely absorbed in the image.

'What is it?' asked Georgia, frowning anxiously.

'Strange, so strange,' she said, and added quickly, 'it's not you, Georgia - it definitely wasn't you...'

'What was it then?'

'It was like – God, it was like a kind of vision! I saw a woman dressed in black, by a graveside. It's connected with that Three of Swords. Like I said, it's not you, but it's something that'll *affect* you. In fact, I have a feeling that whatever it is, when it comes, it's going to affect us all.'

To herself, she was thinking: death. There will be a death, yes, but more than that - a climate of death. And death is the one thing you're not allowed to predict. Trembling slightly, her hand went to the next card. 'Moving on...' she said.

But Georgia was not satisfied. 'No, stop!' she said.

'That's all I can tell you. It's gone,' Tamsin said quietly. 'There was something, something sort of ... I don't know. Leave it for the moment.' And, once again, to herself she thought, something *evil*, and she could feel the hairs standing up on the back of her neck. And immediately, she knew that Georgia had picked up on it, too.

'It sounds ominous,' Georgia persisted. 'Look, I'm covered in goose bumps! Tell me again what you saw.'

'Not now - I'll come back to it later. Maybe.'

Georgia let it go. The reading was making her uneasy. She had a sense of something unpleasant, lurking, waiting to emerge. She wanted to know more, but she could see that there was no point in pressing Tamsin. 'Cassandra,' she said, accusingly.

'No, no,' Tamsin protested with a weak smile, and looked back down at the cards.

'Hopes and fears,' she announced. 'Ah, good - the Empress: love, beauty, creativity, abundance. The Empress is a form of the Goddess - the Great Mother? You should ask for her blessing. The card seems to be saying that all this is waiting for you, Georgia, but before it can manifest, there is -' Tamsin turned over the final card and gasped.

'The Moon,' said Georgia. 'Why did you gasp?'

'Well, it's just that... When *is* the full moon?'

'Tomorrow night?'

'No wonder it was a strange reading! August full moon over Santa Marta – sounds powerful. Better watch out!'

Tamsin gathered up the cards and wrapped them in the purple cloth. 'And that goes for all of us,' she added. She yawned again and got up from her chair.

'Why don't you have a nap?' said Georgia. 'I can look after Poppy...'

'Thanks, but I think I've gone beyond sleep. In any case, she's going to want to be fed any minute now.'

They both looked over at the baby, who had resumed her whimpering. As they watched, her face contorted into a ferocious red grimace and she began to howl in earnest.

'Make that *this* minute!' Tamsin corrected herself, and began to undo the front of her dress. She sat down on the ground and in a graceful movement, reached for Poppy. Leaning her back against the trunk of the lemon tree beneath which Poppy had been lying, she put the baby to her breast. The little rosebud mouth latched on to Tamsin's hard brown nipple and Poppy was quiet again apart from intermittent sounds of contented sucking.

Georgia watched for a moment. A thought came to her. 'I haven't asked about you. What's *your* news?'

'*Nada, nada, nada,*' Tamsin replied sleepily, 'absolutely zilch.' Then, remembering, she added, 'Actually, come to think of it, I have got some news. My darling mother's coming to visit.'

'Really? When?'

'Sometime this week. She's going to call when she's

booked her flight.'

'How nice - and how sudden.'

'Oh, she's been threatening to come ever since I arrived, I just kept putting her off. I needed a bit of space first, to get my head together.'

Georgia felt a stab of envy. Tamsin had it all, she thought: the baby, her mother, a home and family waiting for her in London. She herself felt suddenly terribly alone.

'Will she stay long?' she asked.

'I think she's got some idea she's going to scoop us up and take us back with her.'

'Would you like that?' Georgia asked.

'Not if it's Mum doing the scooping.'

'Still Ben?' Georgia asked.

Tamsin shook her head, and gave an unconvincing little laugh. 'Ben's over,' she replied. Tamsin still couldn't talk about Ben, not even to Georgia. It upset her, even hearing someone else say his name.

Georgia started to collect up her things.

'Wait -' Tamsin stopped her. 'There's something else -'

'Oh?' said Georgia, noticing a new light in Tamsin's eyes.

'I've been offered a job. Richard Devereux's putting on a production of The Tempest in Edinburgh and then touring it if it works out. You know Richard, who I was at RADA with? He's offered me Miranda.'

'Tamsin! When's it all happening?' Georgia asked.

'The plan, as I understand it, is for rehearsals to start in September, and then the play goes on in October. Mum could come in quite handy, actually – you know, with Poppy and everything...'

'Gosh, how marvellous...' said Georgia, struggling to show some enthusiasm.

'You don't seem very pleased for me,' Tamsin commented.

'I *am* pleased, it's just – I suppose I wish something would happen for me, too.'

'It will,' said Tamsin, magnanimously. 'I'm sure it will. Think of the cards...'

'The cards were scary,' said Georgia, getting to her feet.

'Only *partly* scary. On the whole, I thought they were rather promising. Are you going?'

'Yes,' said Georgia. 'I have to get down to the Puerto.'

'Oh?'

'I need to do some shopping in the market. We're having a dinner party tonight – remember?'

Tamsin clapped a hand to her forehead. 'I completely forgot! Will you hate me if I cry off? I've *got* to try and get a few early nights, Georgia - what with mum arriving...' She paused for a moment. 'Actually, I feel really dreadful, all of a sudden'.

Georgia leaned down and kissed Tamsin and then Poppy, who was already falling blissfully asleep at her mother's breast. She noticed that Tamsin's skin looked dull, and there were dark rings around her eyes. It was true; she didn't look well.

'Don't worry about it,' she said. 'You won't be missing much. Same old crowd. Oh, and Cristiane, naturally. Have a good rest. I'll let you know how it goes.'

The sun was high up in the sky: the clear, relentlessly blue sky. You could feel its warmth against your skin and smell the heat in the air. Georgia picked up her things and walked back down to where she had left her car.

CHAPTER FOUR

Georgia wandered around the Puerto restlessly, stopping once or twice to gaze vaguely out to sea. Normally she would have expected to run into someone she knew, or she would stop by at the café in the square where the Santa Marta crowd hung out. But, surprisingly, today she saw no one, and only passing tourists, hot and sweaty, hungry for their holidays, interrupted her view of the harbour. This suited Georgia, wrapped up as she was in her own thoughts and concerns. She was not in the mood for small talk.

The mercado had been packed and noisy, vibrant with colour and movement, and she had enjoyed her shopping, picking and choosing from the stalls she knew and liked best. From a woman about her own age, sturdy and fresh-faced, her hair tied up neatly in a scarf, she bought some big yellow peaches and fat shiny black cherries. Georgia thanked her as she took the bags of fruit, and asked politely after the young woman's family.

'How are the little ones, Maria? Are they all right in this terrible heat?'

Yes, the little ones were fine; their grandmother was taking good care of them, as usual, although probably giving them too many sweets. 'And you,' she asked Georgia in her forthright way, 'when will there be a little one for you?'

Georgia shook her head and gave her usual answer,

'When God wills it, Maria, one of these days!'

And she moved on quickly to the fish market where she viewed the day's catch and ended up choosing a handsome piece of emperador. The fish seller was loud and bawdy, and she made Georgia laugh by pointing out the particular aphrodisiacal effect swordfish had on husbands, and the pleasure and satisfaction Georgia could look forward to that night.

'Not so sure about that...' thought Georgia, and she strolled back into the main body of the market. At a little booth lined with shelves full of exotic spices, she bought a tiny envelope of saffron threads, and a tub of wrinkled black olives, reeking of garlic and herbs, gleaming with oil. She finished up at the panaderia, where she bought a slice of coca topped with pimentos and anchovies to eat on the way home, and a couple of long freshly baked loaves, which she carried under her arm. Her shopping completed, she felt pleased with herself and cheered by the friendly faces, the lovely fresh food. Life was really not so bad.

But almost immediately, the sense of unease that had been dogging her on and off all morning returned, and Georgia found herself at a loss, simply not knowing what to do next. Going back to the house meant dealing with Peter, and she could not face that right away. Not going back meant having to deal with Peter later, which would almost certainly be worse. Her mind went back to Tamsin's tarot reading and the knight in shining armour. If you're out there, she thought, is there any chance you could get a move on?

As she tried to decide what to do next, Georgia gradually became aware of someone standing quite close, looking at her and the things that she was carrying. Taking it all in. He looked to be mid-twenties, slim but well-built, dark brown hair. No sun-tan, crinkly laugh lines round his eyes. He had a London look to him, she thought. He smiled uncertainly as she caught his eye, and there was something about his face, his expression, that she liked immediately.

Quickly, she registered: black jeans, white T-shirt with a smiling Buddha on the chest and some Japanese lettering, an expensive looking camera, dark red sneakers. She hesitated, and for a moment she felt a sudden, unexpected tingle. 'What's this all about?' she wondered. Trying hard to sound casual, she spoke to him.

'It's not as heavy as it looks,' she said, hitching her basket onto her shoulder.

His smile opened up, eager, but still a bit unsure. 'I, er, thought you looked like you might need some help.'

A London accent – yes! She almost hugged him. Georgia suddenly realised how sick she was of Santa Marta. Not just because of the way things were with Peter, but because of the place itself, its self-consciousness, its affectations, the general air of being detached from ordinary reality. Someone had once told her that Santa Marta was like fairyland: you waved a wand and you could be whatever you wanted to be. At first this had seemed a great thing, and it had amused her to find ways of constantly reinventing herself. But now she felt she could not take any more pretence. She needed to put her feet on solid ground.

'That's very kind of you,' she said, delighted to be talking to a real person. 'We haven't met before, have we? Are you here on holiday?'

'Isn't everyone?' he replied.

'I'm not. I live here.'

'Do you now? Well, lucky you! I'm only here a week. A few more days, that's all.' He paused. Georgia wanted to be friendly. He seemed nice...

'And so you really live here, then?' he asked

'Yes. I have a house up in the mountains, in a village called Santa Marta. Have you heard of it?'

'Santa Marta? No... What do you do up there?'

'Not a lot,' she answered. 'My husband looks at film scripts, and I lounge about, mostly.'

'Sounds good to me. It's my specialty, lounging about.'

A flurry of activity in the water attracted their attention.

A motorboat was pulling away from the harbour, bumping out to sea over the waves. Two girls in skimpy swimming costumes sat on the bow, holding onto the rail and shrieking loudly as the boat hit each new wave. The day came into focus for Georgia and started to sparkle, and she smiled happily as the boat and the shrieks disappeared into the distance.

'Have you seen much of the island?' Georgia asked her new acquaintance

'No,' he answered. 'Just this little bit.'

'Oh this!' she said. 'This is just for tourists. The real island - the mountains, the villages, the old part of the city – that's what you should see. It's wonderful, quite magical...'

He was watching her intently, and aware of his look, Georgia felt something inside her melting. And for a moment she was taken over by an inner struggle, knowing that she should be on her way, yet not wanting to leave. Definitely not wanting to leave. Still, they couldn't just stand there, and in spite of what she had said, the basket and bags were cumbersome.

'Tell you what,' he said. 'I'll help you with your shopping, and you fill me in on what I've been missing.'

Georgia thought, oh what the hell! She decided to take a chance and handed him the bag she was carrying, and he took the one from her shoulder and the loaves as well. After all, she was a grown woman. Why shouldn't she do as she pleased? 'Actually,' she said, 'I was just thinking of stopping for a coffee or something...'

'There's a little café across the road there...'

'Oh, I know somewhere much better than that,' she said. 'Follow me.'

Together they walked to the end of the road that bordered the harbour. Georgia led the way along a little path, away from the hotels and restaurants and the tawdry gift shops of the seafront, up along the rocks until they came to a bar set among pine trees, on a flat terrace jutting out over the sea. They sat down at one of the tables and for a moment each of them silently filled their eyes with a panoramic view of sea, sky and curved horizon. The air tingled with the smell of salt and vibrated to the sound of waves washing against the rocks below.

It was too early for the lunchtime crowd, and they found that they were the only customers in the place. For a moment, Georgia felt acutely aware of being alone with a strange man, and it made her self-conscious and slightly guilty, knowing Peter would not approve. But at the same time she felt liberated and rather daring, as if she were taking a first step into an unknown future. It was exciting. She took off the straw hat she was wearing and shook her dark hair loose.

'My name's Georgia,' she said.

'I'm Matt.' He put out his hand. It was long and slim, with well-shaped fingers and fingernails. The veins stood out prominently against the paleness of his skin. Georgia reached out and he squeezed her hand gently, quickly. 'There, that's the formalities dealt with,' he said. 'Now, what will you have to drink?'

'I'll have an *orcherta*, please,' she replied.

'A what?'

'It's a kind of milkshake made with crushed almonds.' The way he was looking at her! Georgia felt her cheeks turn pink, and she was relieved when Esteban, the bar owner, ambled over to serve them.

'I'll try one of those things, too,' Matt said. 'Be adventurous.'

'Dos orchertas, Esteban,' Georgia ordered.

Esteban went away to get their drinks, and Georgia fell silent. She needed to collect her thoughts. She gazed out to sea and focused on a little sailing boat, bobbing up and down as it weaved its way precariously along the coastline.

*

'So,' Matt ventured as they sat waiting for their drinks to arrive. 'What do you do when you're not "lounging about"?'

Georgia was lost for a moment, and fidgeted with the clasp of her bracelet to disguise it. What did she do? Her mind went blank. Come on, come on, she hurried herself, it can't be that difficult! But it was. She was regretting the trite way she had summed up her life in Santa Marta. She had only meant it light-heartedly, but now she realised that she did not want him to think of her as some kind of idle ex-pat who sunbathed her days away, only rousing herself to paint her fingernails, or swallow the occasional gin and tonic while gossiping around the swimming pool with others of her ilk. But why would he think that? He must be able to see that she wasn't that kind of person.

It wasn't that she had nothing to do with her time. Some days were quite busy, when they had friends to stay, which was often the case, and meals to cook and shop for, parties to go to, the house to run. Yet mostly, how she pictured herself, was lying in a hammock with a book, slightly bored and haunted by a longing for something more that she could never quite define. Tamsin's words rang in her ears: you need to have something of your own to do. This was what she was trying to pinpoint. What is my own thing? *Being myself* would be a good start, she thought. But that was something you had to show: what could she possibly say that defined who she was, beyond purely being Peter Gael's wife? Wracking her brains, she blurted out the first thing she could think of.

'I love the sea - it's the best thing about living here, for me. I usually swim every day. Although,' she added, 'this summer I haven't swum so much. They say that every seven years there's a plague of jellyfish, and apparently this is a seventh year. I was badly stung a few weeks ago, which put me off a bit. They're terribly poisonous.'

'Are they?'

'Oh yes, very! The Portuguese Man o' War – that's the worst. They have these great long tentacles, so you don't see the actual jellyfish itself. It feels as though you've scraped yourself against a rock or something. By the time you get out of the sea, you're covered in gigantic blisters and feel like death. They had to cover me in ice to stop the venom moving around the blood-stream. I was actually quite ill for a few days.'

'Nasty,' commented Matt. 'So what have you been doing instead of swimming?'

'I read a lot,' she said. 'And I, er, paint...' Georgia felt her cheeks warming; she hadn't lifted a paintbrush for years. But the lie gave her a mental nudge. 'Oh, and I've been learning to play the guitar,' she added.

'Is that right?' he responded, looking interested. 'We have something in common, then. I play, too.'

'Really? Is that what you do? I should have known – you have the look of a musician.'

'I'm not - not professionally speaking. I get together with a few friends... We do the odd gig, that's all...'

'I see.'

Oh God, he thought, now she's disappointed. What can I say? 'The instrument I studied,' he managed, 'is the flute, and I play the pipes – well, it's the Irish heritage. Obvious, I suppose.' Phew, she was still there, hadn't decided this was all a terrible mistake. He drew in a deep breath. 'But the guitar's my real love,' he said. 'My chosen instrument,' and he smiled as he slowly let the breath out again.

'Ah,' she was saying. 'At first I thought it was a London accent, but now I'm getting that touch of a brogue...'

Matt looked down at his hands and stretched his guitar-playing fingers out in front of him. He was wondering to himself what he was doing here with this girl. And what was she doing here with him? Even for the length of time it took to finish their drinks, he knew he wasn't going to be able to get by on the series of unconnected one-liners and daft remarks that passed for conversation among the kind of people he usually hung out with.

He had first noticed her in the mercado while he was wandering around looking at the stalls. He had his camera with him, and he was about to photograph one of the fish sellers, a mountain of a woman in a sleeveless dress and canvas apron, her upper arms like huge pink hams, raucously calling out her wares from behind a wet, marble slab covered in a dazzling array of newly caught fish. As he aimed the camera, her mouth opened wide in a semi-toothless smile, and her great, meaty hands lifted up a large hunk of swordfish. She leaned forward, and as he leaned with her, the lens picked up her customer: Georgia, in her straw hat, a basket slung over her shoulder, looking cool and hip and slightly aloof. She was smiling as she took the fish, and he got the picture, but amidst the noise and bustle of the market, she didn't notice him. Without thinking about it, he had followed her out into the Puerto. She stopped by the harbour wall and he walked over to where she was standing. It was not the kind of thing he normally did, but something about her had intrigued him, and he had wanted to get a closer look. She was so clearly in her own space; it had not been his intention to disturb her, to try to chat her up. It wasn't anything like that. In any case, with her dark hair and her obvious familiarity with her surroundings, he had assumed that she was Spanish. He was completely taken aback when, as if reading his thoughts, she spoke.

And now they were sitting here together, in a fabulously romantic setting, and he no longer knew what to think or feel. I mean, he thought, did she pick me up or what? He looked up at her, and the beginnings of a smile stopped still on his lips. She was looking back, over her shoulder, at a sailboat about to disappear around the point. He saw her face in profile – skin gleaming, sugar pink lips, black eyelashes squinting against the sun – framed by a cloud of dark, tousled hair and a halo of sunlight. He found himself focussing on her in a way that made him wonder whether he had ever looked at anyone properly ever before. The way she sat, one suntanned shoulder slightly raised to her chin, which she rested on her clasped hands. Her long neck, the casually graceful way she moved her body. He noticed the soft hairs on her cheek, the curve of her spine, her short, unvarnished fingernails. She was extraordinarily pretty, but there was something more than looks that attracted him, and it showed in her face, in her body, in the sound of her voice: a combination of fragility and a kind of underlying force that he found fascinating and irresistible.

'Here are our drinks,' she said, turning back to him, and he quickly tried to do something sensible with the half-formed smile. Esteban placed two tall glasses filled with ice and frothy white liquid in front of them. Georgia watched anxiously as he lurched unsteadily back to the bar.

Matt had noticed, too. 'Is he all right?' he asked.

Georgia shrugged. 'He's usually really sweet and friendly. I suppose he must have his off days, like everyone,' she replied, still looking over towards where Esteban would normally have been standing, busying himself with bottles and glasses, till rolls and receipts. Today, he had disappeared inside the bar. But Esteban's out of character behaviour wasn't a high priority for Georgia at that precise moment. Something more important was happening, and it needed her full attention.

Matt, though, felt uneasy. He wondered if the bartender, knowing Georgia and her husband, disapproved of her being here with a stranger. He was so out of his depth. This was her world; he was just a tourist, passing through. And yet, he felt that if he belonged anywhere, it was here with her, right now. It was where he wanted to be. The thought of going back to his hotel was intolerable. I'm obviously having a funny turn, he thought. Must be the sun.

'Are you here alone?' Georgia asked, sipping at her drink through a straw.

'No, I came with a couple of friends. They've gone to

the beach.'

'You didn't go with them?'

'I get sunburnt.'

'Oh. Bad luck.'

Georgia could hardly take her eyes off him. His eyes were large. Innocent. But his mouth... 'What on earth has come over me?' she wondered. I shouldn't be sitting here. I should go. But somehow she was caught in a moment that was unlike any she had experienced before, and it was like being in a bubble, separate from the rest of her life or from anything that was going on around her. She wondered what he was feeling. Leaning down, she took a cigarette packet and lighter from her basket. She had just thought of something.

'Is anything wrong?' Matt asked, noticing her frown. 'Should you be going?'

'I was just thinking about Esteban,' she replied. 'There's a kind of a ... a situation with his daughter, Isabel. She's been going around with an American who lives in Santa Marta. The playboy type, to put it mildly. She's a pretty girl, quite striking really, but she's only sixteen, a schoolgirl - a bit young to be hanging out with someone like him. I heard the other day that she's been staying at his house down at the beach. I was just wondering if that was why Esteban's looking so moody. His wife's a bit unpredictable, though I don't see her around today. I hope there hasn't been any trouble. The American – Tom Malek – happens to be a friend of my husband.'

'Ah, a bit awkward for you, then?'

'A bit,' she replied. 'Though it's nothing to do with me, really.'

And yet, she thought, it was. She and Peter had rowed after Tom Malek brought Isabel up to the house just a few days earlier. Malek had made a point, it seemed to Georgia, of showing Peter some semi-naked photographs he had taken of Isabel. Georgia knew all about his penchant for young girls and his 'arty' pictures. Everybody did. No voice, of course, was ever raised in disapproval; at the higher moral end, censorship of any kind was considered to be anti-art, and at the lower end, permissiveness reigned supreme. That was Santa Marta. Georgia had tried to challenge Peter on it, not very successfully.

'Do you really think it's all right, the way he boasts about having sex with girls barely in their teens?' she had asked him. 'And takes pictures of them, and shows them to people, shows them to you?'

Peter had just shrugged.

'Does that mean you approve?'

'Don't be prudish, Georgia. It's very unattractive.'

'But,' she had persisted, 'what do you feel when he talks to you about that stuff?'

'What do you feel when you read Nabokov or Jean Genet?'

'Sick, mostly,' she had answered.

'Of course; I should have remembered that. But the fact remains, whether you, personally, happen to like it or not, it's good writing. It's life from a different perspective. It doesn't mean you want it for yourself. But you can't just turn away because something isn't to your personal taste. It's narrow-minded, bourgeois. Think about D.H. Lawrence, Terry Southern, painters - Caravaggio. Do you want them all banned?'

'Literature's one thing, hanging out with a child-molester's something else...' Georgia pressed on.

At which point Peter became irritated. 'Oh, for Christ's sake, Georgia, what is your problem? Why can't you just be cool with it? No-one's asking you to do anything you don't want to, are they?'

'I just don't see how it can be all right. I mean, OK, consenting adults and all that - but not such young girls ...'

'Georgia, just grow up, will you? Please? And give me a break! I'm not Tom Malek's keeper. It's not that important to me. But you, it's like you're obsessed...'

At which point Georgia backed off. She knew what she

meant, and in her heart she was sure she was right, but to argue with Peter was always a losing battle. Santa Marta threw her off balance. She lost the argument because she had not been able to prove her point. Peter had thought out his position on censorship, on other people's sexual preferences, and his own. To Georgia, it was more a matter of instinct, and hard to articulate.

As for Tom Malek, there was no reason why he should care what she thought. He didn't care what anyone thought. All the same, she could not believe he had actually dared to bring Isabel up to Casa Dura, and in the row with Peter that had ensued, she had threatened to speak to Esteban and Dita about it. And, here, she knew, there was an uncomfortable truth she had to face: part of the reason she became so upset was the flirtatious way Isabel had behaved with Peter, and the fact that Peter hadn't exactly discouraged her. She felt furious just thinking about it.

Georgia lit her cigarette and looked at Matt who had picked up a loose pebble and was examining it. It was a perfect oval, smooth and flat, pale yellow in colour and divided precisely at the mid-point by a fine white line. He held it out to her on the palm of his hand, and she reached out and felt its smoothness with her fingertip. For a moment, they both became silently absorbed in their surroundings. The scent of pine, the blue of the sky reflected in the sea, the sea itself, so clear that even from where they sat they could see the sharp, pitted rocks deep below the surface and the little shoals of fish swimming in and out among them, the glittering spiny black sea-urchins that clung to their surface. The sound of the cicadas, constant, clicking, only blended with the silence, suffused it as the midday heat suffused the air, making it dry and warping it so that surfaces and outlines appeared slightly distorted and hazy.

'Tell me about yourself,' Georgia turned to Matt and asked.

'What do you want to know?'

'You could start with the basics,' she said, a bit surprised at herself. 'Married? Single? Live-in lover?'

He kept her waiting for a moment. Then he said, 'I did have a steady girl. We split up a few weeks ago. That's why my pals dragged me along on this holiday. They thought I needed cheering up.'

'Had you been together long?'

'About three years.'

'Three years? Serious, then - what went wrong?'

Georgia had caught Matt off guard. With anyone else, he would have evaded the question, made light of it. Talking about personal stuff didn't come easily.

'She went off with someone else,' he said at last. And seeing Georgia's inquisitive expression, added, 'A Greek waiter she met on a girls' night out at some taverna place in Bayswater.'

He did not look or sound sad or regretful, but Georgia felt obliged to say, 'How awful - were you very upset?'

'No,' he said quickly. 'It had run its course. She wanted to get engaged, I didn't. She was always flirting with other blokes.'

'That's not very nice,' said Georgia. 'Seems to me you had a lucky escape.'

'Yeah, that's me. Lucky guy.' Matt looked down, slightly guiltily. He had omitted to say that he had done his own share of flirting and, on a few occasions, more than just flirting.

But Georgia just laughed, happy that the girlfriend was gone and unmissed. She picked up her hat. 'Let's go and sit by the sea,' she said.

Matt was on his feet, grateful for the opportunity to change the subject and glad to have made her laugh. They picked their way over the rocks and found a flat ledge to spread out on. Georgia kicked off her sandals and dangled her feet in the foamy tide. The water was cool and swirly and tickled the soles of her feet pleasingly. She would have loved to swim, but she had no costume with her. For a moment she imagined jumping in, immersing herself in the waves, being in the water with him... Her thoughts floated like a cloud, drifting skywards.

Matt leaned forward to roll up the legs of his jeans. 'The situation with this girl, Isabel?' he said. 'What do you think will happen?'

Georgia let go of her little daydream reluctantly. Recently, daydreams had become a refuge. Sometimes she became so wrapped up in them, she resented any interruption. Georgia worried about this.

'It's hard to say.' She thought for a moment. 'The local people don't like it. It's definitely causing them to talk. But then, Santa Marta's never exactly been a stranger to scandal. And to be quite honest,' she added, 'I've got my own problems.'

But in spite of what she said, Georgia felt uncomfortable, and looking over towards the bar, she saw Esteban, his face dark and heavy with emotion, staring hard at her. She knew that she should go over and say something, but his expression was so crazy and pained, she couldn't bring herself to. She looked quickly at Matt, whose eyes also were fixed on Esteban. He turned to her.

'I think it's time we made a move,' he said quietly.

Georgia slipped her feet into her sandals and allowed Matt to help her up. As they turned towards the bar, she saw that Esteban's eyes had not moved. He had not been looking at her at all, but past her, out to sea.

Matt put the two glasses down on a table, and underneath one of them, a couple of one-hundred peseta notes. He positioned himself between Georgia and Esteban and, holding her arm, he guided her past the bar and on to the little path which led back to the main part of town.

They walked along for a while without saying much, but Matt's thoughts were whirring through his mind. He was aware of wanting to hold onto this, whatever it was, this rapport that he had found with Georgia. But she was married. She lived in a different world. Her husband - the film scripts... No, he had never met anyone like her. He sensed that she liked him, whatever that meant. But all he knew for certain was that he wanted to see her again. Had to see her! He helped her load her baskets into the boot of her car, and watched her as she lowered herself into the driver's seat and adjusted her rear mirror. She slammed the door shut and lowered the window. He squatted down so that his face was level with hers.

'Well, goodbye,' she said, with what looked to him like rather a sad smile.

'It was nice meeting you,' he replied awkwardly, his heart sinking.

'And you,' she said, starting the engine.

Matt stood back, giving her room to turn the car. She reversed cautiously and then stopped to let another car pass in front of her. It was his last chance. He ran back and leaned into her open window. Without stopping to think, the words tumbled out.

'Georgia!' he said, 'I know this is a bit presumptuous, but I don't suppose there's any chance that we could meet up again? I'm staying at the Hotel Miramar – just along the road there. Maybe we could have another orcherta sometime?'

He waited for the rebuff, but instead Georgia's face lit up.

'Love to,' she replied simply. 'I'll be in touch!' And with that she waved gaily, and pulled away from the harbour, onto the road that led up into the mountains, up to Santa Marta.

CHAPTER FIVE

No sound came from inside the house as Georgia entered. She crossed the large, high-ceilinged entrada to the double doors leading to the kitchen. Putting her baskets down upon the table, she hoped the fish would be all right. Quickly, she put things away, into the fridge, onto shelves, the bread into a deep, earthenware crock. The guests had been asked for around eight-thirty. She guessed it must now be about three. Plenty of time, she thought. What she needed most of all was to sit down alone for a few minutes and sort her head out. And she was longing for a cigarette. Damn, she'd left her pack on the table in the bar. Never mind, there were some in the sitting room. Georgia made herself a cup of coffee and took it with her.

His voice rang out in the empty silence of the room.
'Where've you been, Georgia?'
Peter! She'd completely forgotten about him!
'Where've you been?' he asked again. The tone was menacing. He was sitting in a big, leather armchair, his elbows protruding over the arms, his legs crossed. He looked solemn; she knew that expression.

Peter Gael was a man of striking appearance, and he was well aware of the impression he made. He was tall and rangy, and his clever, sensual face had a lived in look. Against his suntanned skin, his silvering hair and light grey eyes glittered palely, his thin lipped mouth the one feature that seemed to express an unexpected, and unsuccessfully concealed, vulnerability. He was attractive rather than handsome, with a strong physical presence; a man you did not easily forget.

Lately, Georgia had noticed, the drinking was taking its toll. Some mornings the whites of his eyes were veined with red, and you could see the start of crows' feet at the corners. But today, there was something else in his face that Georgia could not define, something she hadn't seen before. And his voice, normally rich and deep, had a hollow ring to it.

'Come and sit down and tell me where you've been.'

Georgia helped herself to a cigarette and he leaned forward to light it. She sat on the sofa opposite him.

'I haven't been anywhere,' she said.

'Well you weren't here, so you must have been somewhere.'

'I've been shopping, if you call that somewhere.'

'Shopping?'

And now for the third degree, she thought. Her defences went up, her mind searched for answers to questions as yet unasked. 'We're having people to dinner this evening, remember?'

'I was up at ten and you'd already left. Now it's nearly three. Should be a pretty good dinner...'

'I hope so. I'm cooking swordfish. Have you seen Antonia, by the way?'

'No. Didn't she say something about not coming till the afternoon?'

Georgia could not remember. She shrugged and leaned forward to flick the ash from her cigarette into a little silver ashtray.

'So, did you go to Palma? Is that why you were so long?'

'No. Only the Puerto.'

Georgia took a sip of coffee. It was sweet and creamy and comforting. She felt a stab of hunger, and remembered she had eaten nothing all day.

'The Puerto? For five hours? What the fuck were you doing in the Puerto for five hours?'

Georgia took another sip of coffee. 'How many times do I have to say it - shopping. I went to the bank. Wandered around. Had a drink at Esteban's…'

'For five hours?'

'Yes, for five hours! Including driving there and back! What is this? Why do I have to be interrogated?'

'Why do you have to lie?'

'I'm not lying! You treat me like a prisoner!'

'Prisoner? Prisoner? What about me? Your husband? You leave the house without a word, you disappear for five hours? You do realise I've had no lunch? So what about some lunch for your husband? Better still, what about having lunch with your husband? It seems to me that if there's anything else you can find to fill your precious time, then that's preferable to doing what you're supposed to be doing, which is looking after your home and your husband!'

Georgia got up from the sofa.

'I don't need this,' she said. 'You're being ridiculous. You're quite capable of getting your own lunch. Anyway, I've got things to do.'

'Georgia!' Peter shouted angrily and leaped to his feet.

Georgia, startled, stumbled back against a low table. He automatically reached forward to help her, but she shrank away from him.

'No!' she yelled. 'Don't touch me! If you touch me I'll scream!'

'You are screaming! What's the matter with you?'

'I'm sick of being questioned and bullied, that's what's wrong with me!'

Georgia felt her whole body shaking. She held her hands over her eyes. Violent, choking sobs caught in her throat, making it impossible for her to speak.

Peter tried to calm her down, alarmed by her reaction.

'Georgia, sit down,' he said. 'Why are you so upset?

Why are you crying?' But she had stopped crying. She wiped her face with her hands.

'I'm going to wash my face,' she said, her voice thin and shaky. 'Then I'm going to try to find Antonia and get her to help me with the food.'

She walked out of the room, crossed the entrada, and ran upstairs. She slammed the bathroom door behind her and sat down on the floor and wept helplessly. After a few minutes her crying began to subside and she felt better. She got up and looked in the mirror. Her eyes were red and puffy, her face was blotchy and her hair hung damply in strings. She leaned over the basin and splashed her face with cold water. Quickly, she brushed her hair, and started to get her mind working on the preparations for the evening. The incident with Peter, she determinedly blotted out.

*

Opening the bathroom door, she heard voices below. Someone was speaking to Peter in Spanish. She stood for a moment, listening, but she could not catch what they were saying. Peter sounded very formal, very controlled. She heard a loud 'Adios', and footsteps in the entrada. When she was sure they had gone, she started to walk down the stairs. Peter was waiting at the bottom.

'Did you get any of that?' he asked.

'No, I just heard voices.' She felt immensely weary, weary of him, of everything. She didn't want to hear what he had to say. Whatever it was, she did not care.

'It was the Guardia,' he said. 'It's the second time they've been here today. They came before, while you were out.'

'What did they want?'

'Two of them are still here. They're waiting outside.'

'Waiting outside? What are they waiting for?'

'Georgia,' Peter said slowly, cautiously. 'Come and sit down for a minute. This is serious.'

Georgia felt a chill in the atmosphere. She had noticed something amiss with Peter when she first walked into the room but she had assumed that it was one of his rages coming on, brought on by her absence that morning. Now the air was laden with an almost tangible feeling of wrongness. It was like an echo, but of what? She had already had this feeling today, but when, where? Her mind was blank. She could not remember.

'Can we go and sit on the terrace? I'd rather be outside.'

She did not want to go back into the sitting room.

'Sure. Do you want a drink?' he asked, holding up his own tumbler of whisky and water.

'No thanks,' she said. She would have liked a drink very much, but not having eaten all day, she decided it was not a good idea. Not with Peter in this peculiar mood. She felt she needed to keep her wits about her and could not risk bring undone by the alcohol.

They both sat down. The afternoon had become stiflingly hot. There was not a breath of air. Everything was utterly still and silent. Georgia felt herself touched by an obscure fear.

'So what's it all about?' she asked, trying to sound matter-of-fact. 'Why the Guardia?'

Peter lit a cigarette and took a deep drag. He blew the smoke out harshly.

'When they first came,' he said, 'this morning, they were a bit cagey. They wanted to question me about when I'd last seen Tom Malek.'

'Well that was fairly straightforward, since you were out on the lash with him all last night.'

'No, I wasn't.'

'But -'

'Wait. We were supposed to meet at C'an Pepe for dinner. Carl was there - Tom had fixed for him to come too. I arrived at nine, like we said, but Tom didn't show up.'

'So?'

'So Carl and I had a few drinks, waited around for about an hour, and then had dinner. After dinner we went to the café to see if anyone there had any word of Tom, but no, nothing. Then we got involved with a whole bunch of people – Anton, Steve and Jules and some friends of theirs who'd just arrived from Berlin. Oh yeah, Randall joined us for a while and then disappeared off into the night, as he does. Tamsin was there…'

'Tamsin? That's funny…'

'Yeah, she'd dragged that poor baby out with her. Typical actress, never thinks of anyone except herself. No wonder Ben Chase dumped her. Anyway, one of the Berlin crowd was a guy she knew from LA. A record producer…'

'Oh, yes?'

'Yeah, but no sign of Tom. I'd intended to drive down to the Cala to see if he was at his house, but it was pretty late by the time we left the café, so I just came back here and crashed out.'

'What do the Guardia want with Malek?'

'Georgia –' he broke off, his face suddenly gaunt and haggard.

'You're scaring me, Peter! Can't you just tell me what it's about?'

Ignoring her question, he asked, 'Was Esteban at the restaurant?'

'Yes.' Georgia was on guard. Peter was looking at her searchingly.

'Did he say anything?'

'No. He was … strange.'

Peter waited for a moment, weighing up what to say.

'Georgia, it's Isabel. She's dead. The maid found her body this morning and called the police.'

Georgia struggled to make sense of his words. Isabel was dead? How could this be? She was found by the maid - she tried to find the sense in this statement.

'What do you mean, the maid called the police?'

'Tom Malek's maid. They found Isabel's body in the house down at the Cala.'

'No!'

'She - the body's - still there. They've got forensic people trying to establish an exact time of death, but it seems like it happened around midnight last night.'

Georgia was stunned.

'What happened to her? Was it drugs? An overdose?'

'No. Apparently she was stabbed. That's all I know. The Guardia were hardly going to tell me the whole story, were they?'

'Stabbed!' It wasn't sinking in. 'They suspect Malek?' she asked.

Peter shrugged his shoulders despairingly. They sat in silence, unable to share what was going through their separate minds.

'Malek and his predilection for young girls,' thought Georgia. 'Still, I wouldn't have thought he could kill. I've never thought of him as a violent type. He isn't. It can't be Malek.'

Above, the sky had darkened. Oh no, she thought, not another sirocco - I couldn't bear it. We'll all go completely mad, if we haven't already. She noticed that Peter was also looking up at the sky, when a sound came from below the house, a car pulling up. They both rose to their feet, and as they did, they heard voices, a woman, shrill and urgent, calling out.

'Señora! Señora!'

Their maid, Antonia, was running through the house towards them, followed by a group of police officers. She grabbed Georgia's hands.

'Señora! Es terrible, es terrible!' She repeated the same phrase over and over.

The officers explained that Antonia had been at Tom Malek's house with her friend Maria, Malek's maid, when Isabel's body was found. It was the day Maria went to do her weekly cleaning and airing, and Antonia had been helping her. Maria was the one who had discovered the body in Malek's bedroom, but Antonia had heard her horrified screams and she was on the scene within seconds.

'Señora, Señora, es terrible! Que horror!' The normally placid Antonia was completely distraught.

'Come into the kitchen, Antonia,' Georgia said, worried by the level of Antonia's distress. 'Come, I'll make you a camomilia.'

And then, turning to Peter, she added, her voice shaking, 'For God's sake, find out what the Guardia are up to. Antonia's completely traumatised. We'll have to cancel this evening – there's no way we can cope with it now.'

Georgia took Antonia into the kitchen and put the kettle on to boil. This is it, she thought to herself, the bolt of lightning that strikes my house and reduces everything to rubble. The Tower from the tarot reading now seemed very specifically to stand for the tower at Casa Dura that housed Peter's study, and the predicted disaster was indeed a personal catastrophe with the potential to shake her own life to its foundations. But why, she thought? It's dreadful, of course it is dreadful, but it's not directly to do with my life, is it? And yet it felt as though it was. Death always has this effect on me, she thought. It always makes me feel sad, stricken. But this is beyond sadness, this is tragic, a real tragedy, and right in our midst. The police here at the house, Malek's involvement, and now Antonia. It's too close, she thought.

She started pouring out cups of camomile tea with a shaking hand while Antonia wept and covered her face with a handkerchief. Peter came back in from talking with the Guardia and sat beside Antonia at the kitchen table. He put an arm around her plump shoulders and spoke to her firmly, reassuringly.

Antonia Coll was a childless widow whose husband had died in a 'flu epidemic that had swept the island during the first year of their marriage. After his death she had gone back to live with her mother in the old family house in the lower part of the village. She had stayed there ever since, content with her cat and her collection of dolls, never for a moment considering the possibility of remarrying. All that was behind her, finished with, she would say with some relief. The single state suited her innocent nature, her tendency to turn away from life's harsher realities. Knowing her so well, Georgia and Peter were protective of Antonia, and now they were both concerned about how the morning's events were affecting her. Peter, realising she would probably feel nervous alone in her house, suggested that she spend the night at Casa Dura; in fact, that she stayed for as long as she wanted to. Georgia would take care of her, he said, she would be safe with them. Eventually, Antonia allowed herself to be comforted. Her sobbing ceased and, tentatively, she took a sip of camomile.

'That's right, Antonia,' said Georgia. 'See, I've put lots of honey in it. You need something sweet when you've had a shock.'

'Yes,' Antonia replied, 'it was a terrible, terrible shock. Never have I seen anything like it! Ah, the poor girl. She was not a good girl, I know, but she did not deserve that. Such a deep cut, so much blood! It must have been a very big knife. I wish I had never gone with Maria. I wish I had never seen such a thing. I will never be able to forget. Never!'

Peter patted Antonia's arm. 'Poor Antonia,' he said. 'You are right. You should never have had to witness such a thing.'

Antonia nodded vigorously.

Peter continued patting. 'But tell me, Antonia, where did you say the body of the girl was found?'

'Oh Señor, she was lying on the bed. But not just lying. No. She had been tied. She was naked, and tied to the posts of the bed. Tied like an animal to be slaughtered. Like an animal, Señor!'

Peter caught Georgia's glance, but she quickly looked away.

'What about the rest of the room, Antonia?' Peter continued his questioning in a gentle voice. Antonia spoke fast and in the Mallorquin dialect, her speech was difficult to follow. He wanted to slow her down a little. 'Was there anything else you noticed? Did it look as if anyone had broken in, for instance?'

'No, no. I don't think anyone had broken into the house. It did not seem so. But there was something else...'

'You saw something else, Antonia?'

'Yes, Senor. And Maria, she saw also. Even though we did not stay long in the room. No, Senor, it was too bad, too horrible.'

Georgia put a plate of bocadillos and some little almond cakes on the table, and urged Antonia to take something and eat. Antonia hesitantly chose one of the cakes.

'What was the other thing you saw, Antonia?' Georgia asked.

'Senora, everywhere there were papers, pieces of paper. Yes, papers and – and – photographs.'

'Photographs?' asked Peter.

'Pictures of the girl. And other girls. Bad pictures. I don't want to say anymore ... I did not look too much.'

Georgia turned to look at Peter, but he had walked over to the window and was staring out in front of him.

'Antonia,' Georgia said, 'I have to go and make a telephone call. Stay here with the Señor, and when I come back we'll decide what to do next. Eat some more of the food, it'll make you feel better. I'll be back in a minute.'

'Yes, Señora,' said Antonia, taking another cake. 'Thank you. I am feeling a little better now.'

Georgia went into the living room and sat down by the telephone. As she picked up her address book her mind went back to earlier that afternoon. It was like trying to recall a dream, a dream from a long time ago. Was it really the same day? She sat for a moment, remembering how she had wandered through the Puerto, reluctant to come home. The meeting with Matt, the orchertas, the sea. And then, all too vividly, she remembered Esteban's face as they were leaving.

'Oh God,' she thought. 'Oh my God.'

*

Georgia put the address book back on the table. Gavin, she remembered, had plans to be in Palma all day. She rang James Parker, and then Anton, but there no was reply from either of them. No-one else who was coming had a phone. Except Cristiane, and Georgia had no intention of ringing her.

'What shall I do? What shall I do?' she thought desperately. Picking the phone up, she tried Gavin's number a couple of times just in case, but there was no response.

'Well that's it then,' she concluded to herself.

Georgia sat back in her chair and sighed. To her surprise, she felt her spirits lift slightly. Perhaps it was a good thing, after all, she thought, that they would be coming. Better than being alone in the house with Peter. The company of friends, some food and wine, maybe it was just what they needed. A bit of normality. Georgia began to look forward to the evening.

'Did you manage to reach anyone?' Peter asked from the doorway.

'No. No-body's home. We'll just have to go ahead as planned.'

'Can you handle it?'

'Yes, but I'll have to get a move on.'

'Do you need any help?'

'No thanks. Antonia'll help me. It'll be good for her to keep busy.'

What now? She thought. Peter never helped with dinner parties or any other kind of meals. He barely knew how to make a cup of tea. She got up to go.

'Georgia?' He said.

'I've got to get on, Peter. I have to cook.'

'Georgia, listen to me for a moment. I'm sorry you got so upset earlier. I really don't know what gets into you. You were the one who disappeared for several hours without telling me where you were going or -'

'Please don't start that all over again! Please! I can't bear it! Haven't we had enough for one day? I can't cope with any more...'

'Georgia, what's the matter with you? I can't understand why you get so het up! All I'm trying to do is discuss -'

'For God's sake, Peter! I couldn't tell you I was going out because you were unconscious when I left. It was you who came in drunk at four in the morning or whatever it was. But, as usual, I'm the one who ends up being in the wrong -'

'Oh yes, poor Georgia, such a little saint! Such a bloody martyr. Too good for this world! Or for her husband. Too -'

Georgia turned and left the room. Her nerves were raw. Anger caught in her throat.

'I can't live like this any longer,' she told herself. 'I just can't. He's driving me insane. Tamsin's right, I've got to get out.'

And that's another thing, she thought. What about Tamsin? She didn't say a word that morning about having seen Peter the night before. She didn't say she'd been at the café. She said she had had a wakeful night with Poppy. What was that about?

'Señora!' Antonia came towards Georgia. Her face, Georgia noticed, was washed and freshly powdered, and in her hands she held the large piece of swordfish Georgia had bought that morning.

'Senora,' she said, 'this is not good! Smell it, it smells bad...'

Georgia sniffed at the fish. Antonia was right, it had gone off. 'Blast!' she thought. 'I shouldn't have had it sitting around in the sun all that time.'

'What shall we do?' Antonia implored.

'Never mind about the fish, Antonia. What else have we got?'

'We have plenty of vegetables, we have ham, we have a lot of eggs, we have salad, we have rice, we have bread, we have fruit -'

'All right,' said Georgia, thinking fast. 'Let's make a gazpacho to start with, then a nice big tortilla. They'll be quite happy with that. You do the tortilla, Antonia, and I'll make the gazpacho. Let's go!'

They went back to the kitchen together and quickly got to work.

CHAPTER SIX

They were seated at a long table on the back terrace, overlooking the Forodada, the strange, mountainous outcrop that protruded several hundred meters out from the coastline, lounging in the sea like a vast prehistoric beast. Moorish lanterns glowed with candlelight in the branches of the trees and above them shone a waxing Gibbous moon. The table was littered with wine bottles and the remnants of the cheese to which people were still helping themselves. The air was heavy and warm, the scent of jasmine and moonflowers mingling with black tobacco and expensive perfume.

Georgia had hardly touched her food and she was beginning to feel the effect of the wine. 'I'll stop now,' she thought. 'I've had enough.' But even as she was thinking it, she reached over to the nearest bottle and refilled her glass.

She listened to the conversation around the table with a frown of disbelief. Were they really as detached and uninterested as they seemed? Georgia had expected the talk to be of nothing but the murder, but she had been wrong: instead, it seemed as if they all wanted to steer clear of the subject.

At the start of the evening, Gavin had been the first to allude to it while standing out on the terrace with his American girlfriend, Donna, waiting for everyone to arrive.

'How's old Antonia bearing up?' he had asked Peter tentatively.

'She's staying here tonight. She was a bit shaken up.'

'We heard she was down there at Malek's place when they found...'

'Yeah - the police drove her back here. We're taking care of her.'

'Of course...'

Peter had proffered a bottle of wine in Gavin's direction.

'Here, try a glass of this new Rioja I've got in.'

Gavin sniffed the wine and then took a drink.

'Yes,' he pronounced thoughtfully. 'These Rioja's just keep getting better. You're right, Peter - good as a claret. Unbelievably good...'

'When you think of that cat's piss we used to get from Binisalem,' Peter had replied pointedly, pouring a glass for Donna.

Gavin laughed raucously. 'Ha! Thirty-five pesetas a litre! It's gone up a bit, but you can still get a couple of litres for less than a quid. Actually, it's not as bad as all that...'

'You're looking particularly lovely tonight, Donna,' Peter had said, turning his attention to Gavin's girlfriend. When he felt like it, Peter could flirt to great effect, and women almost always responded to his attention. Even women who, like Donna, knew him well and were aware of how quickly a caress could, so to speak, become a blow.

'Why, thank you, kind sir,' she had replied, with a flutter of her eyelashes, before taking a sip from her glass. 'And this is divine. You'll have to order some for us...'

'Gladly,' Peter replied graciously, casting his eye around to see where Georgia had got to, the flirting moment over as far as he was concerned.

Georgia was handing round canapés and exchanging a few words of greeting with people as they arrived, glad they were all there, glad to be busy, very glad not to be alone with Peter. Still, she wondered whether it had been a mistake to go ahead with the dinner. It had been such a strange day, she felt unsure of herself and afraid of making the wrong move, saying the wrong thing. She was aware of the need to tread cautiously. As she moved towards the group around her husband, Donna brought the subject back to the events of the previous night.

'It must have been such a shock, Peter,' she said, 'for you and Georgia. I mean, this Isabel business...'

Peter had taken a drink from his glass and looked over towards the door. James Parker was just walking through it, raising a fist in a mock salute at Peter as he strode over.

'I mean, it happening down at Tom's place and all. I was just thinking, Tom being such a great friend of yours...'

'Tom's not involved, Donna,' said James Parker, cutting into the conversation. 'The guy's not even in the country. We none of us know what was happening with Isabel down there at the house – Malek was just letting her use the place while he was away. You know he's been away?'

'We know that she got murdered,' Donna replied. 'And only last night... Brave of you to go ahead with a dinner party, Georgia,' she had added.

'Oh no, not brave at all,' Georgia had replied, aware of Peter's watchful eye. 'There was simply no choice. Trying to cancel at the last minute – it was impossible. We did try to ring around...'

'Well that makes sense,' Donna replied. 'But all the same...'

At which point Cristiane had swept onto the terrace, making straight for Georgia and greeting her with a warm embrace and kisses on both cheeks.

'Darling, how lovely!' she had exclaimed, taking in the whole group. 'But I'm afraid I have some bad news: Anton isn't able to come, poor dear.' She made a sad face. 'He's in Palma, working at the gallery on the arrangements for his vernisage. He sends *mil disculpas*.'

She turned towards her host.

'Now, Peter, darling,' she said, 'are you going to give me a glass of this marvellous new Rioja you've been raving about?'

Later, Georgia wasn't absolutely sure, but she thought it had been Gavin who put forward the theory that the murderer was probably some drug-crazed lunatic Isabel had picked up while Malek was away. James implied that there was another, albeit more remote possibility: that of an honour-killing, on the grounds that the girl was bringing shame on the family name, on the whole village. These things had certainly happened on the island, and in living memory. A discussion ensued on the local cultural mores, and then someone said how sorry they felt for Esteban and Dita, but with a definite implication that Isabel had been allowed to run wild, and for this her parents had to take the blame. This brought them back to the gruesome concept of an act of punishment, which no-one wished to dwell upon. It was very sad, that was all. With that, they closed the subject down and moved on.

Georgia noticed two things: firstly, that everyone was behaving as if what had happened did not concern them; and, secondly, that Peter had said nothing at all. To Georgia, this did not make sense. She, herself, was terribly shaken. So why was nobody else? It was as if there was an understanding between them from which she had been excluded. She felt like a child overhearing adults talking, knowing the words, but not actually grasping the meaning. It was alienating, and added to the general air of strangeness. Georgia sipped her wine and went on listening, the gap between herself and her guests getting wider all the time.

Cristiane, gleaming at one end of the table in a white Moroccan djellaba, her hair wound up in a gold and white foulard, was holding court on the latest books and films. They were talking about a new movie, *1776*. Gavin had been invited to a preview a few weeks earlier in New York.

'Oh wonderful,' she exclaimed. 'I saw the show on

Broadway! Tell us all about it!'

'Well, you know the story - it's about the American Declaration of Independence,' Gavin had replied. 'Huge cast of characters – lots of songs. I didn't think it worked as a movie.' He paused for a moment, thinking about his recent trip to the States. 'It's going to be a big thing, though, when it happens - the 200 year celebrations. A lot of movies, books, exhibitions, in the pipeline. But in a sense it's all been marred by Watergate. No-one knows how the whole sordid business is going to end. There's such a move to get rid of Nixon, but the guy doesn't want to go. Just wants to stay in the White House and keep hammering away at Vietnam. Can't accept it's all over. America's lost the war.'

'It's going take them a long time to recover from the last ten years,' said Peter. 'Since Kennedy. They haven't really got over that yet.'

'America's become so squalid,' exclaimed Cristiane. 'I can't bear it these days. They've lost all sense of style. Last time I was in New York, I just thought, ugh, not for me!'

'Still, it's not good to see the Land of the Brave so down on itself. It's a sad spectacle,' said Peter.

'Now, now, my friend,' said James. 'Never underestimate the U.S. of A. America will get back on her feet.'

'Of course she will, James,' replied Gavin. 'In maybe another two hundred years…'

They all roared with laughter.

'But seriously,' Cristiane said, turning to Peter, 'can you believe it's 1973? I mean, where did the last ten years go?'

Peter looked across at her with a sardonic smile. 'They didn't go anywhere if you're in Santa Marta. This is where the sixties forgot to stop.'

'Oh, no, Peter! What an awful thing to say!' Cristiane scolded. 'You make us sound like Disneyland or something, you horrid man!'

'I think that's exactly what it's become. A never ending

Summer of Love. The happy hunting ground of the Peace Generation -'

'But, Peter...'

'Only they should re-name it Cripple Creek. The jeunesse d'oré has grown up and flown, and now it's just the broken remnants, emotional cripples who've lost the desire to make it anywhere else...'

Peter gave a harsh laugh, and the rest of the table joined in with a collective will to treat his quip as nothing more than a witty piece of British satire and, in the process, avoid any further uncomfortable observations. They were only too well acquainted with Peter's propensity for homing in on a likely target and no-one wanted to risk being singled out in Peter's pitiless searchlight that particular evening. Only Cristiane remained undaunted.

'Oh, Peter, stop it! You're just being naughty and you know quite well that the place is still a paradise for artists, there's simply nowhere else like it. Just look at the amazing work Anton's doing, especially his sculptures, and there's Gavin's new book coming out, and of course your new film -'

Peter shot a warning look at her, and she changed tack.

'- and with all the marvellous help you've been giving him, Luc's been simply churning out poetry – you should see the haikus he's been working on: fantastic!'

Georgia got up from the table, ostensibly to make the coffee, and headed back into the house. She went through to the kitchen and shut the door behind her. Leaning against it, she closed her eyes. The quiet of the empty room cleared her head, like a breath of fresh air. She needed to centre herself, to know where she stood. There was no point, she decided, trying to work out where other people's heads were at. Maybe they were just distancing themselves in order to avoid scrutiny from the Guardia, or any adverse publicity that might arise from a murder case. Perhaps they just felt it was not safe to talk too much about it just yet. Perhaps they were right. But something - instinct? - told her that this was not the case, it was something more than that. But what?

Georgia's moment of solitude was brief. As she was mulling all this over, a sharp rat-a-tat-tat at the door made her start, and on the other side a woman's voice called out to her.

'Georgia, let us in!'

As Georgia stepped back from the door, Donna, followed closely by Ava, hurried in carrying plates and cutlery they had cleared from the table.

'You shouldn't have,' said Georgia. 'You're guests. Go and sit down and be waited on.'

'No way!' replied Donna. Donna was a petite, East Coast fashion writer with big green eyes and short, layered, tortoiseshell hair which she constantly fingered and pulled at.

'The clearing up's just an excuse, for God's sake! We weren't exactly having the best time out there. Peter's on the attack, and speaking for myself, I am not going to be the one in the firing line tonight. Had that experience, thanks very much! But what about you - are you OK, Georgia?'

'Of course – why shouldn't I be?'

'You just seem a bit quiet,' Donna replied.

'Do I?' asked Georgia, her back turned to Donna as she loaded things into the sink. 'Sorry about that. I suppose it's not nice to mention it, but it's just the whole Isabel thing...'

'Don't!' Donna interrupted. 'God, I'm so depressed about it.'

'Me, too,' said Ava, in her lilting Swedish accent. 'How horrible it is! And we all have to pretend it's just sort of normal. Makes it even worse somehow, I think.'

Donna had plonked herself down in a chair, and took a cigarette from a pack she found lying on the table.

'May I?' she asked Georgia, already holding the cigarette between her lips and lighting it.

'Help yourself. And pass one over to me while you're at

it.' Georgia leaned over so that Donna could give her a light, and then offered the pack to Ava.

'It makes me so darned mad,' said Donna, taking a quick puff. 'The way they're all so adamant he's in the clear. But I say Malek has to take some of the blame. I mean, what does he think he's been playing at all summer, hanging out with a little village girl, having her stay over at his house? It's absolutely immoral. How old was she? Fifteen? Sixteen? Way under age. I'm surprised none of the locals have made a denuncia. In the States he'd have been arrested by now, even without waiting for a murder to happen.'

Georgia had started making the coffee and she was putting the coffee things onto a tray.

'Too right,' Ava joined in. 'I wouldn't put anything past Tom Malek. It's really dirty, the way he is with girls. But what I keep thinking of, it's Dita and Esteban. Losing their only daughter – sad, sad, sad! What must they be suffering, the poor things?'

In a strange way, Georgia felt as if a weight was being lifted from her.

'Unimaginable,' she answered. 'What could be worse than to lose a child?'

She went on loading the tray. 'I'd better get this coffee made,' she said, 'or they'll be sending in their complaints.'

'Let them!' said Donna haughtily. 'I'm just so fed up with their macho cynicism. This really is a town without pity!'

Georgia and Ava were nodding in agreement when the door suddenly flew open and Cristiane swept in.

'Here you are!' She looked round at each of them, quickly picking up on their collective mood. 'And what do you call this?' she demanded. 'A wake or something? Is that what it is?'

'We are sad, Cristiane, thinking about Isabel,' Ava explained.

Cristiane looked appalled.

'Oh, no, no, no! No, this will not do at all! We must be strong and keep the darkness at bay! I've already decided - it's the only way to deal with this. We must see it as something completely separate from us and absolutely rise above it. Come on Georgia, what can you be thinking of? You're keeping your guests waiting!'

She gave a little clap with her hands. 'Coffee!' she said briskly. And with another little clap, she added, 'Dépeche-toi, chérie – quick, quick!'

Georgia, Ava and Donna watched, speechless, as she turned and flounced back out to the terrace.

When she had gone, Georgia said, 'If she came to tell me my guests are waiting, then what are you two supposed to be?'

'Women,' answered Donna. 'I don't think Cristiane counts women.'

They digested this and, after a pause, Ava, flicking her waist-length hair over one shoulder, said, 'By the way, I heard she's been sleeping with Anton.'

'Only Anton?' replied Georgia. 'I heard she's been sleeping with everyone.'

'I meant as well as everyone,' Ava giggled.

Georgia kept the ball in play.

'Of course, Anton's sleeping with everyone, too,' she said.

'Ah, isn't that nice, then?' replied Ava. 'Friendly, like...'

Their giggles started afresh.

'Don't laugh,' said Donna, laughing. 'She's a monster.' Taking the tray from Georgia, she added, 'Georgia, why don't you tell her to go fuck herself?'

'Because,' replied Georgia, 'if I ever get started with Cristiane, I might not be able to stop. It wouldn't be pretty.'

'It isn't pretty now, sweetie,' Donna retorted. 'That's not the way you speak to someone in their own home.'

Georgia and Ava picked up what was left to take out to

the terrace.

'I know, Donna,' Georgia replied wearily, 'but I was brought up not to insult my guests. It would go against the grain.'

'Then I'll just have to do it for you,' Donna shot back.

The three of them walked back onto the terrace carrying the trays of coffee and cake.

'At last, ladies!' cried James. 'Where in heaven have you gorgeous young things been all this time?'

'Making your coffee, of course,' replied Ava, a little coldly.

'Why, thank you, my dear. How very, very kind of you,' he replied cheerfully, not the least put off by her apparent lack of interest.

James was the Alabama-born son of African American parents. Before his first birthday his parents had gone off to seek a better life in New York City, leaving him to be raised by his maternal grandmother. They never returned, and from as far back as he could remember, he had made it his mission to find a way out of Alabama too. In the end he found his way to Europe, working for the World Bank out of Paris. He had been invited to the island one summer by colleagues, and before the week was out he had paid cash dollars to an American writer for a little town house where he now spent as much time as possible. Santa Marta, he often said, was the nearest thing he had ever found to home.

James had a lot of style. He was amusing and good-looking with polished manners. He acted pretty macho sometimes, and he was known to be a sexual predator of the highest order. But Georgia suspected him of having more heart than he was inclined to show. She liked him because he teased her - not unkindly - and made her laugh. Some years earlier, James had had a brief affair with Ava, and that night, in the absence of any other available females, it looked as though he wasn't totally averse to the idea of resurrecting their old romance. Ava, on the other hand, was keeping her distance.

Donna, meanwhile, filled with righteous anger on Georgia's behalf, had been chopping the chocolate cake into slices with angry slashes of the knife. Between slashes, she kept raising her eyes to look over at Cristiane who was discoursing on the works of Proust, which she claimed to re-read in their entirety every summer. Finally Donna could contain herself no longer.

'Hey, Cristiane,' she called over to her imperiously.

Cristiane raised her head elegantly and gave Donna an enquiring look.

'You are so full of shit!' Donna snapped in her precise, East Coast accent. 'Why don't you go fuck yourself?'

Cristiane did not bat an eyelid.

'Darling,' she called back pleasantly, 'you know you really must try to hold your liquor. Or just quit drinking! There's a wonderful organisation designed just for people like you.' And silently she mouthed, 'AA'.

Donna's mouth dropped open into a wide O, and she looked as if she might explode. Gavin jumped in quickly.

'Joke, Donna,' he said quickly with a big smile. 'Joke!'

'Oh, ha ha, very funny,' said Donna, and picking up her full wine glass, downed the contents pointedly in one large swallow.

Georgia gave Donna a pained smile, and went on pouring the coffee. She passed a cup to Peter, who looked as though he could do with it.

Gavin was entertaining Peter and Cristiane with a story about a hotel he had stayed in on his recent trip to New York. The room above his head, apparently, been occupied by a couple of newlyweds who kept him awake for three entire nights with the bride's incessant shrieks of passion.

'He'll tire of it by the time the honeymoon's finished,' Gavin ended dryly.

'I should bloody well think he would. If it kept you awake, he must have been half deafened, poor sod,' Peter commented. He fixed his gaze on Georgia. 'Personally, I'm not keen on noisy women,' he continued. 'Georgia, for instance, now she's never been a screamer.'

By now the whole table was listening with amusement, laughing indulgently. Except Georgia.

Still smiling, Peter added, 'In fact, she's so quiet and well behaved, you'd hardly know she was there.'

Georgia blushed furiously.

'Tut, tut, Georgia,' said Cristiane. 'You must know by now that men are so easily wounded when it comes to bed. You have to put on a bit of a show, darling, to let them see you're enjoying it. And,' she added, 'I know you must be enjoying it, because I remember from old experience what an expert lover that delicious husband of yours is!'

Georgia lifted her coffee cup to her lips and said nothing. Even if she had wanted to, she would not have been capable at that moment of speaking. She was suddenly struck by the thought of how good it would be to just punch Cristiane in the face. She could feel the joy of impact in her clenched fist, and the pleasure of seeing Cristiane's perfectly applied makeup splattered all over her face. We could take a picture, she thought, and put it in her stupid gallery and pretend it was a Jackson Pollock.

As the moment passed, Georgia put her hand to her own cheek, horrified to think she could have imagined herself doing something so brutish and, worse still, actually relishing it.

Peter had been unmoved by Cristiane's little speech. But Donna could not resist jumping in.

'It's not all about playing the tart, Cristiane,' she declared. 'We don't all revel in faking our orgasms.'

Cristiane was not remotely ruffled.

'Oh, let's not fib, darling,' she replied, calmly. 'Of course we do! All I'm saying is, with some men, thank God, it isn't actually necessary.'

There followed an awkward pause, which Peter ended by reaching for a bottle and asking, 'Who'd like a brandy?'

As the bottle was passed around the table, a late guest appeared in the doorway. A thin, dark-haired youth stepped down onto the terrace, and weaved his way over to the table.

'Bonsoir, mesdames, messieurs,' he said, with a mirthless giggle.

Cristiane rose to her feet.

'Chéri, darling! How wonderful! Come, come, assieds-toi!'

The boy staggered slightly towards her, his hooded eyelids half-closed, and fell into the chair that Cristiane had quickly pulled up beside her.

'*Salut, fiston,*' Peter called to him in the aggressively cheery tone he reserved for Luc and his ilk. 'Having a good night?'

'Extremely good, thank you,' Luc replied politely.

Cristiane fluttered around him busily, pouring a cup of coffee, taking a piece of chocolate cake.

'Here, darling,' she said, placing both in front of him. 'Come, do have something to eat.' She picked up the cake and tried to feed it to him. Luc waved it away.

From the other end of the table, Georgia asked, 'Luc, would you like me to get you a proper helping of something?'

Luc got to his feet and bowed slightly to Georgia. He pushed a long, dark lock back from his forehead and peered in Georgia's direction as if he was having trouble focussing.

'Non, merci,' he replied in a drunkenly pompous, schoolboy manner. 'I have already partaken well, ha ha -' he wobbled on his legs and collapsed back into his chair.

Cristiane was still bustling, gathering together her bag, cigarettes, lighter.

'Alas, mes amis,' she announced, 'we must take our leave.'

Rising from the table, she encouraged Luc to his feet. But suddenly, without warning, he switched. His eyes took on a dangerous look, and he pushed his mother's hand roughly from his arm.

'Let go of me, you monkey!' he shouted. 'You old ape!' And with that he started jumping up and down in front of her, making grotesque monkey-gestures, scratching under his arms and uttering childish monkey-noises - 'woo-oo-oo, woo-oo-oo,' - while everyone watched, waiting to see what would happen next.

Cristiane stood quite still, her expression unreadable. Then, without warning, she raised her hand and brought it down hard across his face. He immediately burst into tears.

'Why?' he wept. 'Why do have to go? We can stay here. We'll be safe here, won't we, Peter? Tell her, I have to stay. Peter, Peter -'.

Cristiane took his arm again and as she did so, Luc let out a deafening screech.

'I want to stay here!' he shouted. 'I have to stay here! I hate you! I'm not going with you. I refuse!' and with that he ran from the table, into the entrada where he collapsed in a heap on the floor.

'One too many,' said Gavin. 'Let me help you with him, Cristiane. It's late - we ought to be making a move, too.'

Together, they lifted the boy to his feet and tried to assist him as he struggled pathetically into the back of Cristiane's long, black Citroen. Georgia watched them from the doorway.

'That's not just drink,' she thought. 'That boy needs help. God knows we've seen him drunk often enough, but tonight he seemed frightened. Something's scared him. Cristiane should have let him stay. Why did she have to insist on taking him with her? It would have been much better to have left him here.'

She watched as Cristiane started up the car, wishing she had had the presence of mind to intervene earlier. Too late now, she thought.

'Don't worry about us,' Cristiane was saying to Gavin.

Peter stood back and watched, slightly hunched, his hands thrust deep into his pockets. Probably having problems staying upright, Georgia thought.

'We'll be fine,' she heard Cristiane calling brightly. 'Boyish pranks, that's all!'

Gavin came over to say goodnight, and stooping down, embraced Georgia warmly.

''Night, Georgia,' he said. He watched with her as Cristiane drove off, Luc still making a commotion in the back. 'There goes an accident waiting to happen,' he remarked.

Georgia just nodded. What was there to say?

Gradually, the rest of the dinner guests rose from the table, and began to say their good-nights.

'Tatty-bye, Georgia,' said Ava, staggering slightly.

'How are you getting home?' Georgia asked her.

'This nice man's taking me,' she said, with a slightly tipsy smile at James. She seemed to have overcome her earlier aversion.

James enfolded Georgia in a huge bear-hug.

'Good-night, your Ladyship,' he said, 'and sweet dreams.' His expression became serious. 'And Georgia,' he said, 'don't let this shit prey on your mind.'

'It is preying,' she admitted, her thoughts instantly flashing to the murdered girl.

'I guessed. But you let this kind of thing psyche you out, you become a victim yourself. Let it go!'

Georgia automatically took a deep breath and hugged him back.

'I'll do my best,' she said.

'Good girl. And I'll tell you something else, you lovely creature. You listening?'

He looked at her hard and Georgia wondered what was coming next.

'I am,' she said.

'Then it's this: don't hang out at Esteban's – it's bad for the health. You hear me?'

His words took Georgia by surprise. What a strange thing to say! After what had happened, how likely was it that Esteban and Dita would even open the place, at least for a while? But she answered him anyway.

'I hear you, James,' she said.

'Then goodnight, my dear, and thank you for a beautiful evening!'

Georgia stood back and waved as they all drove off, wondering guiltily whether James was referring to her afternoon in the Puerto with Matt. Santa Marta, she knew, was a terrible place to keep a secret.

*

'What was James saying to you?' Peter had walked over to where Georgia stood.

'He said not to let the murder prey on my mind.'

'Not so easy, though, is it?'

'No.'

They walked back to the table on the terrace and Georgia started to pick up the plates and cups. Peter perched on the edge of the table.

'Why don't you leave all that?' he said. 'Antonia can do it in the morning.'

'Don't be silly,' Georgia replied. 'If I leave it out, it'll all be covered in ants in half an hour.'

He got off the table and came up behind her, putting his arms around her waist.

'So?' he said. 'She can hose it all down.' He was drunk, and unwelcomely amorous. Georgia pulled away from him.

'Leave me alone, Peter,' she said

She turned around to face him, and seeing her uninterested expression he hit out with one arm, flinging the things she was carrying from her hands, sending it all crashing to the ground. A stray cat that had been prowling under the table let out a terrified meeow! and fled up the closest tree

Georgia jumped back from the broken crockery.

'How much longer is this going to go on?' she shouted. 'How long are you going to go on behaving like this? You're such a bloody bully! I hate you!'

Peter banged his fist on the table and sent a few more cups flying.

'D'you think I don't know you hate me? It's clear as fucking daylight you hate me! That's why we don't have any goddam sex life anymore! I'm a married man and I have no fucking sex life because I've got a frigid fucking wife!'

Georgia backed away from him, moving towards the house. He grabbed her arm and pushed her down into one of the chairs. Half sitting on the edge of the table, he leaned over her unsteadily. His breath was heavy with brandy and black tobacco, and she had to make a conscious effort not to recoil.

'Sit down – I want to talk about this now!' he said menacingly.

'Well, I don't want to talk about it. I don't want to talk to you about anything.'

'I don't care what you want – I want to know why we don't have a sex life anymore!' He was shouting and Georgia was sure his voice could be heard throughout the valley. It could certainly be heard by the men keeping watch at the front door.

'Will you please keep your voice down?' Georgia pleaded. 'The Guardia are still there.'

'Fuck the Guardia. I want an answer.'

Georgia could see that he was not going to give up. He was too drunk to be reasonable. She was flustered and stumbled over her words.

'Peter, you already know the answer,' she said. 'You know that ever since I came out of hospital, since I lost the -'

'For Christ's sake!' Peter yelled in her face. 'Give me a break! So you had a miscarriage! Women are always having miscarriages - they don't all go off and become nuns! They don't all stop sleeping with their husbands!'

Georgia's face crumpled. She steeled herself not to cry in front of him again, but the shock of his words seemed to vibrate though her whole being.

It looked as though he had even shocked himself. At any event, he stopped shouting and got up from the table.

'Ah, forget it,' he said. 'I'll go and sleep in my study. I've had enough too.'

He stood looking at Georgia for a moment, but she wouldn't look back at him. He gave up and stormed off into the house.

After what seemed like a long, long time, Georgia got up from her chair and walked towards the edge of the terrace. She eased herself into the crook of an ancient olive tree and looked out towards the mountains. The sky was streaked with mauve and clear, limpid blue, the first light of dawn.

'It's tomorrow,' thought Georgia. 'A brand new day.'

She watched for a little while longer, and found herself uttering a short remembered prayer.

'Eternal rest give unto her, O Lord, and let perpetual light shine upon her ...'

She felt comforted, soothed, and wondered why she did not pray more often. She had lost the habit of prayer. Now it only occurred to her to pray in times of crisis, and sometimes not even then. This suddenly seemed like a terrible loss, another part of herself that had dropped off somewhere along the years with Peter; years that had begun with so much joyful expectation, but had brought them to such a miasma of unhappiness.

'But now it changes,' she assured herself.

Close by, an owl emitted its eerie call, and a few moments later Georgia caught sight of it, swooping into the wooded valley on widespread wings.

She went up to her room, laid down on her bed, and immediately fell into a deep, exhausted sleep.

CHAPTER SEVEN

Georgia woke from troubled, murky dreams to sparkling sunlight and the intermittent clanking of sheep bells. She stretched and yawned and rolled onto her back. She had fallen asleep in the dress she had been wearing the night before, and the soft silky material felt like rose petals against her skin. Still sprawled across the bed, she let her head fall back so that her hair flowed over the edge, and as she reached back to run her hands through it, the silk brushed softly against her nipples. She felt them tighten and harden, tingling under the caress of the fabric. She ran her hands over her breasts, enjoying the feeling of arousal that instantly spread down, deep into her body. Unbidden, her mind returned to the previous afternoon, sitting by the sea, her feet dangling in the water. And to the man sitting beside her. And in her mind, it was his hands caressing her breasts; she could almost feel his lips brushing against hers, his body pressed against her body. Her heart began to race and her whole being seemed to come alive with longing. Then, quickly, she rolled onto her front and buried her head in her arms.

'I mustn't think about him like that,' she told herself.

'Why not?' a voice inside her head demanded.

'I just mustn't,' she answered, and jumping up, she grabbed her dressing gown and ran to the bathroom to shower. For several minutes she stood there with the water flowing over her, basking in the warmth and steam as it massaged her into life. It made her feel inexplicably grateful and happy.

'The benison of hot water...' she chanted to herself, trying to remember where the phrase came from. Then, turning the temperature gauge, she gasped as hot turned to cold and set her scalp and skin tingling. Finishing a shower with a burst of cold toned the skin, she had heard. Since turning twenty-six, Georgia had started to take notice of tips like that.

The shower left her feeling fresher, more alert. She dressed quickly in loose white cotton drawstring trousers and a light blue camisole. Still fastening her bracelets and slipping on her rings, she ran lightly downstairs in her bare feet. There was no sign of Peter. On the kitchen table lay a note from Antonia saying that she had gone back to her house and that she would return in the afternoon. Georgia walked out onto the terrace, and her heart gave a jump.

There, sitting with his back to her and seemingly engrossed in the contents of the local newspaper, was Tom Malek.

Georgia, completely nonplussed, could only stand and stare at the back of his head. Malek, sensing her presence, turned in his chair and eyed her casually up and down.

'Looking good, Georgia,' he said

For a second she hoped that he was a product of her hangover, a remnant of her bad dream. To get to the terrace where he was sitting, you had to walk right through the house. Did that mean he had been roaming around on his own while she was getting showered and dressed?

'Who let you in?' she asked abruptly.

'I let myself in. The door was open.'

'You mean unlocked.'

'Isn't that what I said?

'You have such a nerve! You know exactly what I mean. You should have knocked.'

'But, Georgia, your house is my house! Peter told me. In Spanish.'

Georgia turned to walk back into the house and wondered what could possibly be going on. Where were the Guardia? Why hadn't they arrested him, or at least taken him in for questioning? She stopped and looked back at him. His face was not wearing its usual roguish look, despite his banter. He looked tired and haggard, his eyes red-rimmed. She was surprised to find herself feeling slightly sorry for him.

'Do you want some coffee?' she asked him.

'Why, Georgia, you remembered your manners!'

Georgia could have kicked herself for imagining that he was in need of sympathy, and she marched off to the kitchen with Malek following behind.

He watched as she ground the coffee beans, filled the Jolly and put it on to boil. The smell of fresh coffee quickly filled the room.

Malek leaned against a wall, his arms folded against his chest, and looked down at his feet.

'You know about Isabel?' His voice was strained and rasping. He took a pack of cigarettes from the pocket of his denim work shirt. There was one left, which he held to his lips and lit. Georgia watched him, as he crumpled the empty pack in his hand.

'Of course,' she replied. 'The Guardia came yesterday. And Antonia was with Maria when she found the body.'

Malek exhaled a thick stream of smoke.

'I found out a few hours ago. I flew into Palma on a night flight. The Guardia grabbed me as I came through. Immigration had my name on their list.'

'Where were you?' Georgia asked.

'Where was I coming back from? From Kent,' he said.

'Kent?'

'Sure. I'm thinking of getting myself a country pad in England. Peter says Kent's a great place. Don't you think it's a good idea, Georgia?'

Georgia was not interested in Malek's property deals.

'So you were in England,' she said, trying to put the facts, such as she understood them, together. 'That explains -'

'Yeah. I should've been back a couple of days ago, but I kind of got held up. Peter knew I was away. Someone had to, with the whole situation down at the house. Peter was the only one I could trust.'

'What situation?'

'Just that Isabel was down there on her own. Dita had gotten into a rage and kicked her out. She didn't want to go to Esteban – he was mad at her, too. She pleaded with me to let her stay at the house while I was away. But I was feeling like it wasn't a great idea for her to be there alone.'

'Why wasn't it? I mean, obviously, you were right, it wasn't. But why did you think that?'

Malek didn't answer. The Jolly started to hiss and Georgia poured the steaming coffee out into big green breakfast cups. Malek's eyes searched her face, and finding what he was looking for, he said, 'They're holding someone, the Guardia.'

'Already!' Georgia exclaimed. 'Why didn't you say? Who is it?'

The first thought that entered her head was, where was Peter? And the next thought, self-accusing, was how could her mind leap like that, how could she think, even for a second, that he was in any way involved? Confusion claimed her powers of reason, and she stared wildly at Malek as she waited for his answer.

Malek, for his part, observed her with interest. A serious people-watcher, Georgia was one of his favourite subjects. He saw how tense she was, and enjoyed the knowledge that he had managed to give her a bit of a jolt. Malek arranged his features into an innocently impassive expression, gazing steadily at Georgia until she was obliged to speak again.

Working hard to control her voice, she asked, 'Who have they got?'

He stubbed out his cigarette. He had guessed the reason for her embarrassment. For a moment there, she had suspected Peter. In Malek's mind, myriad possibilities exploded. He knew, of course, that they were having a bad time. He had heard Peter shouting at her. But now he wondered, had he ever harmed her? Thinking about this, his desire to taunt her dissipated.

'Hey, is all this bad stuff freaking you out, Georgia?' he asked almost kindly.

She looked at him as if he was mad. Yeah, he thought, like I'm the one she'd confide in!

'Hey, it's OK, Georgia. Guess I'm the one who's all messed up. That was some home-coming.'

'Have you been to the house?'

'Sure. With full police escort. They found a little stash – nothing much, a couple of tabs of acid, a little pot. Not mine, baby. I have no interest in the view from inside a Spanish gaol.'

'It must have been horrific.'

'You bet.'

Georgia collected her thoughts, and poured some more coffee.

'You still haven't told me who they've got,' she said.

'Like to try a guess?'

'It's not a game, Tom,' she said. She felt as if her nerves had been shredded and she hated him for deliberately holding out. 'Why don't you just tell me?'

The front door slammed as she waited for Malek to speak, and seconds later Peter was standing in the kitchen in front of her.

Malek straightened up. 'How did it go?' he asked Peter.

'I was fucking shitting myself,' Peter replied. 'Those guys don't mess about.'

'It's the Guardia, man,' Malek shrugged, and then asked, 'Did they charge him?'

'As far as I know. The clothes he had with him were covered in blood. They didn't find the weapon. They're still looking for it.'

'He's confessed?'

'All I know is that he went in there and gave himself up. A couple of the fishermen saw him going to the house at the time he said he had. Which was around the time it happened.'

He turned to Georgia.

'The Guardia were here early, again,' he told her. 'Someone thought they'd seen my car down by Tom's house the night Isabel was killed.'

Georgia looked at him but did not speak.

'It was the night I went to C'an Pepe with Carl, remember? I thought Tom was going to be back in time for dinner?'

She nodded.

'I was with them at the police station when he arrived.'

'Who? When who arrived?' she asked for what felt like the hundredth time.

Peter and Malek exchanged looks. Malek shook his head.

Peter took a deep breath and blew it out again, hard.

'Esteban,' he said to Georgia.

'Esteban? Esteban killed Isabel?'

'I don't know, Georgia. This is what I picked up. The Guardia didn't go and tell Esteban and Dita about the murder until late yesterday afternoon. They found Esteban at the restaurant. He broke up, collapsed. They had to get a doctor out to him. After that, they left him - I think Dita was there with him by then - and then they went on with their enquiries, which at seven o'clock this morning led them to me. They'd already picked Tom up at the airport.'

'I didn't hear anything,' Georgia said.

Malek gave her a searching look, but Peter let the remark pass.

'Tom was there at the police station when I arrived. Then they hauled in Carl and a few of the people who were at Pepe's to confirm my story. They were just about to take

Tom back to the house when Esteban staggered in, shouting that it was him. He had a cesta full of blood-stained clothes. They took him off on his own to speak to him at that point, and kept me hanging around until half an hour ago. They forgot about me in the excitement.'

As if from far away, Georgia heard a phone ringing. Peter heard it, too, and left the room to answer it.

Georgia looked at Malek, but he was suddenly busy with his cup of coffee. Typical, she thought. He had been with Peter that morning. Virtually everything Peter had just told them, Malek already knew. But he had strung it out, watching, no doubt, her reactions, playing his old games. He had said the situation down in his house was bad for Isabel, that Peter was the only one he could trust. What the hell did that mean? Peter, as usual, was guarded, impossible to read. Georgia seethed as she continued to stare at Malek.

'Something wrong, Georgia?' he asked, suddenly looking up.

Georgia didn't answer. Whatever she said would be the wrong thing at that moment. She was trying to decide what to do next when something clattered noisily onto the stone floor. It was the heavy silver slave bracelet she had been wearing. It had come unfastened and fallen from her wrist. Malek walked over to where she was sitting, picked up the bracelet and clasped it back on for her. Georgia was pulling her hand away just as Peter walked back into the room. He looked at her quizzically, but she couldn't be bothered to explain.

'Who was that?' she asked.

'Jonathan,' he told her and then, turning to Malek, explained, 'My agent in London.'

'What did he want?' Georgia asked.

'The contracts are ready for the New Mexico film. I have to get back to London to go through them with him, and then straight on to California to meet with the people from the studio. I'm going to try to get on a flight today if I can.'

'Today?'

'Yes, today. What do you want to do?' he asked Georgia.

Thinking quickly, she felt the matrimonial chains dropping from her as the slave bracelet had fallen a few minutes earlier. This time she would not allow anyone to replace them. Georgia scented freedom, and it was heady and strong.

'I'll stay here,' she answered.

Peter looked strained and displeased.

'That's not a good idea, Georgia.'

'Why not? It wouldn't be the first time you've had to go away and leave me here.'

'No, but this time's different. You know that.'

Malek joined in the argument.

'Yeah, Georgia, Peter's right. You shouldn't stay here alone.'

Georgia turned on him furiously.

'Keep out of it – it's nothing to do with you!' she snapped.

Seeing that Georgia was on a short fuse, Peter stepped in to try and cool things down.

'Georgia, listen to me. What if it wasn't Esteban? What if there's some lunatic out there that we don't know about?'

'But Esteban's confessed... the clothes... he was seen down there... you said...'

'Yes, yes.' Peter was treading a fine line. There were so many things he hadn't told Georgia.

'All right, then. What about getting a friend to come and stay with you while I'm away? Tamsin or someone?'

'Yeah,' added Malek.

Peter felt like tearing his hair out. He knew Malek could not resist winding Georgia up. Normally he found it amusing, but now was not the best time. Time – he really had to hurry.

'Look, Georgia, do what you like, but I've got to go. This is the only solid thing I've got going for me right now and I have to move with it. Are you sure you won't come with me?'

'Positive.'

'Well just don't say I didn't try to protect you.'

'Protect me?' Georgia laughed hollowly.

Then she turned and walked out of the room, leaving Peter and Malek alone, in very different states of mind. Malek enjoyed being around for glimpses of other people's private moments, especially those of married couples. He himself had never been married, never been in a long-term relationship with a woman. They were situations that fascinated, but never tempted him.

Peter, on the other hand, felt something close to despair. His instincts told him not to leave Georgia alone, but he was exasperated and he had no heart for another fight. If she insisted on being the abandoned wife, he thought, then so be it. Maybe it was time to let go.

Eventually, he walked out to the terrace where she was sitting in the crook of an olive tree.

'Has he gone?' she asked

'Yes.'

She thought for a moment. 'Where's he going to stay?' she asked. 'He can't go back to his house.'

'No. I think he's going to shack up at James' place. Georgia -' Peter was not sure how to tell her the things he needed her to know. The vibe he was getting off her was so closed and unreceptive; so angry.

'Georgia, you know I've got to go?'

'So you say.'

'I have to sort out the travel.' Normally, he would have asked her to make the arrangements for him but now – well, everything had changed, and he found himself unable to ask.

Georgia, who had been staring out at the scenery, turned to face him.

'Will you be allowed to go?' she asked. 'I mean, in the middle of a murder investigation and everything?

'Good point,' he parried. 'I'll have to check with the police, but I still want to book my flight and try to get off today. I've been waiting for this call for a couple of weeks and I can't afford to hold things up at the London end. I don't want to lose this deal, Georgia.'

Georgia bit her lip. She hesitated for a moment, and then asked, 'Why does it feel like there's something you're not telling me?'

Now it was Peter's turn to hesitate, to hold back, wondering how much it was safe to say. Weighing it all up quickly, he decided to take what he assessed to be the least risky option. He could not pretend there was nothing being hidden at all.

'I was going to try to get on the night flight. If I can't get on that, I should be able to get a seat on the late flight over to Barcelona, and then the early one from there to London.'

Georgia waited.

'The thing is Georgia, I need to stop off in Palma and see Cristiane.'

He watched Georgia's face cloud over. He knew how she felt about Cristiane, but now he had to continue. But carefully: it was all so delicate. He was afraid of how Georgia would react. If only he could have her on his side right now. Part of him knew that if he appealed to her honestly, Georgia would help him. It was one of the things he admired about her, her ability to respond to someone in trouble.

But at the same time he could not bring himself to believe that her sympathy would extend to him. The risk of rejection was small, he knew, but still, it was a risk his amour propre would not allow him to take. He decided to compromise with the truth, well aware that it could cost him Georgia's valuable support and, quite possibly, more than that.

'Why?' Georgia asked, trying to keep the ill-feeling out of her voice.

'It's about Luc.'

'Oh?'

'You saw the state he was in last night...'

'It's hardly the first time he's thrown a tantrum.'

Peter thought again. Should I tell her? If he told her, there was a chance she might reconsider her decision and go with him to London. He had a strong feeling that if he went away without her, it could be the end for them. But there was something else. If he told Georgia what he had to tell Cristiane, it could endanger her legally. She could become an accessory. He made up his mind: for her own sake, it was better Georgia did not know.

'True,' Peter replied. 'But all the same, she had her hands full with him last night, and I think the drink and drugs might be getting out of control. A couple of his school mates were expelled last term for dealing pot. Someone's got to take him in hand.'

Georgia shook her head. 'I don't see how that someone can be you. You're just off to make a film in New Mexico. You're not thinking of taking him with you, are you?'

Well, that's that, then, thought Peter. He could not see a way to backtrack to a point from which it would be possible to tell her the truth.

Despondently, he replied, 'No, of course not. I just want to talk it through with her. Let her know I'm there for them if they need it.'

'I see,' she said. And now, she thought, please let this insulting conversation stop.

In the vacant silence that hung between them, a thought arose in Georgia's mind.

'One thing I'd like to ask you to do,' she started.

'Oh, yes?' Peter responded hopefully.

'Randall,' she continued. 'Could you please ask him not to come while you're away?'

The pale flicker of light died in Peter's eyes.

'He's still clearing that lower terrace,' he replied in a thin, tired voice. 'I wanted him to finish it.'

Georgia's voice almost trembled, a sign of the effort involved in mustering the will to persuade Peter of the validity of her request.

'Peter, I can't bear him,' she pleaded.

Peter sighed. 'He's absolutely harmless,' he said. 'And you don't have to interact with him. He knows what he has to do. Just pay him and let him get on with it.'

'How do you know he's harmless?' she demanded.

Peter grasped his head ferociously, his teeth clenched.

'Georgia, why do you do this?' It sounded like a snarl, he was straining so hard not to raise his voice. 'You drive me to the fucking brink! Look, you don't have to stay here. We've been through it. You can come with me or go to London. But if you choose,' - he pointed a finger at her to emphasise his words - '*you* choose - to stay here, then you've got to take responsibility for managing the situation, and that includes Randall. There's a reason why that terrace has to be cleared and I want it done by the end of this month.'

Georgia decided to stand her ground.

'What reason?' she asked.

'Does it matter?'

'Yes it does.'

'Okay. If I'm going to be doing this film – and I am going to be doing it – I'll be away for six months or more. I've been thinking of maybe letting the house out for the duration.'

'What?'

'Come on, Georgia – you haven't been happy in Santa Marta for a long time. Don't tell me you suddenly care what happens to the house.'

'Of course I care - I live here! Anyway, who would you let it to?'

'There's someone, a guy who saw the spread in Vogue. You know, the thing you couldn't see the point of...'

'Oh, was that the point?'

Peter sighed. 'There wasn't a point. It was an opportunity, that's all.'

Peter suddenly looked up at the house, shading his eyes with one hand.

'Is Antonia here?' he asked.

'No,' Georgia answered. 'She's visiting her cousin, Magdalena. Why?'

Peter, still peering upwards, replied, 'Just thought I saw someone at that end window up there...'

'You couldn't have,' Georgia said, also looking up. 'That's the big spare room. Antonia never goes in there unless someone's coming to stay. It's under dust sheets.'

'Must've been a trick of the light, then,'

They looked at each other, both suddenly exhausted and overwhelmed by the weight of their emotions.

'Anyway,' Georgia started to ask, 'sounds like you won't be wanting me to drive you to the airport?'

'No.' Peter was quite emphatic. 'But I want to get moving. You could drive me down to the Puerto and I'll get a taxi to Palma from there.'

'Fine.' Georgia's mind was elsewhere, busily re-thinking her own schedule.

'Georgia?' Peter started again. 'When I get back, let's try and talk rationally. Work things out.'

Georgia nodded, knowing that she had no such intention. Peter might be the one who was catching the plane, but Georgia had already flown.

CHAPTER EIGHT

Georgia pulled up at the railway station in the little port. After loading the cab with his luggage, Peter gave her a tentative hug and kissed her cheek.

'Sure you want to stay here? No shame in having a change of heart,' he told her.

'I'll be all right. Really,' she replied.

Peter's expression softened.

'You're looking very pretty,' he said.

Georgia said nothing; she just smiled slightly.

'I'm sorry, Georgia,' he said. 'I'm really sorry for the way it's been. What d'you think? Is it too late for us?'

Georgia had not expected the question. She thought for a moment.

'I don't know,' she said. 'I feel as if it's all slipped away. I don't even know exactly how or why anymore. It just feels like there's nothing left, it's all gone.'

Georgia blinked back the tears that were filling up her eyes.

'I still love you, Georgia,' Peter said. 'Believe it or not.'

Georgia looked up at him, bewildered by the mix of emotions she was feeling; longing for him to go, hating to say goodbye.

'Have a good journey,' she said at last. 'I hope it all goes well.'

'Thanks.' Peter climbed into the back seat of the taxi.

'Take good care of yourself,' he said.

'I will.'

The taxi pulled away and Peter turned round to wave to her from the window. She waved back, and stood watching until he disappeared from sight.

*

Georgia took a deep breath and walked over to the hotel where Matt was staying. She found him seated at a table out at the back by the swimming pool. He was browsing through the pages of a guide book. She sat down on the chair next to his, and his face creased into a huge smile.

'I was looking up Santa Marta,' he said.

'What does it say?'

Matt pushed his chair closer to Georgia's, so that they could look at the book together. For some minutes it kept them occupied, turning the pages and reading bits out to each other, Georgia commenting on places depicted in the photographs while Matt asked questions. At last, he closed the book and laid it down on the table in front of them.

The conversation petered out, and the two of them sat there slightly awkwardly. Georgia wanted to speak. She felt she should say something, but words would not come. All her attention seemed to be concentrated on the awareness of his presence. Matt himself was painfully lost for words.

'Nice dress,' he ventured at last.

Georgia had changed into a light, pink cotton dress, tied loosely at the waist. The delicate fabric followed the contours of her body and Matt could hardly take his eyes off it.

'Oh, do you like it?' she asked.

Matt, embarrassed by his attack of gaucheness, had lost the thread.

'Sorry?' he asked. 'Do I like what?'

'Er, my dress?' Georgia replied, slightly confused.

'Your dress! Yes,' he said, and found himself adding, 'good colour.'

'Mmm, pink,' said Georgia, with an amused smile.

Matt banged his knuckles against his skull.

'It's the sun,' he said. 'Let's just put it down to the sun. And the fact that I'm a bit of an idiot...'

Georgia laughed. He was so different to the men she was used to, the men in Santa Marta.

'So listen,' he tried again. 'Providing you feel able to put up with my company for a little longer, can I offer you a drink?' he asked.

'No thanks,' she replied, still smiling.

'The company or the drink?'

'Yes to the company, no to the drink.'

'OK, that's good. That's very good. What about a walk then? Would you like to take a walk around the port?'

Georgia nodded her assent, and they got up and left the hotel side by side. The heat was pleasantly broken up by a light breeze coming off the sea. Matt put a guiding hand on the small of Georgia's back as they crossed the road. His touch registered like an electric charge.

Walking past the quays, they came to a low wall overlooking the little beach of boulders and sand. Georgia sat down on the edge of it and looked out at the sea, dark misty blue, mysterious, as it faded out towards the horizon. Matt stood beside her, also looking out, wondering what it was she was seeing, or hoping to see. He noticed with consternation that her face had changed. It seemed that all her earlier gaiety had deserted her, leaving her looking serious and closed in. When she spoke, it was haltingly.

'Something really bad has happened, Matt,' she said, without looking at him.

He waited, not knowing what to say, hoping against hope that whatever the something was, it was not going to completely scatter the bright little drops of happiness that had started to coalesce for them only a few minutes earlier.

'The girl I told you about yesterday – the daughter of the bar owner?' Georgia went on.

'Isabel, was that the one?'

'Yes, Isabel.'

Matt had a flashback to breakfast that morning. At the next table, two middle aged women were exclaiming over an article in the English language daily, The Bulletin.

'Well you don't expect it on holiday, do you?' one woman was saying to the other. 'Drugs and hippies and sex maniacs and I don't know what. You can't get away from them these days. And these young girls, the parents have no control anymore, they don't know what to do with them...'

'It's a disgrace, a down right disgrace,' her companion had responded. 'It spoils it for all the decent folk who just want to enjoy a bit of peace and quiet. Well, she had it coming, if you ask me, and I only hope some of these others like her will take their lesson from it.'

'Oh, Eileen,' her friend had replied. 'That is being harsh. Not that I don't know what you mean. But think on it, dear, she was only a young girl - sixteen it said. And you can't say that anyone deserved *that*. No, it's these hippies and drug addicts that's the problem. Oh, put that paper down, dear, it's too bad for words. Let's go and get ready for our trip to the glass factory. They're giving us a nice picnic lunch to take with us. Now there's something to look forward to!'

The two women had heaved themselves up from the table and, handbags over their arms, made their way out to the terrace.

After they had gone, Matt reached over and picked up the offending newspaper.

Local girl murdered in holiday villa, ran the headline. And below, it screeched, *Frenzied attack by maniac.*

There was a bleary photograph of a white crenulated house surrounded by palm trees with the subtitle, *The exquisite C'an Alora, better known locally as the 'House of*

Drugs'.

It had just looked like typical hyped-up tabloid rubbish at the time. In any case, his thoughts were elsewhere; on Georgia, to be precise. He had no interest in holiday scandal sheets. Now, without knowing how or why, he sensed a grim connection between what he had heard and seen at breakfast and what Georgia was trying to tell him.

'Some people in the hotel were talking this morning. Something about a local girl found murdered in some holiday villa. It was in the paper.'

Georgia turned to look at him.

'That's it,' she said. 'The murdered girl – it was Isabel. The girl we were talking about. Esteban's daughter.'

'God, is that right?' he exclaimed, remembering the bar owner's face before they left, his sudden concern for their own safety. The man had looked so unhinged.

'I don't know what to say,' he stuttered. 'It's hard to take in. I mean, only yesterday we were… Have they caught whoever did it?'

'Esteban's confessed.'

'The father? The guy at the bar?'

Georgia closed her eyes for a moment.

'In the past,' she said, 'that kind of thing happened here. An honour killing, they called it, when a girl disgraced her family. But it's not something you imagine happening in this day and age. In any case, not in that family. They're not a typical Mallorcan family at all – Dita's from the mainland and she lived in London for a few years before she and Esteban got married. And they've lived separately for a while, but of course they still had Isabel and the bar… We're all in shock, Matt. Antonia, who works in our house, she was there when the maid, Maria, found the body.'

'The paper said something about the place where she was found, that it was called the house of drugs?'

Georgia swallowed. 'Tom Malek's house - the American I told you about? It's a nightmare. Even my husband was taken in for questioning.'

'You're kidding -'

'No. We've had the Guardia Civil sitting outside our house for two days. Many of the people I know have been questioned. It's turning our lives upside down.'

He listened attentively, without interrupting, but beneath the surface, he was in turmoil. Since their first meeting, he had found himself thinking about Georgia obsessively, wondering if she really would return, amazed at his own audacity in imagining that she could actually want to see him again. Now here she was, beside him, and again the inner confusion made it difficult for him to judge how to respond. How could so much have happened in twenty-four hours? This was heavy, and he had no idea what was expected of him. And then there was Georgia's mood; she seemed really distressed, overwrought, so different from the day before. He thought carefully before speaking.

'But now,' he said, 'now that there's been a confession, that should be it, right?'

'What, over and done with?'

'No, I didn't mean that. Of course not.'

They got up from the wall and walked in silence for a while. As they drew parallel with a sleek motor launch, a girl with a pony tail, dressed in tight-fitting shorts and a strapless top walked by them and then climbed the steps leading up to the deck of the boat. Matt's eyes followed her, and as they passed, he turned his head, attracted as much by the boat as the girl's revealing outfit. He turned back to Georgia, but she had slipped away from him, and he had to quicken his step to keep up with her.

'Georgia?' he called.

But she just kept walking, away from the boats, back towards the road.

'Georgia?' His voice was strained.

'I should get back,' she answered abruptly.

She was shutting him out, and he did not know what to do. Without another word being spoken, they found themselves in front of his hotel. They stopped for a moment.

He searched her face, but she wouldn't look at him.

'Please don't go yet,' he begged. Still she didn't speak or look.

I've blown it, I've blown it, he thought, flailing around for some way to stop her going.

'Look, Georgia, if you're free this evening – I was thinking – maybe we could do something?'

Georgia turned to face him at last, but her expression was unreadable.

'Like what?' she asked, her voice cool and distant.

No, don't do this to me, he pleaded silently. He decided to abandon any attempt to apologise or justify. He would have to trust to instinct. Having got it all so stupidly wrong, he figured, he could hardly make it worse. He took both her hands in his.

'Come with me,' he asked, and still holding one of her hands, led her into the hotel, through the lobby and into a small lounge furnished with overstuffed, chintz-covered armchairs. It had the look and ambience of a dentist's waiting room, but at least it was empty.

'Time isn't on my side,' he said.

Georgia watched him impassively.

'I'm going back to London,' he continued. 'If I had more time, maybe I wouldn't be saying this now. Meeting you has meant a lot to me, Georgia. If there's any hope that we could spend more time together, then that's what I want to do. There's nothing else about being in this place that means anything me. I know I'm way out of my depth, but tell me, is there any possibility?'

Georgia felt her resolve melting. Her hurt pride ceased to sting quite so sharply and her doubts subsided. She, too, was in uncharted territory. Her head told her to go straight back home and forget all about him, but in some deeper place she knew that it was already too late for that. She decided to take a leap into the unknown.

'Yes,' she said, and he hugged her to him, and Georgia yielded to his hug.

After a moment, she drew back a little and said, 'Would you like to see Santa Marta tonight?'

'I'd love to see Santa Marta tonight!'

'I've got a couple of things I have to do. Do you think you could find your way to my house? You've got the guide book, haven't you? When you get to Santa Marta, just ask for Casa Dura. Oh, and bring a torch! You'll need it for the track up from the road. Come at about eight?'

'I'll be there,' Matt replied.

Georgia drove along the tortuous, twisting mountain road as if it were an empty highway, hardly noticing the bends or the other cars. She headed straight for Tamsin's, effortlessly, easily. In spite of everything, her spirits soared.

CHAPTER NINE

Tamsin was frantic. While Poppy lay screaming in her cot in the bedroom, Tamsin sat on the floor of her sitting room clutching her head and trying to think. Poppy's high decibel wailing was making it impossible for her to focus at all.

'Shut up, Poppy, bloody shut up!' she shouted, and threw a cushion at the door that led to the bedroom. Miraculously, Poppy's screaming ceased, and Tamsin was instantly filled with remorse.

She rose to her feet and walked quietly to the bedroom door. Opening it, she peeped inside. Poppy, transfixed by the shapes and shadows made by the sunlight shining through a lace curtain onto the wall opposite her cot, was cooing and waving happily. Tamsin's heart welled over with love, and she longed to pick Poppy up and cover her with kisses. But, knowing that there was no counting on the current peace and quiet lasting very long, Tamsin crept out and pulled the door to.

Picking up the cushion she had thrown, she sat down again, this time on the divan which, covered in a richly-woven Tunisian blanket, served as a sofa. Tamsin thumped her fist repeatedly into the cushion.

'Why, why, why?' she screamed silently. 'What am I going to do? What am I going to do?'

She tried to calm her thoughts. It's hardly the first big

mess I've ever been in, she thought, though this did not do much to ease her state of panic. She straightened her back and took a couple of deep breaths. And I've always found a way out. I've always survived, she told herself. Certain situations, like her recent divorce, had taken a lot of bottle. Sometimes luck or fate, or whatever you wanted to call it, had come to the rescue. Sometimes she had simply run away. Escaped.

But that was then, in the days before there had been a baby, a Poppy to consider. And it wasn't only Poppy's existence; it was the change motherhood had wrought in Tamsin herself. She could not brush things away any longer. Her old veneer of toughness she saw for what it was, just a veneer. She could still summon it up when required, but now it was an act, not a fact.

Suddenly Tamsin felt sick. A wave of nausea rolled over her and passed, leaving her feeling limp and weak. 'Oh no!' she whispered to herself. Tamsin picked the cushion up again, and holding it against her face, she wept quietly.

Exhausted as she was, Tamsin eventually cried herself to sleep. She lay curled up on the divan, her head still buried in the cushion, for nearly an hour.

When she woke up, all was quiet. She shook herself from her torpor and looked around in a dazed sort of way. Her head was still full of dreams, fragmented images of trees growing on a hill; herself, swimming in a sea full of strange fish; her mother waving to her from a plane.

She got up and opened the bedroom door. Poppy was lying on her back, fast asleep. Tamsin watched for a moment and realised that she was famished.

The kitchen was through an open archway at one end of the sitting room. Tamsin broke off a chunk of country bread that she had taken from an enamelled bread-bin, and sprinkled it with a little olive oil. She spread it with soft white cheese made from sheep's milk, slices of ripe tomato, and a few torn basil leaves. She boiled some water and made a pot of peppermint tea. When the tea was brewed, she laid the meal she had prepared for herself on a tray, and took it to where she had been sitting on the floor.

She started to eat ravenously. The food tasted fresh and delicious, and she relished each mouthful as she ate. When she had finished the bread and cheese, she poured some tea into a cup, and as she sipped it she looked through the newspapers she had bought that morning.

The headlines were all filled with the murder that had taken place down at the Cala in Tom Malek's house. The mixture of tragedy and scandal, fast-living foreigners and ordinary local people - it made a good story and the papers had gone to town.

Each report contained its share of interviews with villagers from Santa Marta. Headline quotes proclaimed Isabel to be everything from a model of virtue who had been considering a religious vocation (from a "close friend" of the parish priest) to a promiscuous wild-child, who had scandalised the village and disgraced her heart-broken parents. One paper reported that Tom Malek's house was known locally as '*la casa de las drogas.*'

"House of drugs" – that'll please him, Tamsin thought. She quickly skimmed through every article. The papers had gone to press before Esteban had made his dramatic confession, and as far as they were concerned, a dangerous murderer was at large on the island. Dire warnings were issued, especially to young women, not to wander around - or even stay at home - alone.

Tamsin sighed deeply. She felt better for her sleep and her meal. The sickness had left her. She put her tray back in the kitchen and while there, wolfed down another piece of bread, thickly spread with apricot jam.

'Tamsin?'

Tamsin looked over at the doorway. It was Georgia. She stood quite still, wearing a pretty pink dress, her hair tied back, looking ridiculously young. There was something different about her. And although she wasn't smiling,

Tamsin had the feeling that she was smiling on the inside. She looked radiant.

'This is a nice surprise,' said Tamsin, wiping jam from her mouth. Georgia walked over to a new painting she had noticed on the wall above the divan, a picture of Tamsin with Poppy in her arms. It was a pretty little painting, washes of pastel watercolour painted over lightly sketched lines.

'Gorgeous, isn't it?' Tamsin said. 'Paul did it.'

'I know, I recognise his style. You're so lucky, Tamsin,' she said, still looking at the picture, 'having Poppy. I so envy you.'

'Don't,' Tamsin replied. 'Your time will come. Lots of people would say you have a pretty good scene going for yourself without kids to complicate things.'

'Well you know that's not the case, whatever other people think.'

Georgia went and sat on the floor. She picked up one of the newspapers and quickly put it down again.

'Oh God,' she said. 'I don't think I can take any more of this.'

'Georgia!' Tamsin exclaimed. 'I've just realised that we haven't seen each other since it happened! I've lost all sense of time.'

'Me too. But we've had the lot - Guardia on the doorstep night and day, Antonia in hysterics, Peter hauled off to the police station at dawn, Tom Malek - '

'What was that about Peter?'

'It was this morning. I was still asleep. Someone had reported seeing his car down by Malek's house the night of the murder. Fortunately he had a whole crowd of witnesses to prove that he had in fact been getting seriously sozzled down at the café.'

Tamsin said nothing.

'Actually, he told me you were there with Poppy.'

'Yes, that's right. I was.'

'You didn't mention it when I saw you yesterday.'

'No. I forgot. Sleep deprivation – it affects the memory.'

For whatever reason, it was apparent to Georgia that Tamsin did not want to discuss her late night at the café any further. Georgia knew she disliked being quizzed about her comings and goings.

Georgia changed the subject and began to describe the events as they had unfolded at Casa Dura after her trip to the Puerto. They discussed the dinner party, Tom Malek's mysterious trip to Kent ('Kent, of all places!'), the gory details of the murder. Tamsin listened passively until Georgia came to Esteban's confession.

'Impossible!' she cried. 'I simply don't believe it. Esteban isn't capable of killing a fly, let alone his trollop of a daughter.'

'Tamsin!'

'What?'

'The girl's been brutally murdered, for God's sake! Don't you have any pity?'

'No, why should I? She didn't have any pity for me, or you for that matter.'

'What are you talking about? Why should she have pitied us?'

'All I mean is,' said Tamsin, quickly back-tracking, 'she didn't care about anyone except herself. She was spoilt and pampered and she thought she could have and do whatever she wanted. You don't know the whole story!'

'What whole story?' Georgia had thought she was ahead of Tamsin on this one, but of course, Tamsin was much more in touch with what was happening in the village than she. Much as she hated the subject, she was curious to find out what Tamsin knew.

'I can't tell you,' said Tamsin, suddenly calm.

'Why not?'

Tamsin lay back on the floor with her arms crossed over her eyes.

'Because...because I don't feel very well,' she said.

'What's the matter?' asked Georgia, looking concerned.

Tamsin shrugged. 'Oh never mind me,' she said. And then, looking questioningly at Georgia, she added, 'Anyway, how come you're looking so happy all of a sudden? I'd have thought you'd be wiped out with all of this.'

'I've made a momentous decision,' Georgia replied.

'Oh? What's that?'

'I'm leaving Peter. I'm packing up and getting out of here as soon as I can.'

'Wow.'

'Now tell me what's wrong.'

Tamsin stretched and sighed. 'If you must know, I think I'm pregnant.'

'Pregnant!' Georgia gasped.

'Ssh - you'll wake Poppy! Look, I don't really want to talk about it. It's all a horrible mistake and don't ask me what I'm going to do, because I don't know. Apart from anything else, I feel so disgustingly sick all the time I can't think straight.

'I didn't know you could get pregnant again that quickly,' said Georgia.

'Oh, yes, you can. I just didn't think it could happen while you were still breast feeding. I thought it stopped you ovulating or something. Evidently not.'

Georgia was wondering. She hadn't even known Tamsin was seeing anybody.

'So who's the proud father?' she asked.

'I'd rather not say for the moment.'

Georgia thought about this. 'Are you going to keep the baby?' she asked.

Tamsin's anxiety showed in her face as she replied. 'I don't know, I don't know,' she said. 'A couple of years ago, I wouldn't have hesitated to get rid. I would never, never have contemplated having a baby with...with this particular person. I still can't. It would be...oh, such a disaster! It would compromise everything. But even so, you feel this little life inside you and...' Tamsin didn't finish the sentence. She sat up and pushed her hair back from her face. 'Back then,' she said, 'I'd have had no qualms about it. It just seemed like a reasonable option, the right to choose and all that. I've had two, you know...it didn't seem that big a deal. But now, now that I've got Poppy...'

'I had one when Peter and I had been together for about six months,' said Georgia. 'I didn't want to. Peter made me. He said we weren't ready. I went to this doctor in Harley Street. He sat there in his consulting room, stuffed with antiques and Persian carpets, walls covered in Canelettos. He made it sound so ordinary. What really got me was that he had all these framed photographs of his own children on the desk and mantelpiece. They seemed to be staring at you, everywhere you looked.'

'Him!' Tamsin exclaimed. 'He's the same one I went to: Bernard Peach, the Harley Street abortionist. Two hundred and fifty quid, cash up front. I remember he tried to make a joke about the horrors of being in the super-tax bracket and the astronomical cost of school fees. Sleek as an otter, he was. Sleek and slimy.'

After a few minutes, it was Tamsin who broke the silence.

'Did you notice how his eyes looked in two different directions?' she said, rolling her own eyes around clownishly as she spoke.

'Oh, don't!' Georgia wailed, and they both started to laugh, reluctantly.

'Tamsin?' said Georgia eventually. 'I think I've met someone.'

'Have you?'

'Well...'

'Who is he, then?'

'He's here on holiday. Staying at the Puerto. I met him there yesterday when I went to the market. His name's

Matt.'

'Oh my God - you haven't descended to picking up tourists, have you?'

'Certainly not!' Georgia protested loudly. 'He's Irish,' she added by way of explanation.

From the bedroom, they heard Poppy whimper and stir.

'Stay and tell me all about it,' Tamsin urged.

'I can't. I have to get ready. I'm meeting him tonight.'

'You know there's a sheep roast up at Anton's later on?'

'Yes. Are you going?'

'I'm considering it. Why don't we both go? You could bring what's his name along...'

Tamsin went to the bedroom and got Poppy, who had woken up in a happy, smiling mood. Tamsin put her down on the divan and started to change her nappy.

'Hello, Poppy!' Georgia cooed, tickling the baby's bare tummy. Now that she had spoken Matt's name to another person, he felt more real. Sparks of happiness seemed to fly off her.

'I suppose we could go up to Anton's. Do you think it'd be all right?'

'Why not?' Tamsin answered. 'We'd make a good double act. Me, preggers. You, openly cheating on your absent husband -'

'I'm not!'

'Not yet...'

Georgia made a face. 'I'll see you later,' she said, getting up and going over to the door. She turned back to face Tamsin, who had finished changing the baby and was getting ready to give her a feed.

'Seriously, are you going to be all right?' she asked.

Tamsin smiled weakly.

'Course I am,' she said. 'Aren't I always? Go on, you don't want to keep your fancy man waiting. Matt!' she said, and rolled her eyes.

Georgia laughed and blew a kiss before disappearing through the doorway. Tamsin looked down at the baby, who was eagerly sucking at her breast. She thought about Georgia and the news she had brought.

'Oh God, sometimes I hate myself so much!' Tamsin said aloud, and Poppy looked up at her, outraged at the interruption to her peaceful feed.

'Sorry, Poppykins,' said Tamsin.

Poppy accepted the apology, and went on greedily feeding.

Dusk was falling and the casita fell into gloom. It matched Tamsin's mood. The upswing had not lasted long. She sat quietly in the twilight, pondering what the future might hold.

*

Careering along the road back to Casa Dura, Georgia took a hairpin bend in third gear and had to slam on the breaks when she found herself meters away from a head-on collision with a mule and cart. She screeched to a halt, and leaping out of the car, she was thankful to see that the farmer driving the cart was Juan, one of her neighbours. He accepted her apology with a friendly scolding, as they both stroked the poor, frightened mule.

Georgia got back into the car gingerly, Tamsin's Tarot warning suddenly ringing in her ears: 'August full moon,' was how she had ended the reading. 'Better watch out!' Right, thought Georgia. She drove on carefully until, with some relief, she parked her beloved, if somewhat beaten-up, old Bristol in its usual space beside the track leading up to the house.

It was still light, and as she looked at the house from the road, she could see the last rays of the setting sun falling upon the upper windows. Its outlines were softened, the sandy-coloured stone melding with the green of the trees and darkening blue of the sky, so that the house itself became a natural part of the rugged landscape. At such moments, Georgia could recapture the love she had once felt for it, the delight it had filled her with. But not now. Now Georgia had other things to think about. Easing herself out of the driver's seat, she felt as if she had spent hours behind the wheel of the car, and she was glad to be back.

Georgia closed the front door behind her and turned on the lights. It was getting dark inside the house. In the sitting room she went over to the hi-fi and found the record she was looking for, a Joni Mitchell album full of haunting tunes and richly-woven lyrics. Throwing herself on the sofa, she gave herself up to the music until she deemed it time to start getting ready for her evening with Matt.

CHAPTER TEN

Back in his hotel room, Matt was in a state of some despair. Looking through the clothes he had brought with him, a choice he had been quite pleased with until that moment, nothing he had seemed suitable for an evening with Georgia in Santa Marta. He pulled from the wardrobe a pair of khaki shorts, his Levis, and a light grey linen suit. 'No way,' he thought, hanging the grey suit back on the rail.

Among the few shirts he had with him, he gave careful consideration to one in off-white Oxford cotton with self-coloured stripes. It was a possibility. But with what? He was wearing a pair of white denims that would probably look OK, but they were a bit grubby and he wasn't happy with the idea of going out in something he'd been wearing all day. Matt was notoriously fastidious about his clothes. He threw the Levis, and a faded blue and white, tie-died t-shirt onto the bed.

'That'll work,' he thought. And he started to get ready.

A few minutes later, getting out of the shower, he heard voices in his room. His friends, Phil and Andy, had come back from the beach, roasted to a deep, lobster pink, and in high spirits. They were talking loudly, haranguing each other in no uncertain terms.

Matt walked in from the bathroom with one towel round his waist, rubbing his hair dry on another.

'What's going on?' he asked.

'He's feeling sick 'cos I scored and he didn't. Pillock! He had exactly the same chance as me. He's only got himself to blame...' Phil had a broad grin on his face. He was obviously pleased with himself.

Matt noticed that Andy really did look ill.

'Go on then, tell me the whole sordid story,' he said, as he fished out a pair of underpants from a drawer.

'Well, there were these two girls. Sunbathing topless, they were. Big girls, too.' He gestured with his hands, indicating the size of their busts. 'You should've seen them, Matt!'

Matt thought of Georgia. Under the thin, soft fabric of her dress, he had been able to see the clear outline of her breasts, her small, hard nipples pressing against the fabric. Hurriedly, he pulled on his jeans, and turned his attention back to Phil, who was being beaten around the head with a pillow by Andy.

'Is this the way for two grown men on holiday to behave?' he shouted at them.

'It wasn't my fault!' Andy was arguing with Phil. 'It wasn't that she didn't fancy me. She was bloody engaged! I was surprised I got as far as I did under the circumstances!' Andy had been drowning his sorrows, and he sounded drunk and stroppy.

'Oh yeah? Well my one was engaged an' all and it didn't worry her. We were well away! I didn't half give her a seeing to, Matt... She'll have something to tell her *fiancé* about when she gets home, ha ha!'

'You didn't bring them back here, did you?' Matt felt distinctly displeased by the idea. He was sharing a room with Phil.

'Nah, went back to their hotel. Not a bad place. Better than this. They had a balcony. Andy saw quite a lot of the balcony, didn't you, Andy?' Andy resumed hitting him with the pillow.

'So what were they called, these two birds?' Matt asked as he fingered his hair into place in front of the mirror.

'Mine was Samantha,' said Phil. 'A little darling, she was.'

'Yours, ha!' interrupted Andy. 'She doesn't even want to see you tonight! I heard her, putting you off.'

'Oh yes she does!' retorted Phil. 'But she can't 'cos your one's bottled out. She certainly didn't hold back this afternoon, did she? Hot stuff, that girl. You could say her fiancé was a lucky man, if she wasn't so partial to other blokes...'

'She said she'd never been with anyone else 'till you insisted on having your evil way with her,' said Andy.

'Yeah, she did, didn't she? But she loved every minute of it, let me tell you! Matt, you know I wouldn't force myself on a woman against her will, would I?'

'Dunno. Would you?'

''Course I wouldn't!' He paused. 'She did get a bit tearful afterwards,' he admitted. 'Said she hoped I wouldn't think she was awful. Silly girl. Must've been the Sangria,' Phil laughed. 'Anyway, didn't stop her agreeing to meet up again tomorrow. Don't know what's going to happen to Michelle, though. That was Andy's one.'

'She doesn't mind meeting us on the beach,' Andy said. 'She just doesn't like being up in the room with us.'

'Oh no, she doesn't mind snogging topless with some bloke she's just met on the beach, does she? But when it comes to -'

'Christ, I feel sick!' announced Andy, rushing to the bathroom.

'A few too many of the old Cuba libras,' Phil commented. 'Drinking from disappointment. Strange - she was that squiffy, I thought he'd have no problems. She was keen enough on the beach. All over him, she was! But then she went a bit maudlin. My one did, too, I suppose, but not 'til after -'

Matt pulled his T-shirt over his head, tied the laces of his sneakers, and fastened his watch strap. He picked up his wallet and sun-glasses from the dressing table, and tied a cotton jersey round his neck.

'Well, see you later, guys!' he said.

Andy could be heard vomiting in the bathroom. Phil looked surprised.

'You going somewhere?'
'Yep.'
'Where?'
'I've been invited out for the evening. Enjoy yourselves!'
'Wot - ?

Matt closed the door of the hotel room behind him and leant against it for a moment. He took a deep breath and walked down to the lobby. A few minutes later he arrived at the taxi-rank by the railway station. The cab drivers were standing by their cars, smoking and chatting to one another. He went up to the first one in the line.

'Santa Marta, por favor?' he asked.

'Muy bien,' the man answered, opening the back door for him.

Minutes later, the lights of the hotels and bars were far behind him. The scent of the night air was clean and sweet. Matt leaned back in his seat and enjoyed the swerving motion of the car as they drove along the road that zig-zagged upwards, higher and higher into the mountains.

CHAPTER ELEVEN

The journey took longer than Matt had anticipated. Looking it up on the map, he had reckoned on fifteen minutes, max. In the event, it was closer to half an hour. The road was steep, a series of sharp bends winding up the side of a mountain. To the left, there was rock, to the right, a sheer slope to the sea. It was narrow, too, and careful manoeuvring was required when meeting a vehicle coming from the opposite direction. At one point, they found themselves stuck behind a rusty old truck travelling at around five miles per hour. The chances of overtaking it were zero, and so they crawled on behind until its driver pulled in at a natural lay-by, allowing them to pass.

Matt realised that he'd cut it a bit fine. But there was nothing he could do about that now, so he sat back, gazing from the window, looking out onto the darkening night. Even from the confines of the taxi, he could feel the magic of the place. In the glare of the headlamps the ancient olive trees looked like illustrations from a book of Grimms' fairy tales, all twisted twigs and branches, bent up like goblins or crones. Above him, the sky was crammed with stars, sparkling and shining and lively. He leaned out of the window and looked up, and something inside himself also sparkled and shone and silently clamoured for expression. Totally caught up in the moment, he barely noticed the taxi pulling to a halt.

'*Aqui, Santa Marta!*' announced the taxi driver.

Matt paid the man, and getting out, he found himself in the main drag. On the opposite side of the street were old, stucco fronted houses with long wooden shutters and wrought iron balconies. On his side of the street, he found himself standing by the steps leading up to a large terrace covered by a canopy of palm leaves. Above him, between two pillars, hung a sign: '*Bar/Restaurante*', and underneath that, '*C'an Pepe*'.

Walking along the middle of the narrow street towards him were two girls dressed in ankle-length skirts. One of them had long fair hair styled into little braids and tied with ribbons. The other girl's dark brown hair fell long and straight about her shoulders, and around her neck hung a heavy copper necklace. Between the two girls a bearded man with a rose between his teeth was playing fast and noisily on a pair of castanets. They passed by, laughing and talking as they went, and Matt climbed the steps to the café.

He threaded his way through the tables to the bar itself. In the dark interior, the bartender stood pouring a measure of dark green liqueur into a shot glass. He looked up briefly at Matt.

'*Hóla*,' he greeted him, with a casual glance. '*Que quiere?*'

'Hóla,' answered Matt, and hesitated for a moment. He wondered if he would be able to make himself understood. His Spanish was limited to a few basic phrases. Yeah, we'll forget the pidgin Spanish, he thought, and asked, 'I'm looking for Casa Dura?'

'Ah, Casa Dura,' the barman repeated.

'Si,' said Matt, nodding his head.

Beside him stood a girl with a heavy, shoulder length mane of tawny brown curls and a golden tan heavily sprinkled with freckles. She wore a skimpy pair of cut-off jeans, hand-tooled gaucho boots and a little emerald green, embroidered waistcoat over a white tank top.

She turned to him, and in a cut-glass English accent said,

'Don't tell me, you must be Matt.'

Matt was taken aback, but tried not to let it show.

'That's right,' he said. 'And you are?'

'Tamsin,' she replied.

He noticed she did not smile, but looked at him with interest.

'I'll take you as far as the road up to the house, if you want,' she said. 'It's not too far.'

'Thanks,' said Matt. 'I'd be grateful for that.'

'No sweat,' she replied, picking up a pack of cigarettes and a lighter from the bar.

'Adios, Pepe,' she called to the barman over her shoulder, and headed off towards the steps leading down to the street.

They walked back in the direction from which Matt had come.

'I hope you've got a torch,' she said, noticing he hadn't.

'Damn!' he exclaimed. 'Georgia told me to bring one - I forgot.'

'You're in trouble then. It's not a very good road if you don't know it. More of a track, really. Death to ankles.'

Matt cursed silently, and was just wondering how hard it was going to be to make his way up to Casa Dura, when suddenly she stopped at an obscure turning off the main road.

'Looks like you won't be needing a torch after all,' she remarked.

As their eyes followed the track upwards, they could see that it shone with tiny lights. Little candles had been placed along the path at intervals of a few yards. The rough stony track snaked upwards, and at the end of it, just visible, were the lights of the house itself.

'So it would seem,' said Matt totally taken aback by the sight of the candles, and the fact that Georgia must have put them there for him.

'Have a nice evening, then,' said Tamsin. 'And tell Georgia I'll catch her later.'

'I will,' said Matt. 'And thanks again.' And turning off the main road, he started to climb the path.

*

Georgia, meanwhile, was putting the final touches to her make-up and slipping into a dark blue and white tunic-length kaftan. She fastened a woven leather belt around her waist, slipped on a pair of sandals and slid her silver bracelets onto her wrists. She shook her hair loose, letting it fall in dark waves around her shoulders, and sprayed herself lavishly with scent. In front of her full length mirror, she viewed herself from every angle, making miniscule adjustments to her hair and clothes.

Finally, looking down at her hands, she slowly, gravely, removed her wedding ring. Perched on the end of her bed, she turned the ring over and over, examining it closely. It was a slim, pale gold band, and since the day she and Peter were married, it had never left her finger.

Georgia took a handkerchief from the top drawer of her dressing table and wrapped the ring in it. She thought that she would never wear it again. She tucked the hanky under a pile of underwear and closed the drawer with a slow intake of breath.

Turning away from the dressing table, a framed photograph caught her eye. It had been there for years, and she realized that she had not actually looked at it for a long, long time. It was a picture of herself and Peter on their honeymoon in Provence. They were sitting under a cherry tree, eating the ripe fruit from a basket. She looked at them, those people that she and Peter had once been, their lips stained with cherry-juice, grinning at the camera. No matter how she tried, she could not remember who had taken the photograph, or how the two of them had come to be sitting there, under that tree. There were so many things like that now, times that had gone from her memory, erased by all that came after. How sad, she thought. Where had it all disappeared to?

As Georgia sat, lost in her thoughts, it came to her mind that Peter was away, and she was alone in the house. And at that moment, she realized that she did not want to be on her own. The thrill of being unexpectedly free had dissipated, and she felt a shiver of fear. Silly! But the house felt big and empty now, and she found herself dreading the prospect of spending a solitary night in it. In the stillness, she heard a noise coming from downstairs, from the entrada. 'Matt?' she thought. But surely he wouldn't just walk in without knocking?

She went quietly to the top of the stairs and peered over the banisters: nobody. Then she noticed a shadow falling across the floor. Someone was there, standing directly beneath the landing where Georgia stood. Her heart began to pound.

'Who's there?' she called out quickly.

A man stepped out into the middle of the entrada. It was too dark now to make out more than his shape. As he came into focus she saw that he carried a knife with a cumbersome wooden handle and a long vicious blade. He looked up at her. Then she recognized him.

'Randall!' she cried. 'You frightened the life out of me! For God's sake, put the light on.'

Randall went over to the light switch and turned it on, but did not speak.

'Have you been working outside?' she asked.

He stood quite still, sun-streaked hair flopping down over his eyes.

'Nope,' he said. 'Only just got here.'

'Oh,' she said. 'I didn't think you were meant to come today.'

Randall made a swiping motion in the air with the knife.

'Careful!' Georgia called. 'That thing looks lethal!'

'Just came to leave some tools for tomorrow,' he said, and he started to jump around, thrusting with the knife as if it were a sword.

'Thought I'd come and finish off that back terrace.'

'Stop it, Randall, please! You shouldn't play around like that. It's dangerous. And actually, could you leave it - tomorrow?'

'Sure. When d'ya want me to come?'

'I don't know. Peter had to go to London today. Let's wait till he comes back.'

Randall suddenly became jittery.

'Peter's gone to London? Why? Why's he gone now?'

'Business. What's the problem?'

'Why didn't you go to London, too? Why didn't you go with Peter? You'll be all alone...'

'Look, Randall, I'm fine. In any case, someone's coming over this evening, and I haven't quite finished getting ready...'

Randall, still agitated, walked over to a cupboard built into the wall of the entrada and hastily put the knife away inside.

'Guess I won't be needing that,' he said, and started towards the front door. 'But Georgia, can we talk? It's important, *real* important. I need to talk with you alone...'

Georgia was about to answer when they heard footsteps outside, and she walked forward to open the door. It was Matt, looking fresh and solid if slightly awe-struck by his first encounter with Casa Dura.

'Matt,' Georgia said. 'Come in!'

Matt walked into the house, and then stopped when he noticed Randall. The two men looked at each other with instinctive hostility.

'Matt, this is Randall, Randall this is Matt,' she said.

They nodded and said 'hi' to each other.

'Well, I guess I better be going,' said Randall. He turned to Georgia with a troubled look. 'Remember what I said? About talking...' he asked.

'I remember. Will you be at Anton's tonight?'

'Sure will.'

'Well, I'll see you there, then?'

'Oh you'll see me - you can bet on it.' And on that parting note, he turned and left.

'Did I interrupt something?' asked Matt.

'No. Randall's our sort of odd job man. Emphasis on the 'odd'. He's my husband's little helper. He seemed a bit upset that Peter's gone to London without telling him. I'm afraid he's a bit unbalanced. A combination of drugs and a bad tour of duty in Vietnam. They had to ship him out after six months. He arrived here with the Sixth Fleet and just sort of stayed.'

'Poor devil,' said Matt.

'Oh, let's not talk about him – he's not exactly one of my favourite subjects. What would you like to drink? I've got a bottle of white chilling in the fridge...'

They walked into the kitchen, and Georgia opened the wine.

'Cheers,' she said, handing him a glass.

'Cheers,' he raised his glass to her, and drank. 'The candles were nice,' he added.

Georgia blushed. 'I thought you might forget to bring a torch', she explained.

'I did.'

As Georgia led the way into the sitting room, Matt took in the details of the house: the enormously high ceilings; the beams, some made out of entire tree trunks; the deeply-set shuttered windows, the flag-stoned floors. He noticed the paintings, the old dark wood furniture, and through a doorway he glimpsed a table made from a gigantic circle of grey, pitted stone.

'Unusual dining table, you've got there,' he said.

'It's a mill wheel,' she explained. 'This room's part of the original house. It's what they used to call the tafona – the olive press. That stone was used for crushing olives, to make the oil. Over there, the ring in the far wall, that's where the donkey would be tethered, and the groove beside it was the manger.'

'Wow. It must be amazing to live in a place like this,' he said.

'I'm not going to be living here much longer,' she replied. 'Peter and I are separating,' she added, with a combined sense of guilt and elation. God, she thought, I could have had the decency to inform Peter first. Oh, well...

Matt looked disconcerted. 'I'm sorry,' he said.

Georgia gazed into her wineglass.

'Where will you go?' he asked.

'Back to London. I've got a flat in Holland Park.'

Matt's face lit up. 'Is that right? We'll be neighbours, then. I live in Shepherd's Bush, just the other side of the Roundabout – what's that if it isn't fate?'

Georgia laughed.

He came up to her and took the glass from her hand. He placed it with his own over on the table and coming back to her, he held her in his arms. She nestled against him and he held her closer.

'Georgia?' he said.

'Yes?'

'Can I see you in London?'

Georgia hesitated for a second. She felt his body tense slightly.

'If you'd like to,' she answered.

Matt's arms encircled her, and his cheek was warm against her face. For a long moment, he was quite still. Georgia could feel his breath rising and falling, as if he were asleep. His hair and skin smelt clean, masculine, virile. She touched the side of his neck with her lips, and she felt his arms tighten around her. She kissed his cheek, and then his ear, softly, silently, as if in a trance, and then he started to kiss her, too. At last, after what seemed like an age of waiting, his mouth found hers, and the kiss was gentle and slow and insistent at the same time, and his warm breath was intoxicating. They were like that for so long, so lost in each other, so aroused and so absorbed, that neither of them noticed the face at the window. Neither of them realised that they were being watched.

Eventually, Georgia pulled away a little. They moved apart, though still touching, smiling and then laughing, unable to take their eyes off one another. And when at last they separated, blinking against the light like two people just waking from a dream, the face at the window had gone.

CHAPTER TWELVE

Santa Marta put on a good show that night. The leading players had gathered at C'an Pepe, together with a full supporting cast. Georgia always thought of it like that: as a play, a piece of theatre, and it was how she had described it to Matt.

Centre stage, at one of the more prominent tables, sat the old poet, Godfrey Spence, his wife, Anne, and his much younger mistress, to whom he had given the mythic name, Ceridwyn. All three were obviously and eccentrically English, their manner as restrained as if, despite their mad, raggedy clothes, they were politely taking tea in a respectable and rather old-fashioned Bloomsbury hotel.

'Isn't he the poet laureate?' Matt whispered to Georgia.

'No,' she replied. 'You're mixing him up with Betjeman. Easy mistake to make. Actually Godfrey's far more famous.'

At a corner table, Tom Malek was sitting with James Parker and Dominique, a vivacious French ballerina with feline eyes and a turned-up nose. Dominique was James' date that night, but she was already a little drunk and flirting outrageously with Malek.

Only one table in the room was unoccupied, and Matt and Georgia made their way towards it. They passed a couple dressed all in white, both with long, straight, sun-blonde hair, the girl's light green eyes rimmed with thick black kohl. In her lap she held a tiny golden baby, wrapped in a white kimono. The man rose as Georgia approached, and held out his hands.

'Georgia,' he said, in a laid-back mockney accent. 'Good to see you, girl!' and he kissed her on both cheeks. 'But what's been happening here?' he went on. 'We just got back and like there's all this bad energy...'

'I know,' agreed Georgia. She crouched down beside the girl and baby. 'How are you, Jools?' she asked. 'Glad to be back?'

'We're good, Georgia,' Jools answered. 'But, Esteban's daughter - I mean, how can something like that happen in Santa Marta? And it was so far out, because just before we left for the States, like three weeks ago, we had this friend, Solomon, staying with us, and Solomon's an aurologist. We were with him down at the Cala one morning, and Esteban's daughter was there with Luc - you know, Cristiane's son? When Solomon saw her he was like, *"Who is that girl?"* And then he said he could see her whole aura, and it was deep, deep red – like blood red! And now when we heard what happened, it just totally freaked us out!'

'Yeah, totally, man. Solomon's too much. We were eating at Esteban's one evening, and just looking at him, Solomon knew right away that Esteban was epileptic,' echoed Steve. 'Well I never knew that, so I checked it out later with Pepe, 'cos I knew they'd, like, grown up together, and Pepe said, yeah, that's right, Esteban has that problem. Far out, man.' Eyeing Matt up and down, he added, 'Anyway, Georgia, where's ol' Pete tonight?'

Georgia was still leaning down, stroking the baby's cheek.

'He's in London,' she replied. 'By the way, this is Matt. Matt, Steve and Jools. And this adorable person is Jezabel.'

'She doesn't look a Jezabel,' said Matt, gently touching the baby's hand. 'Not yet, anyway.'

'Will you be at Anton's later?' Georgia asked Steve.

'Yeah. We have to take this little lady home first. Jools'

mum's come over to help us with her. We'll make our way up after that. You've gotta come over to the house, Georgia. Come and have dinner soon.'

'You, too, Matt,' said Jools. 'You have to see our Zen garden, we've just finished it. It has the most amazing vibe, doesn't it, Steve?'

'Yeah, amazing, man,' answered Steve.

'Sounds great,' said Matt.

'Come on, Matt,' said Georgia. 'Let's get that table before someone else does.'

'Georgia,' said Matt when they were seated, 'Steve Southern's wife just asked me to dinner!'

'Are you into his music?' asked Georgia, looking around her.

Matt was almost jumping with excitement.

'Am I? Doppelganger's one of my favourite bands! I saw them at the Rainbow a couple of years ago. I mean, they're legends! Superstars! I've been invited to dinner by a superstar!'

Georgia laughed. 'Calm down,' she said. 'He's off duty down here. Just think of them as neighbours.'

Apart from its illustrious clientele, C'an Pepe was a typical Spanish restaurant of the time, with whitewashed walls, tiled floors, starched white napery and candles on the tables. The furniture was plain and solid, and the air was permeated with the scent of wood smoke. There was no pretence to the décor, and not to the food either, which was good local home cooking.

At one of the longer tables, Carl Frankel was having a raucous time with a large group of friends. Seeing Georgia, he called over to her.

'Hey, Georgia, why don't ya join us? Come and grab a seat!'

Georgia waved and smiled. She could see his party was getting ready to go. A couple of them were pushing back their chairs.

'How 'bout we catch up with each other later?' Carl

called. 'You goin' up to Anton's for the sheep-roast?' He ambled over to where Georgia and Matt were seated.

'We'll be up there later,' said Georgia. 'Oh, Carl, this is a friend, Matt. Matt, this is the infamous Carl Frankel.'

Matt recognised Carl as the man with the castanets and the rose. They shook hands.

'New in Santa Marta?' Carl asked.

'I am,' said Matt. 'My first visit.'

'Well, you certainly picked your moment, Matt. August full moon, man!'

He slapped Matt on the shoulder. 'Make the most of it - the time's they are a-changin' - even for Casa Dura, right, Georgia?'

Georgia had no idea what he was talking about. She put it down to the wine.

The rest of the party were waiting to settle the bill. 'Take it easy, you guys!' he called as he and his group crowded hectically out of the door.

Carmen stood patiently waiting for their order. She had placed a carafe of red wine, a basket of bread and a bowl of olives on their table. James Parker noticed them and waved, and Georgia smiled back at him.

'That's James. He's an old friend of Peter's. And mine,' she said.

They looked at the menu together.

'The fish is always good,' she said. 'Tonight they've got fresh tuna or *arroz marinera*. It's like a spicy fish stew with rice.'

'Well, I love fish and I love rice, so I think it'll have to be the – what did you call it?'

'Arroz marinera.'

'Arroz marinera, por favor!'

Carmen smiled, and told Matt in Spanish that he had made a good choice. He seemed to understand.

'I'm just having a salad,' said Georgia. 'I like fish and rice, too, but I can't eat in this heat. My appetite's deserted me.'

'That's a shame,' he replied. 'Georgia, who's the guy sitting with your friend, James? He keeps looking over at us.'

'That's the dreaded Tom Malek,' she said.

Matt glanced over briefly towards Malek's table. Malek caught him looking and stared back. It was a mean, challenging stare which continued, to Matt's discomfort, until Malek was distracted by Dominique's attempts to spoon ice-cream into his mouth. He pushed her hand gently away, but by then Carmen had arrived with Matt and Georgia's order. Matt was more interested in the food than in playing staring games with Tom Malek, and he began to eat hungrily.

'This is very, very good,' he told Georgia, with his mouth full of rice. 'Try some?'

He held out his fork, and Georgia leaned forward to taste. As she did so, Malek appeared beside them.

'Hey, Georgia,' he said. 'Leave some room for the sheep roast.'

'Isn't it crazy?' she replied. 'Everyone's going to the sheep roast, but we're all having dinner here first…'

'The sheep roast isn't just about eating, Georgia,' he started saying, but he was interrupted by Dominique who had followed him over and, grabbing his arm, dragged him out with her.

'God - that man!' said Georgia with a mock shudder when they were alone again.

She looked out of the window beside her. Below, in the street, Malek was still talking to James and Dominique. Santa Marta was buzzing that night, and other people passed by and spoke or called out to each other. James and Dominique strolled over to the café, James' arm draped casually around the pretty dancer's shoulder. Malek stayed lounging against his Jeep. He looked as if he was waiting for someone.

After a couple of minutes, the someone arrived. It was Randall. Georgia watched as both men got into the Jeep and sat there talking. There was some movement, and it looked to Georgia as if Malek was giving something to Randall. She saw Randall hold up the jacket he had slung over one shoulder and search through the pockets. Malek grabbed the jacket away from him and started feeling around the pockets himself. Then he flung the jacket back at Randall, started up the engine, and drove away.

'I wonder what that was all about,' said Georgia, almost to herself.

'What was what?' Matt was chewing on a large prawn.

'Oh, nothing,' said Georgia. 'Nothing important.'

Matt finished eating.

'That was terrific,' he said. 'Would you like something else?'

'Ice cream?' she suggested.

'Yeah!'

Magdalena cleared their plates away. From all around them came the sound of conversation, the clatter of cutlery and the clink of glasses.

'Is it like this every night?' asked Matt.

'In the summer, pretty much. It's the only restaurant in town.'

Strawberry ice cream arrived, piled high in glass bowls and scattered with slivers of toasted almonds. They ate in silence for a few minutes.

Then Matt asked, 'So, Georgia, how did it all strike you, when you first got here?'

Georgia took a sip of wine. Balancing it in the fingers of both hands, she looked down into her glass. She saw a brief vision of her first glimpse of Santa Marta: the turn in the bend of the old sea road, and there it was, rising up before her, crowning the Puig, the hill which itself was dwarfed by the heights and peaks of the Tramuntana mountains. Santa Marta had seemed to float magically on a cloud of early morning mist. It had taken her breath away.

'It's beautiful,' she had said to Peter, in wonder. 'I hadn't realised...' 'Oh,' he had replied. 'Did I forget to mention that?' And she had laughed. They both had. It was the one thing about Santa Marta he had omitted to tell her.

Looking up at Matt, she said, 'Oh, mixed feelings. More than anything else, I was scared stiff.'

'Scared?' Matt looked surprised. It was the last thing, at that moment, that he had expected her to say, and far removed from what he himself was experiencing.

Georgia hesitated for a moment. Matt was looking at her expectantly, his expression unguarded, his eyes shining in the candlelight.

'Can I trust you?' she was thinking, and the realisation dawned on her that it was a long time since she had allowed herself the luxury of trusting anyone. 'This is to do with breaking away from the past,' she thought. 'And I don't want those old hang-ups to stop from me enjoying something new, something different. What's the worst thing that can happen? That it could turn out to be a mistake, trusting him? Well, God knows, that wouldn't be a new experience. But even so, please don't let it be a mistake!'

'It was a step into the unknown,' she said aloud. 'I'd heard so much about it from Peter, it was like some mythological land, somewhere that had previously existed only in stories, and it was about to come to life. So maybe apprehensive, rather than scared. And then, there was something else - a former girlfriend of Peter's who I knew would be down here. Actually, even now, she still has a bit of a hold on him, she's that kind of person. Back then, I didn't know if I could handle it.'

Matt was wondering how this Peter bloke could be hung up on someone else when he had Georgia. What must this other bird be like?

'Ex's are always a bloody pain,' he said.

'And this one's been a constant factor in our life,' Georgia went on, warming to her subject. 'She has an art gallery in Palma. She's very glamorous, very sophisticated, she knows everyone. It made me feel a bit like a spotty schoolgirl.'

'I can't see that at all, Georgia,' replied Matt with a look of complete disbelief.

'But I did - I know it sounds pathetic, but you haven't met Cristiane. And back then, it really clouded my whole experience of Santa Marta. I never felt free to enjoy it, to just be myself. I always felt her shadow on me.'

Georgia took a sip of wine, and leaned forward to light her cigarette from the candle. As she did so, Matt gently held a wisp of her hair away from the flame in a protective gesture.

'Thank you,' she said softly.

For a moment their eyes locked, and then she continued her tale.

'She's got a teenage son called Luc, from her marriage to Frank Ewald - the English artist, you must have heard of him?' she continued.

Matt nodded. 'I've seen his stuff in the Tate,' he said.

'Well, you know, he committed suicide. It was when Luc was two years old. He came home one day with his mum to find his Dad hanging from the banisters.'

'God, that's terrible,' said Matt. 'A cousin of mine tried slashing her wrists once, but they managed to get her to hospital in time. She's OK now. Got married a couple of years back, in Galway. It was a great little wedding -'

Georgia looked perplexed.

'Sorry,' he spluttered, aware of the redness spreading upwards from his neck. 'Not relevant.'

'The point is,' continued Georgia, eyeing him uncertainly, 'it must have scarred Luc quite badly. And now, well, there's something not right. You can see he's suffocated by his mother, and he's definitely over-attached to Peter. It's like a fixation. Sometimes it really spooks me out. I've tried talking to Peter about it, but he doesn't listen.'

Now Matt was hesitant.

'You and Peter,' he said. 'Do you have children?'

'No,' she replied.

'I see. So when you say you were afraid, then, was it that this ex and her boy would come between you and Peter?'

'They have come between us,' she answered emphatically. 'But that wasn't what worried me to begin with. Peter was getting on for forty when I met him, so I expected him to have a past. Just not such an on-going past.'

The restaurant was beginning to empty. Georgia caught Carmen's eye and made a sign for her to bring the bill. When it came, Matt took it and insisted on paying.

'Gracias,' he said, as he handed the plate and payment, together with a hefty tip, back to the waitress.

'De nada,' she replied, impressed. Many of the regulars who frequented the restaurant had trouble scraping together even the required amount, never mind a tip.

'Buenas noches!'

Georgia gathered up her things, and together she and Matt stepped out of the restaurant, into the Santa Marta night.

CHAPTER THIRTEEN

The café below was packed to overflowing, every table taken. Matt was struck by a vision of suntanned skin, guys, young and old, in loose, Indian type pants and cotton waistcoats, beaded necklaces, rainbow coloured wish-bracelets, bangles and rings of silver and turquoise; girls in long dresses, filmy kaftans, sandals, earrings that looked like they had come from far away soukhs and bazaars; not ordinary girls. These girls had originality, style. They knew how to wear their exotic clothes with an air of graceful nonchalance. Matt had not encountered anything like it before. There was an exclusive, members-only feel to the gathering which was daunting, but at the same time he could see that it was quite relaxed and welcoming if you had the right introduction. His interest was definitely aroused.

It was a very different crowd to the one he had seen sitting around with their Cuba libres and piña coladas in the garish bars and cafes of the Puerto. Sunburnt, overweight bodies squeezed into sweaty synthetic fabrics or swathed in oversized T-shirts bearing vulgar, unfunny slogans; tarty teenage girls and their brassy mothers done up to the nines, vying for the leering attention of greasy waiters; tourists, mainly German and English, on their worst behaviour, noisily displaying the least attractive of their national characteristics.

On the night they arrived, Matt, and his friends, Andy and Phil, had tried out the disco in the basement of a hotel not far from where they were staying. The heat had been almost intolerable. The music, a mixture of tourist trash and mindless disco, the kind of stuff Matt loathed, pounded from gigantic speakers while strobe lights flashed relentlessly in time to the beat.

Reeling from an excess of heat and noise and cheap rum-and-coke, Matt had manoeuvred himself, with no effort at all, into a hard-core clinch with a not bad-looking girl whose yellow mini dress had ridden up almost over her knickers and slid down from her pink, peeling shoulders. The girl, whose name he hadn't been able to catch above the noise, wriggled and panted beneath him on a banquette at the side of the dance floor. The hem of her dress reached waist level, and Matt's hands were all over her fleshy buttocks, her hard little breasts.

Then suddenly the music changed to a slow ballad, and the strobes ceased their incessant flashing to be replaced with soft pink searchlights. As a rosy beam of light fell upon them, Matt looked at the girl lying sprawled under him. Her face had become sweaty and smeared with lipstick and mascara, her hair and dress were in rumpled disarray. He noticed one or two of the dancers looking at him, and suddenly he didn't feel so drunk or aroused anymore. He got up and asked the girl if she would like a bit of fresh air. She stared at him uncomprehendingly and shook her head. He left the place without looking back and staggered out into the street.

The next morning he could not remember getting to bed, but he was relieved to discover that he had spent what was left of the night alone. The next evening he had pleaded sunstroke, and his mates went clubbing without him. He spent the night out in the courtyard of his hotel, contentedly engrossed in a book he had brought with him, completely undisturbed. He was in no great hurry to repeat his disco experience.

All this Matt remembered as he took in the scene at the Santa Marta café. Here the atmosphere crackled. It was very enticing. But he sensed that Georgia was not keen, and he himself felt a need to connect with her, to be alone with her for a while. Together, they decided to give the café a miss and to walk on up to the sheep roast.

'Is it far?' asked Matt as they strolled along the main drag.

'It's on the way up to Casa Dura,' she replied. 'Anton's my nearest neighbour. About twenty minutes, that's all.'

Soon they had left the main street behind, and Matt slipped his arm around Georgia's waist. The wine made him feel mildly, pleasantly high. Georgia's body was slim and graceful and when she looked up at him her face was more than just pretty. He wondered what he had done to deserve this amazing woman, this incredible evening, and he had a sudden rush of fear that he would not have her for long, that she would slip away as quickly and mysteriously as she had appeared.

'If I could have a wish right now,' he said, 'it'd be for this evening to last for ever...'

'I don't know if I believe in for ever,' she replied.

'Then we're different,' he said. 'I believe in it very firmly.'

They came to the place where they had to turn off towards Casa Dura. The path was covered in loose stones and full of treacherous little dips. Georgia took a torch from her basket and shone the light on the ground in front of them. They followed carefully in the beam of the torch and then, as they turned a bend in the path, Matt took the torch from Georgia and switched it off.

'No longer necessary,' he said.

In front of them loomed the encircling mountains, and rising above the crest, dead centre, was a perfectly round and gleaming, pearl-white moon. In the midst of the deep black sky, bursting with stars, they saw constellations flash into view, comets streaking silently across the heavens.

They stood still and watched, their faces bathed in moonlight. From the distance, the murmur of voices and the strumming of a guitar floated towards them. Matt dropped the torch into Georgia's basket, and they walked on up the hill.

CHAPTER FOURTEEN

Tamsin said goodnight to Ana, the neighbour who had come to baby-sit for Poppy, and set off for Anton's place. Her dress was so long she had to hold up the hem to avoid tripping over it. It was a stupid dress to have worn, she thought, and wondered whether she should go back and change into something more practical. The alternative was to see if someone could give her a lift when she got to the café. Tamsin did not like driving on the mountain roads, especially at night. But one thing was sure: there was no way she could climb the path to Anton's in that dress.

She had put it on, a dramatic metallic grey and silver confection she had bought from a little boutique in Laurel Canyon, in the hope that it would get her into the party mood. It had not worked. She would have preferred to stay at home and she felt envious of Ana, sitting quietly in the soft glow of the casita, surrounded by her music and books and Poppy's sweet, sleeping presence. Tamsin had a sudden yearning to be with her baby, a longing so powerful she turned back to face the direction from which she had come. The moon was up, and shining brightly on the stony street, casting long, shapeless shadows across Tamsin's path. From the dark of one such shadow, she heard a voice call her name.

Tamsin could see the figure of someone sitting on a low stone wall at the side of the road. It was a woman, dressed in black, a lace mantilla covering her head. Tamsin walked over to where the woman sat, small but upright, her face sorrowful, without expectation of sympathy. Tamsin crouched down beside her and took one of the woman's hands in both of her own.

'Dita,' she said quietly. 'Dita. I'm so, so sorry.'

The woman allowed Tamsin to hold on to her hand as if it were she, Tamsin, who needed comforting. She spoke in Spanish, her voice young, tremulous, at odds with the grotesque mourning clothes.

'Tami,' she said, 'we have to talk. I have so much to tell you. And you, you must help me, Tami.'

Tamsin was unnerved by the woman's bizarre appearance and the desperation in her voice. In her own uncertain, disconnected state, her instinct was to shy away.

'I'm on way up to Anton's place, Dita,' she said. 'I'm supposed to be meeting Georgia there.'

'Georgia!' Dita exclaimed. 'Of course! You must tell me, what does she know about Isabel?'

Tamsin was determined to stay cool. At the same time, she felt it was probably wise to humour Dita, who at that moment was scrutinising her, ready to pounce at the smallest hint of deception.

'Georgia's maid, Antonia, was with Maria when they – when she - found Isabel,' she replied cautiously, 'and the Guardia went to Casa Dura to ask Peter about Tom Malek.'

'Ah, so they do not know about Peter and Isabel?'

Tamsin chose her words carefully. 'They took Peter in for questioning this morning,' she said, 'but they didn't keep him for very long. I've no idea what he told them. And no, Georgia knows nothing about…about that. Peter left for London this afternoon,' she added.

'He's left her alone?'

'Georgia? Yes - '

'We must act fast,' Dita muttered. 'Come with me,' she

said.

They walked to a clearing at the side of the road where Dita had parked her car. Sitting inside, Dita started to talk.

'I have seen her, Tami,' she announced. She paused for a moment, letting her words hang in the air. 'She has come to me twice, the night she died, and again this evening.'

Tamsin felt her scalp tingle and her heart start to pound uncomfortably.

'Isabel?' she asked.

Dita nodded.

'Tonight, I was sitting on the rocks, watching for the moon to come up. She sat beside me. Like the first time, when she stood by my window in the dark, her face and body were translucent, shimmering. Again, she came to reassure me. She is peaceful now. Completely at peace. Thank God.'

Dita rearranged her mantilla and looked straight ahead through the windscreen at the bent and twisted silhouettes of the olive trees. Tamsin listened in silence.

'I did not hear her voice. But as I looked into her eyes, I understood. Without words, she explained to me that the purpose of her life had been to give meaning to my life and to Esteban's, to draw us together and enrich us in our emptiness. But we were unable to appreciate this treasure that was given to us, this precious child. Alas! Esteban and I, we were so poor and stupid. All we could do was spoil her and make it possible for others to use and corrupt her. Her death has released her from what her life had become. Now, now she is pure, so pure! She is in heaven, Tami. And I am happy that she has been taken. We did not deserve her, Esteban and I.'

Tamsin kept her silence, torn between dislike for Isabel and pity for Dita.

'But, Tami I am troubled, all the same! We must make known the one who killed Isabel. She must have justice! I knew, of course, that it was not Esteban. How could he kill the daughter he loved?'

'Then why did he confess?'

'Why? Because he thought he was guilty! Now he is beginning to doubt. The police also, they do not believe it. But it is convenient for them to have Esteban locked up. They are cunning, the Guardia - while Esteban is held, they are able to track down the real killer, who thinks he has escaped.'

Where is this leading us? Tamsin's mind was whirring. Was it just going to be a long stream of demented babble, or did Dita really know something? Either way, it was not good for Tamsin. Tamsin was too enmeshed. For the moment, she decided, the only option was to go along with Dita.

'Do you have any idea who it was, Dita?' she asked.

'Oh yes, I have an idea. And more than an idea, I have proof! I have it here with me. I brought it to show you.'

'Tell me, Dita.'

'Constantly, constantly, I have been thinking. Who could it be who committed this savage act? It was the act of a madman, wasn't it? That is why Esteban confessed.

'Late that night, the night of the murder, he went to Malek's house to find Isabel and to bring her home. We knew Malek had left the island, and Esteban did not want her to stay there by herself. But he was not angry, he was calm. He was worried - of course, he was worried.

'He went to the police and confessed because, from the time he parked his car outside Malek's house, he could remember nothing until he woke up in his own bed the next morning. He had no memory at all! When the police told him what had happened, he went back to his room. He found his clothes, stained with blood. He decided that he could not remember because he had suffered a fit of madness, and in his crazy state, he had killed Isabel.

'You see, as a child and in his youth, Esteban had suffered from epilepsy. He was so frightened of the fits. When he was very young, they were quite frequent. They had stopped by the time we married. He did not like to even talk about it, but he told me once that the worst thing was not remembering what had happened afterwards. He was left to imagine all kinds of monstrous scenarios. Of course, all that ever happened was that he would fall to the ground for a few moments. But the people here, they are so stupid. He would come round and find himself surrounded by faces, their expressions filled with disgust and horror. He would feel as if he had done something bad. When he lost his memory that night, all his old nightmares returned. And then, of course, at the time he made his statement, he was truly mad with grief. He did not know what he was confessing to.'

'Poor Esteban,' Tamsin said with feeling. 'What do you think actually happened, Dita?'

'It's very simple. I think he went into the house and found Isabel, dead. The shock must have been such a tremendous blow, so unbearable, his mind rejected what his eyes had seen. The memory was instantly eradicated. Maybe there was a seizure. He knows only that he went to the house at the Cala, and that the next morning he was shaken and unwell, and his clothes had marks of blood on them. He has been able to tell the police nothing else, even under the most rigorous interrogation. No-one could be more innocent than Esteban.'

'I knew it couldn't have been Esteban,' Tamsin said. 'When I heard about his confession - no, I didn't believe it. It just didn't make sense. I wondered if they were trying to set him up.'

Dita turned to face Tamsin, and Tamsin almost recoiled in shock. For a moment, Dita's face appeared to have aged frighteningly. Her normally firm, pale skin looked withered and deeply etched with a network of lines. The shiny black eyes were sunken into darkened sockets; her lips, shrunken into a hard, thin line. Swathed in the bizarre black, she exuded an air of mad determination.

'Georgia's Tarot reading!' The recollection suddenly hit Tamsin. 'The woman at the graveside – why didn't I see it before?'

The vision passed, and Dita's appearance returned to normal. She spoke quietly now, conspiratorially.

'Tami,' she said, as if reading Tamsin's mind, 'you must help me. Will you read the cards for me?'

Tamsin hesitated.

'You are afraid?' Dita asked.

'I don't see how -' Tamsin, faced by Dita's fanatical determination, was lost for words.

'Tamsin, we have to do it! I know the murderer, and it is possible he may kill again! I told you, it can only be a madman. Now that the taboo of killing has been broken, what will stop him?'

Tamsin stared, not knowing what she could safely say.

'When I saw Isabel tonight,' Dita continued, 'she wanted to tell me who it was who did this terrible thing. Even in her peaceful state, I understood that it was vital to find this person quickly, because until he is found, others are in danger. One other in particular, and it is one whom Isabel herself is guilty of having harmed, although that one is not aware of it yet.'

Tamsin drew in her breath.

'Georgia?' she said. 'Is that who you mean?'

'Yes. Georgia.'

Tamsin's voice was shaking.

'Dita, who would want to kill Georgia? You don't think it's Tom Malek?'

'No.' Dita was dismissive. 'Malek is bad, but not in that way. He would not kill unless his own freedom was in jeopardy. Isabel was never a threat to him, and nor is Georgia.

'Listen: Isabel indicated that she wanted me to know who this monster was. After she disappeared, I came to look for you. I thought you could read the cards for me, and at such a powerful moment, the cards would reveal the killer to us. But you were not there. So I went into Santa Marta. I was walking towards Pepe's, when I saw Tom

Malek driving towards me. He stopped, and I went to ask him if he had seen you. As we were talking, I noticed another man in the car. It was that boy, the American who has been working at Casa Dura. When he saw me, he became afraid, but I looked at him and then, then I saw it. I saw the face of the man who killed my child!'

'Randall?'

'The crime was written on his face. In the flash of a moment I knew everything.'

'Dita, you must be mistaken. Randall's a bit mixed up, that's all. And anyway, what possible reason could he have to - to hurt Isabel? They were friends...'

'Ah! You don't know? The reason is connected with Isabel's association with Peter Gael. This is what led her to her death!'

Tamsin interrupted. 'Did Isabel talk to you about Peter?'

Dita took an embroidered handkerchief from her sleeve and wiped her eyes with it.

'Yes - and you know from Malek, of course. Am I right?'

'He mentioned something...' Tamsin did not want the conversation to digress to her own connection with Malek. Dita knew too much. Isabel had obviously spoken freely to her mother, and Tamsin felt uncomfortably exposed. 'What did Isabel say?' she asked quickly.

'She said she was in love with Peter. She told me some weeks ago that she had fallen in love with him. I told her not to be silly, but she wouldn't listen to me. She was convinced his marriage was over. She believed that they would divorce soon and that she would be with him. Foolish girl! Of course she was right that things have gone badly for Georgia and Peter. Tell me, Tamsin, you are sure Georgia knows nothing?'

'Positive! Georgia was devastated when she heard what had happened to Isabel. But go on, Dita, tell me about why Randall would have done this?'

'At first I thought, maybe he wanted her for himself. Or

maybe he thought she threatened his friendship with Peter. But now, now I know the real reason.'

'Which is?'

'From the evidence, Tamsin, it appears that this devil has an obsession with Georgia. A crazy obsession! And in his madness he decided to destroy Isabel, to punish her for daring to take from Georgia what was rightfully hers.'

Tamsin tried to work out whether there could be any truth in this. Certainly Randall had a bit of a thing for Georgia. She and Georgia had joked about it often enough. But there was no way she could see Randall as a murderer. What he liked was gardening and nature and poetry. He sometimes came across as something of a lost soul. He could get a bit hyper. But there was nothing nasty about him, nothing she had ever seen. Dita, however, was utterly convinced, and her voice seethed with accusation.

'Isabel had no possibility of taking Peter from Georgia. Am I right? Tell me! All he wanted from her she had already given him, presented it to him as a gift, wasted it on him.'

Tamsin stayed silent. There was no acceptable response. For a moment they sat without talking. Tamsin felt the night closing in. Her head was spinning and she felt sick again.

How could she repeat to Dita what she had heard from Malek? That Peter had had Isabel one night when he was too drunk to know what he was doing, that it was unlikely he would ever have laid a finger on her even then had it not been for Malek egging him on?

Was there any point in telling Dita that if there was anything that could have been described as an affair between Peter and Isabel it was there only because after that first drunken encounter Isabel, with Malek's encouragement, had emotionally blackmailed Peter with tears and threats and pleading letters into continuing to see her, while all the time Malek gloated in the background?

'And whatever I say,' Tamsin thought, 'it's going to be

bad for Peter, though God knows why I should protect him, except that I've also been holding out on Georgia.' Tamsin didn't even want to try to think about what would happen when Georgia finally found out. Suddenly she remembered something.

'Dita!' she exclaimed. 'You said you had evidence?'

Dita smiled. It was a cunning, ugly smile.

'Yes, I can prove everything. How could I make such an accusation without proof?'

She reached behind her and produced a piece of paper from a coat lying on the back seat.

'This evening, while I was still speaking to Malek, the murderer got out from the jeep. Naturally, he could not bear to be in my presence. He jumped down and told Malek he would see him later. I noticed that he had left a jacket on the seat in his hurry to get away. When I finished speaking with Malek I pointed out the jacket. "Isn't that Randall's jacket?" I asked him. "I guess so," he said. Then I offered to take it to him. I said I would be passing his place.

'Malek did not want me to have the jacket, but I insisted. And I think he too was afraid of me because he gave it to me in the end. That's it on the back seat.'

Tamsin looked over her shoulder and saw a patchwork denim jacket lying in a crumpled heap. Dita was staring at I too, her eyes filled with hatred, as if the jacket somehow shared its owner's guilt.

'I went back to my own car and drove here,' she said. 'When I was sure nobody could see me, I looked into the pockets of the jacket. Sure enough, I found the evidence, even though I had no idea what I was looking for. Here it is!'

Tamsin unfolded the sheet of paper and began to decipher the inky scrawl that covered it in a series of short lines. She saw that it was a poem. Of course, she thought. Randall was a poet, or at least, he aspired to being one. He'd even read her a couple of things he'd been working on at the Cala one day. She'd tried to be encouraging, but actually she had not been able to follow the embarrassingly bad stream of consciousness that he stumbled over at great length.

This, though, was terrifyingly clear. It told its story with unflinching frankness. Tamsin read it slowly, stopping from time to time, registering the fact that she was reading an account of a murder, told by the murderer himself. In a wild but strong hand, which itself came as a shock, it seemed so uncharacteristic of Randall, the poem read:

the sound of the moonshrieks
flooded the room
they shook up my HEAD
she was there on the bed
tied to the 'stead
you have to destroy her
that's what the voice said

blood from her neck
splashed over the knife
blade cold as ice
held it up high
her last breath choked out
death rattle sigh

it was what she deserved
she was nobody's friend
plotting to get and to take
and to break

the half-written letters
KNOW who they're for
Stuffed them into her MOUTH
When she tried to scream OUT

NAKED like her

and covered in BLOOD
It caked up like mud
But the sea WASHED it clean
washed off the crud

did it for YOU
DID IT with love
The moment had come
it wasn't no DRUGS
Star Silver Lady shining above
too HIGH to reach
arms crippled and WEAK
too limp to beseech
had the power to stab
and to slash and to KILL

these DARK little deaths
offered to you
unworthy gifts
but a sacrifice still
dedicated to you
dedicated to you
DEDICATED TO YOU

When she finished reading, Tamsin folded up the paper again, and as she did so she noticed some words scribbled on the other side. Tamsin deciphered the words, doodled haphazardly:

Casa Dura sunset
NO MORE BETRAYALS!!!

'Deaths,' Tamsin said to Dita. 'At the end, he says "deaths". But there's only been one death, as far as we know.'

'That's why we must hurry, Tamsin. Whose death is he offering? Who is to be the next sacrifice? Come, Tamsin, you must read the cards! They will give us the answer.'

Tamsin was overtaken by a wave of panic. She was shaken by the poem and now horrible images flashed before her eyes: a young girl, naked and bound, the passive participant in someone else's sick game. Who, she wondered, had initiated Isabel into this kind of scene? The answer was obvious. Malek, it must have been him.

Malek, the father of the baby she, Tamsin was carrying. She felt a terrible revulsion; she was disgusted with herself, with her own body, ashamed that she had allowed a man like that to touch her, to make love to her, to make her pregnant. She wanted to scream, to howl! Everything started to bear down upon her: her condition, the murder, the danger that could be lurking in wait for Georgia.

'Dita,' she cried. 'Drive me back to the casita. Please hurry!'

Dita started the engine and revved hard a few times. She turned the car sharply in the road and, as she turned, the headlights caught in their beam a startled pair of eyes. The breaks screeched as Dita slammed her foot down and the car stopped abruptly. Dita cursed, changed gear and drove on while Tamsin, looking back, just glimpsed the white under-tail of a young deer as it leapt over the bank and up into the densely wooded hill.

CHAPTER FIFTEEN

Loose scree scrunched beneath the tyres as the car drew up outside the casita. The drive had taken less than five minutes: time enough for Tamsin to realise that Dita's plan must be abandoned. Fortunately, driving required all Dita's attention, leaving Tamsin free to think. The obvious thing to do was to take the hideous poem and the jacket straight to the police. Someone had to make Dita report what she knew without delay. Someone, thought Tamsin, but not me.

Something else had happened during the short journey. Tamsin had noticed that she was no longer nauseous. Normally, even when a bout of sickness had passed, she would still be left struggling miserably against the constant queasiness which blighted the early months of her pregnancies. It had been exactly the same when she was expecting Poppy. Now, somewhat ominously, it had lifted, leaving her clear-headed and alert. She snapped effortlessly into present time as Dita opened her door.

'Stop.'

'What? What's the matter? Let's hurry, Tami, hurry!'

Tamsin closed her eyes for a second, determined not to let Dita pressure her. The night air was light and fragrant. Mountain air, pure as spring water. Tamsin inhaled deeply, and her breathing steadied her.

'Wait, Dita,' she said. 'Let me speak.'

Dita glared at her impatiently, still holding onto the door.

'A reading would only waste time,' Tamsin reasoned. 'You already have all the evidence you need to take to the Guardia.'

At first there was no response. Then, gradually, Dita's face crumpled into an expression of bewilderment. She tried to remember why she had come to Tamsin at all, but her thoughts just swirled around in an abstract haze of disconnected words and colours. Her confusion rendered her helpless, unable to follow the simple reasoning behind this new course of action. She frowned sadly at Tamsin, speechless, drained.

'Wait here,' Tamsin said gently. 'I'll call Ana - you know Ana, the wife of Miguel, the fireman? She's looking after Poppy. I'll ask her to drive with you to the police station. You can explain everything there, show them the piece of paper. I'll get Ana right away.'

Tamsin swung her legs out of the car and winced in pain. A stab, low in her belly, left her momentarily breathless. As it abated, she turned to see if Dita had noticed. But Dita was gazing blankly into the darkness of the night, her eyes devoid of understanding or perception. Carefully, Tamsin got out from the car and walked as quickly as she dared to the door of the casita.

As she entered, Ana jumped up from the sofa where she had been looking at the pictures of Casa Dura in the copy of Vogue Georgia had given to Tamsin.

'*Que pasa?*' she asked, 'What happening?'

Tamsin gave Ana a carefully expurgated version of what had transpired during the drive to the casita with Dita. Ana listened carefully. She was a practical young woman, sensible and not too alarmed by Tamsin's story.

'I'll go with Dita,' she said, picking up her bag. 'I'll ask Miguel to come, he knows everyone at the police station. But what about you, Tamsin? You look sick ...'

'It's a stomach ache, that's all,' Tamsin replied. 'Just

take care of Dita, you can tell me everything later.'

She listened for Dita's car to start up and drive away. When the sound had faded into the distance, she staggered to the bathroom and pulled off her clothes. As she had known they would be, her knickers were soaked with blood, and there were a few splashes on the back of her dress. She threw both into the wash basin and sat on the lavatory where the pain and bleeding continued for a few dull minutes.

Eventually, she got up and washed herself. The cramps had stopped, leaving her tummy feeling hollow and weak. Tamsin dried herself and slipped into a nightdress. She wondered whether she should call a doctor, but decided against. It was early, no more than eight weeks. She would see it through on her own. Calling Alfonso, the village doctor, would be tantamount to broadcasting the news to the whole of Santa Marta.

In the kitchen, Tamsin made herself some tea, which she took back to bed with her. She put the cup down on the bedside table, and going to the cot where Poppy slept, she lifted the baby out and took her into her own bed. Propped up on her pillows, Tamsin sipped her tea. When she had finished, she laid her head down next to Poppy's.

'My beautiful girl,' she whispered. 'My own, sweet, little Poppy - I love you so much, so much.' Gently, she wiped away the tears that had fallen on Poppy's face.

Tamsin lay awake for a long time that night, too upset to sleep and too shattered to tell for certain whether she was weeping for sorrow or relief.

CHAPTER SIXTEEN

'I wonder what's happened to Tamsin.'

Georgia was watching in disbelief as Matt polished off a plateful of roasted lamb.

'She definitely sounded like she meant to be here tonight,' he replied, still chewing.

'Aren't you full?' Georgia asked him.

'Yeah, but this so good. I wish you'd have some, Georgia. You eat like a bird.'

They were sitting on a low, stone parapet at the edge of the terrace. All around, people lounged or stood in groups, talking, eating, laughing, passing joints, playing music. Matt recognised many of them from the restaurant.

'Who's that guy over there, the one you were talking to when I went to get the drinks?'

He looked over towards a dark-eyed man, his chest hung with a necklace of painted shards, sitting cross-legged on the ground. Beside him knelt a doll-like Vietnamese girl, her silky black hair hanging over one shoulder, her head bent in concentration as she painted a stripe of opium along a perfectly rolled joint.

Georgia sipped at her wine. 'That's Angel,' she replied. 'He's a South American artist, from Chile, I think. He wants me to tell him my dreams so that he can paint them.'

Matt pulled a mocking face and Georgia smiled.

An older woman, her silver hair pinned up in a tight chignon on top of her head, came over to them.

'Maya,' Georgia greeted her, and the two women embraced warmly.

'This is very nice, isn't it?' said Maya, a smile spreading across her lined face. She wore a long cream coloured linen tunic over loose, matching pants, the neckline picked out in a geometric pattern. From her earlobes hung dark silver Balinese earrings, and her wrists were encircled with a number of plain silver and ivory bangles. He noticed her bony but elegant fingers, the long fingernails, painted scarlet, as she held Georgia's hands in hers.

'I was quite uneasy about coming here tonight, you know,' she was telling Georgia. 'I had a lovely swim down at the lagoon this morning, and walked home the long way, enjoying every step. Sshh,' she hissed, a finger to her lips, 'I picked a few figs from the garden of the big finca on the way up to my casita. The owners are always away and the fruit is left to rot. Do you know that tree? It has the most wonderful, tiny green figs, sweet as honey. I had a feast when I got home!'

'I know the path, but not the fig tree. I must remember that,' said Georgia.

'Indeed! And, after that,' Maya continued, 'I was so comfortable, I thought, I'll stay here now. I'll spend the evening on my terrace, and watch the moon from there. It's a powerful moment, the August full moon – the Hunter's moon. So that was my plan.'

Maya looked up at the moon, and Georgia and Matt looked up too.

'But as I sat there, alone on my terrace, I had a tremendous sense that something was happening that I needed to know about. For the last few days, I have been very quiet, on my own. You know, Georgia, don't you, that's what I like the best. But suddenly, I felt that I must be with the other people of Santa Marta, that something was happening, and we needed to be together.

'At that moment, a little bird flew down – can you imagine, it was already dark! – and it sat on the table in front of me and looked into my eyes, its little head cocked to one side. I looked back and said, so, my friend, what have you come to tell me? The bird looked at me with such sadness in its eyes.

'Ah, I said. A death, of course. And is that all? But the bird remained a little longer, and I said, well, what do you want me to do? And the bird turned and flew off in the direction of the place where we are now standing. So of course I came, and here I am, and now I have heard the news of the death of the young girl, Isabel.'

Matt looked at Georgia quizzically. But she was intent on what the old lady had to say.

'My dear,' she said to Georgia, 'this place is also very close to where you live. Isabel is gone, but we don't know what is yet to come. Be very careful. Watch every step. And, above all, don't be alone!'

Georgia gave Matt a worried look, and he moved nearer to her. Maya noticed, and held out her hand.

'I am Maya,' she said.

Matt took her hand. 'Matt,' he responded.

'Matt,' she repeated. 'But not English?'

Matt shook his head. 'My people are from Ireland,' he said.

'Ah, Matthew, then,' she went on. '"Gift of God", I think it means. A good name. And a good heart, also.' She smiled warmly at him. Then she took his hand and Georgia's hand and held them together.

'You are safe,' she said to Georgia. And then turning to Matt, she said, 'Take care of her.' Her look was solemn, even stern. At her touch, Matt felt a bolt of energy course through his arm.

'And now I must go,' she said. 'Angel and Kim have promised me a lift home, and I see they are getting ready to leave. Remember what I said. Good night!'

Matt looked at Georgia.

'It's okay,' she said. 'Maya's the real deal.'

'I got that,' Matt replied. 'But what does it all mean?'

'I don't know. I didn't like the bit about it not being over. You weren't embarrassed, were you?'

'Embarrassed?' Matt echoed. 'The bit about taking care of you, you mean?'

'Yes...'

'Will you let me?'

'I won't stop you...'

'Good. Because she said you'd be safe with me, and with everything that's been going on around here, and the full moon, and your husband off in London, it seems to me that safety could be an issue.'

Georgia noticed that he wasn't smiling. She snuggled up beside him. Then he smiled.

They sat in silence for a while, Georgia reflecting on Maya's words, and Matt observing the other guests. Not far from them, a girl with Pre-Raphaelite features dressed in harem pants and a tiny bikini top was dancing alone. From a hi-fi system in the house, dreamy, druggy music pulsated out into the surrounding atmosphere, filling it with a sound that seemed to mould itself to the night and its colours. The girl was joined by a tall, graceful man, barefoot in baggy yellow dungarees, who moved sinuously in time with her, his darkly tanned skin gleaming in the moonlight. All around, the smell of wood smoke and charred meat mingled with the sweet, slightly sickly smell of hashish, and the embers over which the sheep had been cooked still smouldered and glowed hotly.

Beneath them, on the other side of the wall, the moon lay supine, reflected in the water of the deposito, the large tank which held the water supply for the house. It was fed directly from a *fuente*, a mountain spring, and it was full, deep enough for two or three people to swim in. Built into the terrace below, surrounded by trees, Anton had left it uncovered that night in case anyone felt like a dip, and in the darkness the water was still and black.

Unexpectedly, Georgia felt a sudden catch, a contraction, and her hands went straight to her belly. It lasted only a moment, but at the same time the thought of Tamsin came into her mind.

Turning to Matt, she said, 'I'm worried about Tamsin.'

Matt was distracted by a shuffling sound in the trees behind the deposito. As he glanced over his shoulder, he noticed a movement in the undergrowth, and quickly turned away.

'Sounds like someone's having their own little party over in the trees,' he said.

Georgia ignored his remark. 'She wasn't well when I went over to her house this afternoon,' she said.

'She looked fine when I saw her.'

'The thing is,' Georgia said, lowering her voice, 'she's pregnant.'

'I thought you said she had a baby?'

'Sssh! She does. We have to keep quiet about this - she doesn't want anyone to know.'

Matt put his plate down. 'What do you want to do?' he asked.

'I was thinking - would you mind if we looked in on her?'

Matt was thinking, too. He could not gauge whether Georgia meant him to stay the night. He gulped down some wine.

'Of course I don't mind,' he said. 'But it's getting late, it's past midnight.'

'Do you have to get back?' Georgia asked.

'I don't know. Do I?'

'Not if you don't want to. You can stay at Casa Dura. There's masses of room,' she added quickly.

'In that case, let's go and check on your friend.'

They got up and strolled over to where Anton was sitting, strumming a guitar.

'Leaving so early, Georgia?' Anton asked. He spoke in a quiet, American drawl with just a hint of an accent that Matt could not quite pinpoint.

'Yes -' she replied.

'For ever?'

'Maybe…'

'Sheep roasts have that effect sometimes.'

Georgia smiled. She had a soft spot for Anton.

'I'm just so tired,' she explained. 'It feels like I haven't slept for days.'

'Yeah, I know what you mean. Oh, by the way, Georgia, I noticed a couple of real big ruts in the road where it turns up to your place. Got your torch with you?'

'I did - but where've I put my cesta?' Georgia looked around for her basket.

'You probably left it over by the wall,' Matt said.

'I hope so,' Georgia replied. 'I keep mislaying things just lately.'

She and Matt walked back to where she had left the basket. Matt got there slightly ahead of her and leaned down to pick it up. As he did, he noticed something.

'What's that?' he said, peering over the wall.

'The deposito,' she replied.

'Yeah, but what's that floating in it?'

Georgia leaned down over the wall in time to see a long dark shape drift slowly into the circle of moonlight. She let out a terrified scream as the body of a man appeared below them.

Matt grabbed her round the waist and pulled her back from the wall.

'Hey!' he shouted in Anton's direction.

Several people, including Anton, had already heard Georgia's scream, and hurried over to where she stood. Anton took a quick look, and followed by Gavin Johnston and Carl Frankel, he ran down to the deposito. Matt and Georgia watched as Anton jumped into the water and pulled the floating figure to the side of the tank. The other men reached down and heaved the body out.

A number of people had gathered at the wall to see what was happening. As the body was dragged out of the water, people craned their necks to see who it belonged to.

'I think it's Randall...' a female voice exclaimed.

'Is he, like, dead?' someone else asked.

Georgia clung to Matt, shaking. He held her head to his chest.

'Don't look,' he said.

But Georgia pulled her head away and saw the men below lifting Randall's limp body away from the side of the deposito. Anton turned Randall onto his front and began pumping with his hand between the lifeless shoulder blades. The body twitched and jerked and several tense seconds later a stream of vomit spewed from Randall's mouth.

James Parker came striding over to where Georgia stood.

'Ambulance on its way, Anton!' he called down.

Anton looked up.

'That means the Guardia, people!' he called back, and immediately the crowd above the deposito began to disperse.

'Are you all right?' Matt asked Georgia.

'I want to see if he's going to be okay, if there's anything we can do to help...'

To James, a crisis like this was men's work. The adrenalin was pumping, and in his view, this was no place for a girl. Seeing Georgia's pale, horror-stricken face, he wanted her out of the line of fire.

'There's nothing you can do, Georgia. Look, the guy's breathing. He was probably drunk or drugged up or more likely, knowing Randall, both. Leave it to the medics, my dear, and get yourself home. Enough's enough. You need to take it easy.'

Georgia looked at him, questioningly. James read her thoughts.

'Look,' he said. 'Peter left me a message. He told me he had to take off for London and he asked me to keep an eye out for you. But it looks like you're going to be taken care of - right?'

'Right,' Matt replied, his arm still around Georgia protectively.

'Then take the lady home, my man. We've all been having a hell of a time these past few days and we need our beauty sleep.'

He pecked Georgia on the cheek and Matt steered her away towards the front of the house.

As they reached the path which branched up towards Casa Dura, Matt asked her, 'Are you sure you still want to check on Tamsin? That was a nasty shock there...'

Georgia turned back to where she could see James.

'James lives right up by Tamsin's place,' she said.

'Hey! James!' Matt shouted. James turned and walked towards them. 'Georgia's worried about Tamsin. She should have been here tonight.'

'It's OK, Georgia,' James called back. 'I'll look in on her on my way home. You go and get some rest and try and forget about this mess till tomorrow. Things usually look less gruesome in the clear light of day.'

Georgia tried to smile, but the smile would not come. Matt noticed that her lips were pale, almost white.

'Are you feeling faint?' he asked.

She shook her head.

'OK, then, give me the torch.'

Georgia did not move.

Matt took the torch from the cesta and switched it on.

His arm still around her shoulder, he said, 'It's all right, Georgia, it's OK. You'll soon be home.'

They started to walk along the narrow, rutted track. After a couple of minutes they were able to make out the shape of Casa Dura in the moonlit darkness. From the road below, the wail of sirens pierced the silence, and an owl, disturbed by the sound, fluttered clumsily out of a high tree and flapped away on its great, feathery wings a few feet from where Matt and Georgia were walking, stopping them in their tracks.

'Christ!' gasped Matt.

Georgia looked at his surprised face and in spite of everything, almost laughed. She felt the life coming back into her body.

'It's just an owl,' she said.

'I don't care, let's get into the house!'

They pushed the great door shut and stood close together in the cavernous entrada. Georgia's earlier sense of fear suddenly returned as the darkness inside the house seemed to loom menacingly about them. Matt picked up on her nervousness, and also felt uneasy. From the floor above, he heard a sound, a movement.

'Was that someone moving about upstairs? A door closing?'

'The house is full of creaks and groans,' she said. 'It's the old beams. And mice.'

'It sounded like a door being closed.'

'There's no-one else here. Only us.'

'Well, if you're sure...' he said, still looking about cautiously, listening for noises.

They stood there without speaking for a few moments.

'Would you like anything?' Georgia asked, her voice echoing slightly in the silence.

'Would you?' he answered.

She shook her head. 'I just want to go to bed,' she said.

'You'll have to lead the way.'

He took her hand, and together they climbed the staircase that led to her room. The door was ajar, and Georgia walked in. Matt stopped at the door way.

'Stay with me,' she said. 'Don't leave me alone.'

Closing the door behind him, Matt went to her, and took her in his arms.

'I won't leave you,' he said. 'I'll stay as long as you want me to.'

He held her more tightly, until it felt like she could hardly breathe. All she could do was cling to him. She looked up, searching, but his eyes were closed, and his expression was hidden from her. But then his lips found hers, and his kiss was warm and full, and in it she found what she had tried to see in his face.

They stumbled over to the bed, pulling at each other's clothes until they lay naked, frantically entwined. Their hands roamed wildly over each other's bodies, their kisses becoming ever more intimate. Georgia was intoxicated, drunk with the scent and taste and feel of him. She felt a thrill at the weight of his body upon hers. His mouth buried in her neck, she could only just make out his muffled words, 'Do you want me, Georgia, do you really want me?'

'Yes,' she said, 'really... really...'

Then all she was aware of was the mad gush of excitement and pleasure running through her, as if he was possessing every part of her, filling her completely.

'Georgia, Georgia,' he groaned helplessly, and she felt the spasm, the tremor inside her, and then she was lost, and her own cry seemed to come from a long way off.

Their bodies still joined together, they turned onto their sides, face to face, both of them hot and breathless, slippery with sweat.

'Georgia,' Matt whispered.

He pushed the damp tendrils of hair away from her face.

'You're beautiful,' he said. 'So beautiful...'

She touched his cheek gently. Her eyes were closing, and he asked, 'Tired, now?'

'Mmmm,' she answered drowsily.

'Sweet dreams, then,' he said softly, kissing her eyelids.

Georgia did not answer. Lying sated in his arms, she was already fast asleep..

CHAPTER SEVENTEEN

A few brief hours later, Georgia, still blinking the sleep from her eyes, was wrapping her dressing gown around herself and hurrying down the stairs.

She had been woken by the urgent clang of iron against wood; someone knocking insistently at the front door. She had just had time to register Matt's sleeping form sprawled in a state of bliss beside her, when another couple of clangs reverberated loudly through the house.

She pulled the door open. It was James.

'Sorry to disturb you at this early hour, Georgia dear,' he said by way of a greeting.

'What time is it?' asked Georgia, yawning.

'Ten after seven. We were on our way back up to Anton's place when we found this young lady at the bottom of your drive, so, naturally, I escorted her up here.'

The "young lady" in question was Antonia, who came blustering along behind him.

Georgia stood aside as Antonia entered the house and made her way into the kitchen. She was thinking, I'd better get Matt out of my room: Antonia's had enough shocks lately. James was still standing in the doorway.

'Gosh, you look grim,' she told him.

'Quite possibly,' he agreed. 'Some of us haven't had the benefit of a night's sleep.'

'Poor James,' she said. 'Come in and tell me about it.'

They went in to the kitchen, where Antonia was busy putting the coffee on. The freshly ground beans smelt good. But Georgia noticed that Antonia was frowning.

'Que pasa, Antonia?' she asked.

'The lady's mislaid her door key. That's why we had to wake you. I do apologise for that.'

'Ah, this morning, I cannot find anything! And no, I did not mislay the key, Señor Jaime,' she replied, searching through one of the kitchen drawers. 'When I left here yesterday morning, around eleven o'clock, then I could not find my key. It was not in my bag, and of course I always put it in my bag. Señora, you know that I never, never mislay my key, isn't it true?'

'I don't remember you ever losing it...'

'Ah! There you are. So what happened to my key? Why did it disappear from my bag where I always put it?'

'Could it have fallen out?' asked Georgia.

'No,' replied Antonia firmly, continuing with her search. 'Where can it be?' she muttered in annoyance.

'Now what are you looking for?' Georgia asked.

'The knife, to cut the bread. How can I cut the bread without the big bread knife? It was here yesterday. I used it to slice the old bread to take home for my sopas.'

'I've no idea. It must be there. Or maybe you took it home in the bag with the bread?'

Antonia answered her with a withering look, and went on rummaging through the drawers. The coffee pot began to gurgle and whistle. Georgia took it off the stove and poured out a cup for each of them.

'Here, this'll make you feel better,' she said to James, who accepted the coffee gratefully. 'Will you excuse me while I throw some clothes on?' she added. 'I won't be long.'

'Take your time, my dear,' said James. 'But I have to be honest with you, Georgia. I didn't make the journey just to accompany the lovely Antonia. I need to have a word...'

'I'll be right back,' Georgia replied quickly.

With Georgia upstairs, Antonia took the opportunity to harangue James with a catalogue of complaints regarding her lost items. Too exhausted to resist, he listened patiently but inattentively. One elbow on the table, his chin resting on his cupped hand, he was on the point of dozing when Antonia broke off her monologue with a sudden shriek.

James leapt up and rushed over to where she was standing, in front of a window that looked out onto the terrace.

'What the hell was that, Antonia?' he called.

'Out there, out there!' she cried.

James peered through the window, just in time to see a figure jump down from the terrace to a path leading off through the olive groves towards Anton's place.

Barefoot, a hairbrush in her hand, Georgia came racing down the stairs.

'What's going on?' she cried in alarm. 'Antonia? Are you all right?'

James was already heading out to the terrace. 'We'll just see what this guy's playing at -' he called back to Georgia as he disappeared through the door.

'It - it was the boy!' Antonia was saying, wringing a tea towel in her hands.

'What boy? What are you talking about?'

They both stood looking out of the window, watching as James nimbly followed the path that the figure had taken. Antonia was starting to calm down.

'Señor Pedro's boy,' she said. 'Luca...'

Georgia was non-plussed.

'For God's sake, Antonia, you almost gave me a heart attack! If it was only Luc, why did you have to scream like that?'

Antonia's face was aghast.

'It was his eyes,' she answered. 'He looked crazy, like a wild man! Loco, loco! He was staring at me, and I was frightened. His eyes, they were red, like fire! I looked at him, I was shocked, and then, suddenly, he turned round and ran!'

Georgia looked towards the window where Luc's face had appeared. What was he doing there? And why did he run away?

'Mother of God!' Antonia was exclaiming. 'What is happening in this place? Everyone is going crazy!'

You included, Georgia was just thinking, when a crash sounded from the floor above, and both women jumped, startled. Georgia felt her heart thudding and she held her hands against her chest. Then she remembered.

'It's all right,' she said quickly. 'We have a guest staying. I expect he must have dropped something.' Antonia's face was white and she stood tensely still, but Georgia noticed her eyes move in the direction of the open door.

'Good morning,' Matt said as he entered, freshly showered and dressed. 'I'm afraid one of the paintings just fell off the wall on the landing. I had a look – the string was all frayed. And the picture's come askew in the frame – it's going to need to be re-hung.'

Georgia hardly heard what he was saying. Her heart was beating wildly, and she felt her cheeks redden as flashes of the previous night flooded her mind.

'Oh,' she said quickly. 'What a nuisance. Never mind, meet Antonia. Antonia, this is my friend, Matt.'

Georgia had to drag her eyes away from him. It was as if she was seeing him for the first time. He looked quite different, although it was difficult to say in exactly what way. And then she knew: before, he had looked like a stranger, someone passing through. Now, she thought, he has a look of belonging. It was not a matter of location, that he was now more familiar in the Casa Dura setting. It was personal: he belonged with her. This knowledge came to her both as a surprise and a conviction. We're meant to be, she thought. It was foretold, Tamsin saw it in the cards. The goodness that was waiting to become manifest, and here it is. Here *he* is. And then she remembered all the other things Tamsin saw, and a shiver ran through her.

In the meantime, Matt's arrival had galvanized Antonia

out of her state of shock and into action. Pouring from an tall jug, she turned her attention to Matt.

'Buenas dias,' she said.

'Buena dias,' he replied.

Antonia held out a glass of freshly squeezed orange juice to him. Matt thanked her and drank it down.

'Very good,' he said.

Antonia advanced with her jug and poured him some more. She pointed outside, indicating that the juice had come from the fruit of the orange trees belonging to the house.

'Ah,' was all he could think of to say in response, but he smiled and Antonia smiled shyly back and, for Georgia, a little fragment of simple ordinariness rescued the morning from a descent into the madness that had been reaching into every moment since the news of the murder at Malek's house had first reached them.

She noticed the way Antonia was eyeing them both, looking from Matt to Georgia and back again, intuiting that this was not just 'a friend', as Georgia had implied. Oh God, thought Georgia, I have no idea how to handle this, as Antonia nodded her head with a knowing look. Saved by the bell, she thought, as the phone started ringing in the sitting room.

'I'd better get that,' she said, and quickly left the room.

'Hello? Diga me,' she said into the receiver.

'It's me,' Peter's voice came back on a crackly line.

'Peter!' Georgia's heart jumped into her throat.

'What's happening?' he asked.

'What's happening with you?' she replied, stalling. 'Where are you?'

'I'm still in Palma.'

'In Palma?'

'Is everything OK?' he asked brusquely.

'Depends what you mean by OK...' she answered.

This is not right, she was thinking. He should be in London. She had not counted on him still being on the island.

'Why aren't you in London?' she asked.

'Because ... because I had some stuff to sort out. Georgia, I have to talk to you.'

'Go on, then,' Georgia replied hesitantly.

'Not on the phone. Can you come and meet me?'

'What, now?' she asked. 'Where?'

How does he do this, she wondered. Where did he get this power to rock the ground she was standing on with just a few words?

'Can you meet me at the airport, at about three? I'm flying First, so we can use the VIP lounge.'

'Three o'clock?' Georgia repeated.

'Yeah...'

She thought for a moment. She did not want her whole day to be disrupted by this unwelcome meeting. What could it be that was so important?

'Are you sure we can't talk now? Peter? Peter?'

Damn! The line had gone dead. Now what was she supposed to do? Had he gone deliberately? Would he be expecting her at the airport? I don't think I actually said yes, she thought. She stood, biting her fingernail, wondering what to do, when she heard the sound of someone outside.

As she walked back into the entrada, Anton entered through the open door flanked by two police officers, smart and brisk in their navy trousers, boots, and shining white short-sleeved shirts, the sun glinting off their mirrored sunglasses.

'Buenas Dias,' barked one of them.

Georgia returned the greeting and turned to Anton.

'What's all this?' she asked.

'Can we go in and talk?' he asked.

His look told Georgia it was serious: God, she thought, if I hadn't just spoken to Peter on the phone, I'd have sworn they were coming to tell me I was a widow.

'Of course,' she said, and noticing Antonia peering round the kitchen door, led the way into the drawing room.

Anton closed the door behind them.

'So -' Georgia looked at the three men.

'What it is, Georgia,' Anton explained, 'is there's some new evidence.'

'Evidence?'

'Yes...' he looked towards the police officers.

One of them shifted on his feet and prepared himself to address her.

'Senora,' he said in a flatly formal tone, 'we have come in connection with the murder of the young girl. We are looking for the murder weapon and we have a warrant to search your house.'

She turned to Anton.

'This is just routine, right?' she asked him. 'They're searching everywhere, all the houses?'

'Not exactly...' he replied hesitantly. 'This evidence I was telling you about - it kind of implicates Randall. It's something Randall had written.'

Georgia was looking at him questioningly, expectantly. He started speaking in Spanish, so that the officers could understand what he was telling her.

'How much do you know about what happened to Isabel, Georgia?' he asked suddenly.

'Well, that she was stabbed, that it happened in Malek's house. That Antonia, our maid, was there when Isabel's body was found and then she came up here and told us what she'd seen. But I imagine everyone knows all that by now?'

The three men were watching her intently, waiting for her to continue.

'And I know that Estoban confessed to the murder, though I found that hard to believe. Peter didn't believe it either. He thought...' Her words tailed off as she felt the intensity and anticipation in the three pairs of eyes, all focussed upon her.

'What did Peter think?' Anton prompted.

Georgia faltered. 'He – he didn't want me to be alone in

the house when he left for London yesterday. He said it might not have been Estoban, it might have been some lunatic still out there.'

The men exchanged glances.

'Why are you asking me all this?' she questioned.

One of the officers spoke.

'Did your husband make any suggestion that the murderer could have been this American who worked for you?'

'Randall?' Georgia exclaimed. 'God, no! Randall was here in the house last night! I had no idea -'

'So, your husband, you don't think he suspected this man, the young American?'

'No, absolutely not! He said nothing about him. I mean, why? Why would Peter suspect Randall? I don't understand -'

Georgia felt the panic rising in her throat. She could hear her voice becoming thin and taut, a line of sound streaming out into the ether.

The door opened, and they all turned round as James, slightly breathless, walked in.

'I lost him,' he said to Georgia. Then turning to the three men, he spoke in Spanish. 'Luc,' he said. 'He ran off for some reason, but I couldn't catch up with him. Headed down towards your place, Anton.'

'We can attend to that later,' Anton replied, brushing the issue aside.

'Does Georgia know about -?'

'We're getting there,' said Anton.

'Georgia, dear,' said James, taking command of the situation. 'This is going to be difficult. Why don't we all sit down?'

Georgia responded at once.

'Yes, of course - please, everybody -' she said. James sat down on the sofa and patted the place beside him. Georgia went over and sat next to him nervously, placing herself on the edge of the seat, and Anton took an armchair opposite. The officers remained standing.

'Now, I'm going to say this right out, Georgia, so brace yourself,' James began.

Georgia nodded, her heart pounding painfully.

'Randall had a thing going with Isabel. Did you know that?'

Georgia shook her head.

'No,' she said. 'I thought she and Tom -'

James seemed to ignore the remark.

'Listen, Georgia, Randall was seeing Isabel, like I said, and then,' he looked into her eyes, so that she had to look back, 'and then, that night, he went to see her, and he found her writing a love letter to someone else.'

Georgia waited. The silence was so heavy she could almost feel the weight of it bearing down upon her. Her mouth was dry, her nerves so raw it hurt. 'Why are they looking at me like that?' she wondered. What am I supposed to say? And then, somehow, calm descended, and the question came to her.

'She was cheating on him?'

'That's right,' James answered.

The next question was ready and waiting, too, she found. And before she asked it, the answer leapt at her, spelled out in large letters before her closed eyes. Knowing allowed her to keep her composure, for which little she was thankful.

'Who else was she seeing?' she asked.

James drew in his breath.

'I'm going to give it to you straight, Georgia. Randall said - and I'm afraid it checks out - he said it was Peter.'

Georgia sat very still

'Peter,' she replied flatly.

'Yes, Peter. Did you have any idea?'

'No. None at all.'

Anton leaned forward towards her, a concerned expression on his face.

'We just thought, maybe - we know there've been a few problems -'

'You don't need to be so delicate,' Georgia interrupted. 'It must be common knowledge our marriage is on the rocks. But no, I knew nothing of this, nothing at all.'

'I'm sorry, Georgia. We had to tell you. They had to find out how much you knew...'

'You said it checked out? How? How do you know it's true?' she asked.

James answered carefully.

'The letters Isabel was writing – they were to Peter. They were pretty graphic. And there was -' he stopped, noticing the look on Anton's face. Too late.

'What?' asked Georgia.

James looked like he wanted to kick himself, but he could not see a way to avoid answering.

'There was a photograph,' he said.

It was the final blow. Georgia covered her face with her hands. She had seen Anton's expression. And James'. They had both seen the photograph. They didn't need to tell her - one of Malek's, no doubt, and she knew the style. Squalid Polaroid shots of stupid, shameless girls. Only this one included the image of her stupid, shameless husband.

Georgia burned with anger and revulsion and the searing pain of betrayal. He betrayed me, she thought, with that little slut. How could he? Words she had heard flew back at her: Antonia - 'There were pictures, bad pictures, I didn't look too much...' and Tamsin - 'She had no pity for us!'

Georgia felt the sting of tears in her closed eyes, and James' arm went around her shoulder.

'I'm so sorry, dear, so sorry...' he said.

Georgia felt such hatred at that moment, hatred for Isabel, hatred for Tom Malek - yes, certainly for him! - but hatred most of all for Peter who had betrayed her and disgraced himself so horribly. He hadn't even covered his tracks. They all knew! Everyone - except her.

Georgia wiped her face with her hands, and looked at the police officers. 'The knife,' she said, her voice muffled and shaky. 'Randall came here with a knife last night. I just thought it was one of the tools he used for clearing the terraces, for pruning.'

The men all looked at her. One of the officers spoke.

'Do you know where he put this knife?'

'Yes,' she said. 'It's out here.'

They all followed her out into the entrada. Georgia went to the cupboard in the wall where she had seen Randall put the knife the night before, and knelt down to open it. She reached inside.

'NO!' the two police officer shouted in unison.

Georgia drew back fast, as if her fingers had been burnt. The officers rushed forward. One of them helped Georgia to her feet. The other, taking a pair of plastic gloves and a plastic bag from his hold-all, removed the knife gingerly by its heavy wooden handle. Once encased in the plastic bag, he held it out to show his colleague. They conferred briefly, and then, satisfied, turned back to Georgia.

'Thank you for your help, Señora,' the more senior officer ventured. 'I am sorry we have had to disturb you.'

'Will you be all right if we leave you, Georgia? You won't be alone?' James asked discretely.

'No,' she replied. 'I'll be all right.'

The men started to walk towards the front door.

'Wait!' she called. Another question had presented itself.

They stopped and turned round.

'What's happened to Randall? Is he still in hospital?'

Anton exchanged a look with James before replying.

'Yes, he's still there,' he said. He noticed Georgia's face cloud over.

'So what will happen?' she asked nervously, imagining Randall, crazier than ever, staggering back to Casa Dura. 'I mean, will they let him go till he stands trial or what?'

Anton was emphatic. 'No way. He's under armed guard. As soon as the doctors give the say so, he'll be carted off by the police. I can promise you, Randall's not going to be roaming round these parts again.'

'That's good,' she said, with relief. There were no more questions left. Not for the time being, anyway.

Anton put his arms around her and held her for a moment.

'Come by anytime you want,' he said. 'If there's anything I can do...'

She nodded, and watched pensively as they walked away.

*

Georgia went to look for Matt in the kitchen, but he was no longer there. From somewhere in the house she heard a faint strain of music, and followed the sound to her workroom at the far end of the entrada. Matt was sitting on the floor, playing on her guitar, singing softly. She stood at the door, listening, until he looked up.

'A Rodriguez,' he said approvingly. 'Beautiful instrument.' He held the guitar up and looked at the wood, the shape, the workmanship. 'Hope you don't mind?'

'No,' she said, 'I don't mind at all. You play beautifully. Will you teach me?'

'It'd be a pleasure.'

'This is my room,' she explained. 'Where I keep all my things.'

Matt looked around him. He had already noticed that it was quite different from what he had seen of the rest of the house. It had the same high ceiling sloping down to the windows, the beams, the whitewashed walls, the stone flagged floor. But it lacked the austere starkness of the other rooms. They had a feeling of being stripped down; this room was the opposite. For a start it had colour; the other rooms seemed to have been arranged to reflect the outside, the landscape, almost to merge with it. But this room reflected Georgia. A couple of bright kelims on the floor, an old record player and a collection of LPs, books on shelves and in piles everywhere, a sheaf of music, a desk covered in writing paraphernalia, photographs in little silver frames. On the wall, paintings, drawings - hers? he wondered - a wind chime hanging in front of the window. A feathered black and gold Venetian mask hanging from a nail in a beam. On the floor, an old bean bag and a few scatter cushions; a wood burning stove. It was the only room that had curtains at the long, deep windows, curtains made from the material that seemed to be a local speciality, woven in a pattern of pale blue and white chevrons. Coloured glass paperweights stood on a side table, and there were lamps with fringed shades. He noticed a rosary with wooden beads hanging from a corner of a framed picture of the Madonna and Child. The wall opposite the window was mainly occupied by a psychedelic John Lennon poster and some prettily faded Japanese prints of snow-topped mountains and cherry blossom. It was a good room, he thought, it had a good feeling. Like she said, it was where she kept her things.

'Will you keep me, too?' he asked.

Georgia smiled.

'Come here' he said, and she went over to where he sat.

He pulled her towards him, and she leaned in close against his chest.

'So, what was that all about?' he asked, nuzzling her neck.

'It was the police,' she said. She hesitated for a moment, and then she said, 'It was Randall. Not Esteban. It was Randall who killed Isabel.'

She extricated herself from his embrace and walked over to her desk, and started randomly picking up objects from it: letters, pens, a picture of her parents and herself as a small child.

Matt stood up quickly and went over to her.

'The freak that was here last night? The one who nearly drowned in the tank?'

Georgia, her back to him, nodded. She showed him the photograph she was holding.

'This is the only photo I have of myself with my parents,' she told him.

'Really?' he asked. 'Why's that?'

'They separated shortly after it was taken, when I was three. My father married someone else and he has a whole other family now – wife and three kids in Toronto. Mummy married again as well, but it didn't work out. She died of cancer when I was sixteen.'

'You look very like her,' was all he could think of to say.

Georgia put the photo down.

'It was quite good, really, with the police,' she said. 'I was able to show them where he'd left the murder weapon. It was the knife he used for cutting branches and things - pruning. He'd been swinging it around like a toy just before you arrived. I made him stop, and he put it away in the tool cupboard. That's how I knew where it was.'

Matt was thinking: this is crazy stuff all right. He felt a kind of panic, rising in his throat; was it his own, or was it coming from her? Either way, he thought I have to get a grip here. I made a promise I'd take care of her...

'How are you feeling?' he asked gently.

'I don't know. There was something else - I don't know how to say it...'

'I always think the best way is just to spit it out,' he said coaxingly.

Solemnity did not come easily to him, even in a crisis. What could she have to tell him that was worse than what had already occurred?

'My husband was sleeping with the girl who was murdered,' she said.

'They told you that? And he really did it, and got himself caught out into the bargain? Well he's got to be the biggest arse of all time then, hasn't he?'

He couldn't help it. It was out of his mouth before he had time to think. Uh oh, he thought, that probably wasn't the right response. But then again, maybe it was, because it had made her laugh.

He put his arms around her.

'That's bad. I mean, I don't know the all the facts, but whatever they are, that's bloody awful. He must be some kind of a madman. At least he's gone. He's out of your life.'

'If only,' she replied. 'He rang up just before the police came. He's still on the island. He wants me to meet him at the airport this afternoon.'

'Are you going to?'

'I have to. I have to hear him out. I probably won't like it, but that's not the point.'

'Okay...' And then he remembered. 'Shit!'

'What?'

'I'm going back to London today! The flight's about five. I'm going to have to make my way to the Puerto.'

Georgia looked at him for a moment.

'In that case,' she said, 'we'll have to move fast.'

Matt looked at his watch.

'It's quarter to ten; I don't need to be back there till about two. All I have to do is throw things in a suitcase.'

'Good. That means we've got time for a swim.'

'A swim?'

'Yes. I refuse to let my entire life be messed up by all this. There's a place I want to show you, in case I never come back here. In case I never see it again. When I remember it, in years to come, I want you to be part of the memory.'

'We'd better get going, then,' he replied.

CHAPTER EIGHTEEN

'Peter.'

Gavin sauntered through the door, his handsome face sporting the easy boyish grin that he was famous for, the disarming smile that enabled him to effortlessly seduce numbers of breathless young women; elegant, older (often married) women; clever, brittle, challenging, career women. It also helped him to engage with ease all the hard-bitten, hard-living male journalists, agents, war-mongers, publishers, newspaper editors, politicians, mercenaries and other red-blooded types who populated his full and busy life. Gavin Johnston was as well-known for his laid-back charm as he was for his promiscuity. He liked to think he came across as a relaxed, fun type of guy. He did, on first meeting, but it was an illusion. Gavin's smile was the foil for a fully signed-up workaholic who never went anywhere without his little black book and a good supply of expensively engraved business cards.

'Got stuck behind a water truck this side of the mountain - they've become a bloody traffic hazard. If it doesn't rain soon, the next thing'll be rationing.'

'We've been rationing at Casa Dura since the beginning of July. Five-minute showers and I piss out on the lower terrace to save flushing. Haven't managed to persuade Georgia yet...'

'Ha!' Gavin gave a croaky, schoolboy laugh.

They lapsed into temporary silence and turned their eyes to a large portrait in oils. The subject was a woman, seated on an ornate, high-backed chair, dressed in an ankle-length black evening dress with long, full sleeves and a plunging neckline. Her face, turned to one side, was partly in shade, but a thin shaft of light illuminated her yellow hair and her rosy white decolleté. The flashes of gold and white rosiness stood out against the background of formless shadows thrown against darkened walls. Her bare feet rested on the floor, and next to them stood a bottle of red wine and two glasses. The painting exuded a sense of bohemian sophistication and pleasure-weariness. The woman's pose, her manner, suggested an easy familiarity with her setting, though her half-concealed facial expression gave nothing away except an air of languor or boredom. The painting's title was The Artist's Model, but everything about it, Peter was thinking, implied that there was a lot more to the relationship than that.

'One of Paul's,' said Gavin.

'Yes,' answered Peter.

'Cristiane,' said Gavin.

'Hmm...'

'Good picture. Always liked Paul's style.'

Peter responded with a barely audible grunt. He was standing absolutely still, his posture stiff and straight, arms folded across his chest. His posture reflected a resolute determination to defend himself against the inner turbulence that was smashing at his very core. Inside, a shout of anguish reverberated through his body: This cannot have happened! This cannot be happening! But outwardly, outwardly no-one must see, the shout must not reach his throat, the inner tumult must never be glimpsed. It would be the end, annihilation, and he hid the full extent of fear and shame even from himself.

So he stood there, his face a mask, staring intently at a painting that he would happily have put his foot though.

They were inside Cristiane's little gallery in the old part

of the city. It consisted of two interconnecting ground-floor rooms. The upper floors of the house had been converted into apartments, one of which Cristiane kept as her pied-á-terre, her hideaway, as she like to call it.

The gallery was cosy and intimate, with paintings and tapestries carefully hung close together on plain white walls, pieces of sculpture displayed on plinths rising up from the ochre and lapis tiled floor, velvet curtains sweeping against the arched doorway that separated the two rooms.

Against one wall, a deep sofa draped in a hand-embroidered Indian throw invited customers to sink back comfortably as they sipped a tiny cup of thick sweet Turkish coffee or a glass of sherry while they discussed the pieces on sale and decided which they would buy. Peter called it Cristiane's casting couch. He had often enjoyed listening to her sales pitch: 'Cheri! But it's the most precious thing in the whole gallery! I can hardly bear to part with it, and really the price is ridiculous - it's like giving it away! But I can see it's chosen you, darling, and you must have it, c'est tout...' Once lured to the sofa, her victim would not easily leave without making an expensive purchase.

Gavin had entered the gallery hurriedly, and it was only as he turned back toward the door that his eye was drawn to a piece looking toward him from the corner of the room: an olivewood carving of a naked girl. It reminded him of a Dégas ballerina: the small, pointed breasts, the gently curved hips lightly draped in a wisp of gauze. And then he looked again. 'How the bloody hell,' he asked himself, 'did I miss that?'

The head of the girl was thrown back in a carefree gesture, long hair tumbling down in a wild cascade of curls and tendrils, tilted eyes looking out questioningly, lips parted capriciously somewhere between a smile and a pout. The warmth of the wood, its golden sheen, gave the carving a disturbingly life-like aspect, so that from a glance out of the corner of one's eye it seemed about to move, as if a tiny wood-nymph had strayed into the gallery from some secret, sunlit mountain grove and might skip lightly back there at any moment.

As he looked, Gavin began to feel a slight twinge of uneasiness: the slim arms, the firm little buttocks, the small hands and feet belonged to a girl whose childhood was not far behind her. The model for the carving seemed so present; she seemed to inhabit the statue, her youth and vivacity glowing through the wood, imbuing it with the radiant freshness of young skin. Combined with the unmistakable sexual invitation in the girlish face and the clean, pubescent body-shape, the effect was disconcerting.

Peter had followed Gavin's eyes over to the statue with resignation. Well, there was no way he could have avoided seeing it, was there? He had arranged to meet Gavin in the gallery not realising the piece would be on display.

'Come on,' he said quickly. 'Let's grab a coffee.'

'Sure,' said Gavin, still looking at the carving. 'Bloody hell, that gave me a start.'

'Cristiane should have taken it down,' Peter replied. 'I don't know what she thinks she's playing at. Let's get out of here.'

'Probably part of Anton's new exhibition. Where is Cristiane, anyway?' Gavin replied, walking towards the door and casting a last backwards glance at the carving.

'Up in her apartment. She asked me to shut the place up after us. She's not opening today.'

'Old Cristiane, eh?' said Gavin. He wasn't sure whether Peter knew about his own brief *affaire* with Cristiane the previous summer.

'Yeah,' Peter replied, turning the key in the lock.

'So what'll it be, the Formentor?' asked Gavin.

'Christ, no,' Peter replied. 'We'll run into half of Santa Marta in there. No, there's a little place off the Plaza España, OK?'

'Fine by me.'

They walked along the narrow street which eventually brought them into a large square, lined with palm-trees on one side and dominated by a church with a tall bell-tower, at the front of which a series of broad steps lead up to an impressive entrance. Peter passed the church purposefully, and turned down a cobbled passage way at the far side of it. Halfway along was an obscure little bar. He led the way inside.

'I know this place,' said Gavin. 'I came here once with James...'

'You're kidding,' said Peter.

'Not recently. I don't know if anyone comes here these days. It was about ten years ago. We were checking out the night-life, doing a little tour. We were fairly loaded by the time we made it this far. I just remember the name: La Brasileña. They used to have music here at night, a little samba group. It was when the whole bossa nova thing first came out...' Gavin gave up on his reminiscence in the face of Peter's resolute lack of interest.

Inside the bar was long and dark and narrow. There were a few leather-covered stools at the bar which ran along one wall, and a row of booths along the opposite wall. Peter and Gavin went and sat in one of them.

'Fancy something to eat?' asked Gavin. 'What about a few tapas and a couple of beers?'

A swarthy, moustachioed waiter garbed in the standard white shirt and black trousers, black apron falling from his waist to his Cuban-heeled boots, ambled over and took their order. Within a couple of minutes a basket of bread and a bowl of olives arrived together with two bottles of San Miguel. Peter took a long swig straight from the bottle.

'That first gulp, when it hits the back of the throat, it's the best,' he said pouring the rest of the beer into his glass. For a minute or two they drank their beer and helped themselves to bread and olives. Gavin drizzled olive oil and vinegar from long-spouted carafes onto a side plate, sprinkled some salt on the mixture and dipped a crust of bread into it.

'*P'am boli*,' he said. 'Food of the gods,' and laughed as he took another bite.

Peter joined in the laughter, unconvincingly.

'I thought you were just supposed to rub oil and garlic on the bread,' he replied.

'Everyone's got their own way of doing it. I like it like this,' Gavin said.

Peter took another swallow of beer, put the glass down on the table, and lit a cigarette. Gavin noticed that his hand was shaking.

'It's a bit of a mess, isn't it?' he said, his face now serious.

Peter stared across the table at him.

'I should have seen it coming,' he replied. 'Not this,' he added hurriedly, 'but something. I didn't take it seriously enough. It's all been so bloody grim with Georgia, anything else seemed like light relief.'

'Hey, come on, Peter,' Gavin countered. 'You're not going to stick the blame on Georgia?'

He gave a short defensive laugh to take the bite out of the question.

But it was exactly what Peter had in mind to do. He had practically convinced himself that if it had not been for the issues with Georgia, for which he absolutely blamed her, none of the recent events would have occurred.

'Gavin...' he replied half-heartedly. 'Look, you don't know what it's been like. Georgia's so bloody insecure, she's impossible. It'd drive anyone over the edge. I mean, what the hell does she want? She has everything, but nothing makes her happy. You can't reason with her. She's hyper-sensitive. Do you have any idea what it's like to live with someone that neurotic? I make allowances, of course, but if you want to know the truth,' he lowered his voice, his tone more deeply confiding, 'Georgia's pretty unstable mentally. She never properly got over her mother's death, and that was when she was sixteen, for God's sake. Between you and me, Georgia has some problems. Serious problems.'

Gavin was not easily roused to anger; there was not really anything he cared that much about. But he realised, at that moment that his hackles were rising. To conceal it, he broke off a piece of bread, dipping it around in the oily mess he had made in his side plate. He was thinking back a few years, seven years to be precise, when he had been responsible for that first meeting between Georgia and Peter. As is the way with so many a life-changing moment, it could all so very easily not have happened.

*

It had been an evening in April. Gavin was at his mews flat, just about to leave for a party, a book launch being given by his publishers, when Peter turned up in a dark mood. It had been brought on by his - just that day - having turned thirty-nine.

Gavin, a couple of years behind him, could not see the problem. But for Peter it meant one year left to the big Four O, as he put it, which he deeply dreaded as the gateway to old age. Gavin was reluctant to exchange what might well be an interesting party for a morbid drinking session with Peter, so by way of commiseration, he had persuaded him to tag along.

'Come on,' Gavin had coaxed him. 'Angus says he's just taken on an absolutely stunning girl – French, I think he said. I'd say it's our duty to go and check her out - and free champers, to boot! It's only down the road, just round the corner from the V and A. What are we waiting for?'

Peter was persuaded and, strolling along the smart, leafy London streets that led from Gavin's Gloucester Road flat to the Victoria and Albert Museum, even he brightened up as they joked and chatted and, inevitably, ended up recalling other such events and romantic interludes that had ensued.

Arriving at the party, they spotted her the moment they walked into the room. Well, she was unmissable, and Gavin was absolutely knocked for six. Beside her, all the other women there paled into insignificance. Long tan suede boots, white mini dress clasped at the waist with a gold chain belt, shiny black shoulder length hair, and the most strikingly pretty face he had ever seen.

Angus, the editor who had worked with Gavin on his latest book, came over to them with a couple of flutes of champagne. He followed their line of vision.

'That must be the girl you were talking about, Angus. Am I right?' Gavin asked.

'It is indeed she. And I suppose you'd like to meet her? Well just remember that a) she's only nineteen, and b) I saw her first and c) I am completely head over heels, so hands off, you predatory pair of bastards.'

The girl, sensing, perhaps, that she was the object of their attention, turned round at that moment, and walked over to them. She smiled, slightly unsurely, as Angus made the introductions.

'These men,' he told her, 'are pirates. Adventurers of the worst type. They give no quarter, so be warned! And this, gentlemen,' he added, his voice softening, 'is Georgia.'

Angus had become embarrassingly soppy-faced, but neither Gavin nor Peter noticed. They were too busy looking at Georgia, eating her up with their eyes.

'So, Angus tells me you're French,' Gavin ventured.

'No,' she answered, in the voice of a well-bred English girl. 'But I've just come back from a year in Paris.'

'Ah, maybe that's why you're looking rather French,' he continued. 'Or at least, much too *soignée* to be strictly English...'

'Well, *strictly*, I'm not. My mother was Armenian,' she answered.

'There you are, I guessed it was something exotic! I was in Armenia a few years ago – amazing country. I remember my first sight of Mount Ararat, covered in snow...'

Gavin was just getting into his stride, but Peter cut him out ruthlessly.

'Never mind all that Armenian rubbish,' he said. 'I've been there myself, and it's the back-end of the bloody universe. Tell us what you were doing in Paris, instead.'

'Erm, French and art and that sort of thing,' she said, a bit startled.

'Now that sounds much more interesting,' Peter replied, fixing her with a piercing eye. 'Come and tell me all about it.'

And, leaving Angus and Gavin open-mouthed, he steered her off to an empty sofa at the far end of the room, where they proceeded to spend the remainder of the evening, deep in conversation. Gavin, and more so, Angus, never forgave him for it.

*

Peter frowned sadly as he spoke. 'I've done everything I can to look after her. To try to keep the marriage together...' He swallowed a large gulp of beer.

'Peter,' Gavin responded, 'you were screwing Isabel.'

Peter drew on his cigarette and blew out a stream of smoke. 'That's not exactly how it was...'

Gavin crushed another piece of bread onto the table. 'Oh, sorry. How was it, then?' he asked.

The door to the bar opened and Peter, facing towards it, looked up sharply. It was a local couple, pleasant-looking, smartly dressed, obviously regulars judging by the waiter's familiar welcome. Peter scowled and took a drink of beer.

'It was just something that...occurred. I didn't look for it or pre-plan it. I was down at Tom's one night. We'd been having a drink with a few other people, and Isabel turned up. We went on drinking and then it was like all of a sudden everyone else had gone, and I was alone there with her, and she was telling me all about her problems with her mad mother. She was coming on to me, man! I didn't mean it to go that far, but I suppose I must have been pretty drunk. When I woke up in the morning I was in bed with her, and Tom had made us all coffee.'

He lit another cigarette and glanced up at Gavin through the smoke. 'I know,' he said. 'It's not good.'

'Have you talked to Georgia about it?'

'Are you kidding?'

'It's going to come out.'

'Not necessarily...' he said. 'Where have those bloody tapas got to?' He called the waiter over and asked for two more beers and whether they could hurry up with the food.

'Anyway,' he said, turning back to Gavin. 'This isn't what I wanted to talk about. There's something else.'

'Hang on a minute,' Gavin interrupted. 'Where does Randall fit into it?'

'I don't know if he was having a scene with Isabel. I don't think so. I mean, they smoked a bit of dope together. Randall's fairly well in with Malek, he's often down there at the house. So, who knows?'

'And Tom?'

'Well, obviously, Tom. But that was a while back.'

'How far back?'

Peter attempted a smile, but it died on his lips. 'Six months, maybe more. Possibly a year. Something like that.'

'Bloody hell, that's jailbait territory...'

The waiter arrived with an assortment of little dishes. He started to place them on the table with a glance of dislike at Peter: grilled squid, prawns in garlic and parsley, fried potatoes, smoked mountain ham, asparagus with mayonnaise. For a moment the two men forgot the direness of the situation and gave their attention to the food. As soon as the waiter had gone, they tucked in.

'Mmm, good,' said Gavin.

'And less than six quid, including the beers,' Peter boasted.

Gavin wiped his mouth on his napkin, and resumed his former, more serious expression.

'So,' he said. 'Who's next?'

Peter hesitated. 'Luc may have had some involvement,' he said at last.

'Luc?' Gavin thought for a second. To his ears, this was the most sinister news so far. 'I saw them together once or twice, down at the Cala,' he said slowly. 'But I have to say, I don't know the kid well. He floats about like a will o' the wisp, but he never really seems to engage. Off in his own space, isn't he?'

'He's very introverted, and he's always been a bit secretive. Cristiane thinks he may have got into some kind of homosexual scene. I think she's wrong, but she says he never shows any real interest in girls. And he's started hanging out in some pretty sleazy places, back-street clubs packed with all sorts of dodgy types, according to Cristiane.'

'So what's the connection with Isabel?'

'He knew her through Randall. The three of them spent time together. Apart from that, I don't know. Except for something that I think I'm going to have to tell the cops about...'

Gavin shifted in his seat and lit another cigarette. The more he heard, the less comfortable he felt. Curious as he was, he would have preferred not to be privy to these particular confidences. But over the years, Peter had helped him out a few times, and he was aware that he owed him. He had to stay and hear the rest.

'It was the night of the murder,' Peter went on. 'I was in the café with Carl and James and a whole crowd of people. We'd just finished dinner and we'd had a few drinks. I guess it was about half-eleven. Luc suddenly appeared.' Peter pushed away his plate and lit a cigarette.

'He came over to us. Seemed fine. Said something about checking out a new nightclub in the Puerto. Asked if he could borrow the car. I gave him the keys.'

Gavin was listening intently.

'Okay...' he said.

'An hour later he was back. I know it couldn't have been more than half-twelve, because that's when Pepe shuts up shop, and he was just in the process when Luc walked in. He gave me the car keys and he was gone again.'

Peter sat in thought for a moment. Gavin waited.

'The thing is,' said Peter, 'when they picked me up yesterday, the cops said my car had been spotted down at the Cala round about the time Isabel was killed. And it's a one-off in these parts, isn't it? I mean, an MG – it's not like I drive a Seat or a Jeep. If someone saw a car that answers to that description, then it's pretty well got to be mine.'

'Have you spoken to Luc?'

'No. Cristiane's beside herself. He's been missing since his appearance on the terrace at our place night before last. Cristiane got him as far as the main drag in Santa Marta, but then he took off again. No-one's seen him since.'

'Christ, Peter, you've got to tell the police! Why didn't you tell them when they had you in?'

'It slipped my mind.'

Gavin shook his head in disbelief.

'It's true - I meant to, but after Esteban came in and confessed, it all got a bit disjointed. They left me for a while, then sort of picked it up again, but their attention wasn't in it; they'd got their man – or so they thought. Then they just said, fine, you can go. I said, that's it? They said, sure, that's it. Muchas gracias. Now fuck off.'

'So what now?'

'I spent last night talking it through with Cristiane, and we drove around trying to find him. Everywhere, we just drew a blank. But now I need to get to London fast to sign the contracts for this movie. If I tell the cops, they may not let me go. I've got a plane ticket for a flight at four-thirty, and the Guardia've given me clearance to go. If I get snarled up in this, I could just end up stuck on the island for weeks, months - and that is *not* going to happen, Gavin.'

Gavin shifted in his chair uneasily.

'What do you want to do?' he asked.

Peter dragged heavily on his cigarette. 'Gavin,' he said quietly, 'I'm going to call in a favour.'

'Right...'

'I've written out a statement and signed it. You just have to give it to them. You don't have to say we discussed it. You don't have to say anything. It's in a sealed envelope. It's pretty vital they get it soon, only not so soon they stop me from leaving.'

Gavin looked at his watch. It was coming up to midday.

'It's a delay of four hours, Gavin, that's all.'

'Peter,' Gavin replied, 'you don't mess with the Guardia Civil. This is fucking serious. You've got to go and tell them yourself.'

Peter got an envelope out from his jacket pocket.

'Look, I understand. Really,' Gavin said, his voice now a hoarse whisper. 'But you're not thinking straight. I'll do it for you, sure, but we can't play around here. If there's any suspicion Luc's got anything to do with what happened to Isabel, then we haven't got four-and-a-half hours. Randall was half-drowned last night, possibly because he knows something. I heard that Dita's come up with some kind of evidence, God knows what. It's all getting pretty intense. This isn't the time to hold back, man.'

Peter was breathing heavily. He ran one hand through his hair in a desperate gesture. Then he took his wallet from his pocket. He put a couple of one thousand peseta notes on the table and placed the envelope on top of it.

'Please, Gavin,' he said. 'Do this for me. I've got to be on that plane.'

Pushing the money and the envelope towards Gavin, Peter got up from his chair and walked out of the bar without looking back.

Gavin sat holding his body so stiffly he wondered briefly if he was ever going to be able to move any part of it again.

There was no sign of the cheerful smile now: his face looked as if it had been cast in stone. He waved over at the waiter.

'La cuenta,' he said.

While he waited for the bill, Gavin sat looking at the envelope, turning it over in his hands. And by the time he had settled up and thrown a few coins down onto the table for a tip, Gavin had decided what he was going to do.

CHAPTER NINETEEN

Matt's heart was full, as they drove towards the port, his mind flooded with the events of the past three days. But all the same, it was a strain to focus on anything other than the moment he was currently in. One hour ago, he recalled with some effort, I was down in a secret cove with this extraordinary girl, not another human being for miles, swimming naked in a deep turquoise sea, so deep you couldn't see down to the bottom, surrounded by immense crags of mountain thrown up by oceanic earthquakes that took place hundreds of thousands of years ago.

High above them, golden eagles had circled, and the only sound had been the sound of the surf, splashing against the rocks. They made love in the waves, and dried out under the pine trees, talking quietly, sharing confidences, laughing together. All too soon, it had been time to take off for the port, and they had dressed and walked the twenty minutes uphill to where they had parked the car in the shade of a carob tree, preoccupied and silent, knowing that the drive had to end in a parting. It was all about Georgia: he was completely hooked, and leaving her now was a hard thing to have to do.

They passed the turning down to the Cala and, more to distract himself than for any other reason, he started thinking of that other girl, the one now presumably lying in a morgue somewhere, her bloodied body cold and stiff. How could something so sordid happen in such an astonishingly beautiful place? Where's the sense in that? he asked himself. And amidst all the talking and the investigations, where was the regret for what had happened to her? Why did no-one seem to care that what had actually occurred here was that a young girl had had her life taken? Out of the side window, he watched the scenery slip by as the car descended towards the Puerto.

'Poor kid,' he uttered, thinking aloud.

'What?' Georgia asked.

'The girl - Isabel. I was just thinking, it's like she's incidental to the whole thing. As if she didn't matter.'

'Didn't matter?' His words triggered a sudden and ferocious rage that took Georgia by storm.

'Georgia! Look at the road!'

Georgia swerved out of the path of an on-coming coach and continued downhill, her driving fast and erratic.

'What are you talking about?' she demanded. 'I told you what they said. Poor girl! All she cared about was getting what she wanted or thought she wanted. Now look at the mess!'

'Come on, Georgia! Malek, Randall, your husband - they held the power, not her. She got into something that was too much for her to handle, and now she's dead. Do you really think that's what she wanted?'

'No - what she wanted was a bit of the high life, and she obviously saw Malek or Peter or Randall and God knows who else as a potential ticket.'

'Georgia, the girl's dead, she's been murdered -'

'So what are you saying? I should be sorry for her? What kind of girl behaves like that, allowing someone to tie her up and take pictures? If she hadn't been so keen to flaunt herself she might not have ended up the way she did.'

'It was wrong, of course it was wrong. But things happen, Georgia -'

Georgia turned sharply into the main road of the Puerto

and screeched to a halt at the kerb.

'What 'things' are you talking about exactly?' she asked, her voice quiet now, and strained.

'Well, you know...sex games. People do stuff like that. You know what I mean.'

'No, I don't know, actually. Tell me about it. You, for instance, what kind of things do you do?'

Matt felt confused, but obliged to answer. They were running out of time. He wanted to finish this, to talk about what they were going to do next, to make plans for when they got back to London.

''Look, Georgia, what do you want me to say? You must know what I'm talking about - just playful kind of stuff. Messing around. You know, sometimes you just try something different. It's nothing - just a bit of fun...'

'What, tying girls up, taking dirty pictures, that sort of fun?'

'Georgia, come on, you know the sort of things people get up to -'

'I don't care about people! I'm asking about you! Is that what you like to do?'

'Georgia -'

'Get out!' she shouted.

'Georgia!'

'No! Get out, get out of my car!'

She leaned across him, flung his door open and pushed him out. He jumped onto the narrow pavement and she slammed the door shut.

'Georgia, please -' he called, but she put the car into gear and swung it round in the road. Matt could do nothing but watch helplessly as she drove furiously back towards the mountain road, scattering pedestrians in her path.

He stood there, stunned, as the car disappeared from view. When it was out of sight, he turned disconsolately back towards the main road. Alone and desolate, his heart thumping hard against his chest, he walked in the direction of his hotel. He passed a small gift shop, and then, remembering something, he turned back and went inside.

'Hóla!' the girl at the counter ventured brightly.

Matt fished inside his wallet and handed her a ticket. She took it away with her and returned a few seconds later holding out a packet of photographs.

'End of holiday?' she asked, in a strong Catalan accent.

'Yeah, end of holiday,' he replied.

*

Outside, on the terrace of the hotel, Phil and Andy were lounging with a couple of girls, the men swigging Spanish beer straight from the bottle, the girls clinging to large glasses of rum and coke, clinking with ice cubes, the bubbles dancing in the sunlight.

'Matt, where've you been?' Phil called with a big grin.

'The coach'll be leaving half an hour, mate!' Andy chimed in.

'Yeah, yeah,' Matt responded, barely glancing in their direction.

'Get a move on then - you haven't even packed! Hurry up and I'll get you in a drink.' Phil took a large gulp from his bottle and added, 'Good night was it?'

Matt walked past them. Over his shoulder he said, 'You enjoy yourselves. I'll be down in a bit.'

'Ah, don't look so glum, mate,' Phil called after him. 'Everyone knows these holiday romances don't mean nothin' serious!'

He winced as his own bleached blonde provider of holiday romance thumped him on the arm.

Matt kicked the door of his room closed behind him, and threw himself onto the bed. He tried to compose his thoughts, but couldn't, and rolling onto his side, he opened the packet of photographs.

He sifted deftly through a series of snaps of Phil and Andy larking about in over-sized sombreros, a few shots of boats in the Puerto, pictures of the hotel. And then he found it.

Lying on his back, he held the photograph out in front of him, his eyes fixed on the glossy image. There was the fish-seller, beaming broadly as she held out the impressive swordfish; and there, in front of her, was Georgia, smiling under her straw hat, the first time he saw her. Matt looked until he had absorbed every detail of her clothes, her posture, her face. Still holding the photograph in his hand, he buried his head in the pillow and for the first time in his adult life, he cried.

CHAPTER TWENTY

As the familiar bends and twists in the road back to Santa Marta flew past, it occurred to Georgia that something was wrong with her. The main symptom was the shivering. Her skin felt cold and clammy and her teeth chattered, yet it was another blazing hot day. The midday sun flashed through the windscreen, making her giddy, and there was a chill in the pit of her stomach.

'What's the matter with me?' she wondered. 'There's something wrong - what can it be?'

She had to struggle to concentrate properly on the road. Her camisole clung to her skin and the pulse in her right temple throbbed heavily.

'Please,' she prayed, 'let me get back in one piece.'

At last the signpost for Santa Marta came into view. She drove past it, through the main street, and wondered whether to stop at Pepe's or to drive up to Tamsin's.

'No, not Tamsin's,' an inner voice seemed to say.

So she kept on driving and, not knowing where else to go, she followed the turning up to Casa Dura and continued, slowly and bumpily, until she reached the fork in the track. Without giving it much thought, she took the path that led to Anton's place.

She pulled up in the shade of a palm tree, not far from the front entrance. Anton, hearing the car, came to see who it was. He found Georgia sitting in the driver's seat, holding onto the steering wheel, the engine still running, her head drooping forward. He quickly opened her door and, reaching into the car, switched off the engine.

'Is the handbrake on, Georgia?' he asked.

She nodded weakly.

'Come on, then.' He helped her out from the driving seat and shut the door. Georgia leaned back against the car.

'I'm not well,' she said. 'I feel all broken up.'

Anton pulled her towards him and held her gently. 'Ah, girl!' he said, holding her more tightly, taking the weight of her body in his arms.

Georgia straightened herself up a little. She was not sure what she wanted from him or what she expected to happen next.

'Come inside,' he said. 'We'll make it all better. Put you together again.'

Georgia allowed him to take her by the hand and lead her into the house. They walked through the cavernous entrada into the equally large but well lit studio, the naked walls hung with Anton's canvases, niches stacked with ceramic pots and bowls of every shape and size, glazed in vivid cerulean blues and earthy oranges, greens and golden browns shot with bronze and gleaming silver, the colours of the Santa Marta landscape. Olive wood carvings stood on the floor and on plinths, and in the middle of it all, an easel bearing a large canvas, its painted surface hidden from view under a paint-spattered sheet.

A pair of Siamese cats mewed and purred and sinuously weaved their way around the room, their sapphire eyes focussed on Anton's every movement. Indian music was playing on the stereo, the beat of the tabla and the drone of the tamura throbbing though the air.

The room smelled richly of incense. Sticks of patchouli and sandalwood exuded wafts of aromatic smoke which weaved itself into the room's native scent of weathered stone over-laid with white spirit, oil paint and French tobacco. Georgia curled her legs under her comfortably on an old velvet sofa, and Anton wrapped a light cashmere blanket around her. She shivered, and he rubbed her arms and back. It felt good, and Georgia allowed him to carry on for a while.

'So what'll it be?' he asked, now gently massaging her neck and shoulders. 'Flower remedy or Fundador?'

'Fundador,' she replied, without hesitation.

Anton poured them each a wine-glass of honey-coloured coñac, and came to sit next to her.

'God, I needed that,' Georgia said, after taking a large sip.

'Don't drink it too fast,' Anton said, and then, rethinking, 'what the hell, drink it as fast as you like.'

He smiled and downed the rest of his own glass.

'Would a little grass help?' he asked.

'No, thanks, I'm not into it. As you know,' she replied with a small smile.

What Georgia would have liked most at that moment was to be left alone to drink another glass of coñac and then fall into oblivion. But at that moment she was still too strung out, and the brandy's initial warmth was turning to fire in her empty stomach. She looked over at the shrouded easel.

'What are you working on?' she asked.

'I'll show you later,' he replied. 'You look shattered, Georgia. Do you want to sleep?' he stroked her arm gently, and pushed the hair back from her face.

'I don't know what I want,' she answered, her eyes half-closed, her body responding to the touch of his hand.

'I have another suggestion,' he half-whispered, his lips close to her ear, his hand moving down her back which arched to his touch.

Georgia turned towards him and sleepily laid her head on his shoulder while his hands continued their adventurous journey. Then, reluctantly, she made him stop.

'Don't,' she said.

He stopped stroking, but still held her close to him. He

was breathing heavily, and she could feel the tension in his muscles. He was bare-chested, naked apart from a sarong knotted around his waist.

'I made love with someone this morning, Anton,' she said quietly.

'The guy you were with last night?'

'Yes.'

'Ah, so that's where the sexy vibe's coming from. And I thought it was me turning you on,' he said with a wry smile.

'It's not that you I don't fancy you, Anton,' Georgia offered, in case he was offended, 'it's just...'

Anton laughed. 'Yeah, yeah,' he said. 'It's OK, Georgia, you don't have to pander to my fragile male ego. It's cool. I hope he deserves your loving.'

Georgia did not reply. Still wrapped in her blanket, she got up and walked over to the easel, and picked up a corner of the sheet that was covering it.

'May I?' she asked.

'Go ahead,' he replied, lighting a cigarette.

Georgia drew off the sheet and took a moment to integrate what she was seeing.

'It's me,' she said.

'Yes, it's you.'

'It's - it's amazing.'

It was a picture of Georgia standing against an open window, and through the window, a full moon rising in a dark night sky over the Tramuntana Mountains.

She said, 'But I didn't sit for you...'

'I've been looking at you for years Georgia. I didn't need you to sit. In any case, it's my fantasy Georgia, it's not really you at all.'

'It's such an incredible picture. It's a bit spooky...'

'That's how I see you. You're a spooky lady sometimes. I like it...'

Georgia was excited by the picture. It was like looking in a mirror, only through someone else's eyes; seeing a self that she vaguely recognised but didn't quite know. She stood for a long time, looking at the Georgia in the picture, wondering about her.

'Anton, can I buy it from you?' Georgia asked impulsively. It seemed terribly important that no-one else should have the painting. It had to belong to her.

'Difficult,' he answered. 'It was commissioned by your husband.'

'No!'

'Yes.'

'But he never told me. He never said anything.'

'He asked me to do it a while back, about a year ago, and I haven't had the time till just recently. It was Peter who asked for the full moon. The rest, he left to me.'

As Georgia considered this, James' words came back to her in repeated fragments, "I'm so sorry, dear, it was Peter - it was Peter - I'm so sorry - so sorry - Peter - it was Peter -", over and over, in a monotonous loop, until she thought she would scream.

It was all hopeless; what was she doing here with Anton, anyway? He was standing behind her now, his arms clasped around her waist, moving his hips to the rhythmic beat of the tabla, his body slyly dancing closer and closer to hers. No, I don't want this, she thought. It's all wrong. Moving swiftly but gently she danced away from him, looking into his eyes the whole time, the hint of a smile playing on her lips. My God, she thought, another one who can't take no for an answer. Her body felt stiff and cramped, and she had pins and needles in her foot but she kept moving towards the door that led to the terrace. From a window recess, the Siamese cats eyed her suspiciously. Don't look at me like that, she thought. I'm not one of his women.

All the while, Anton was watching, fascinated, wondering if it was really possible that she was rejecting him. It had never happened to him before, as far back as he could remember. Certainly not in Santa Marta. Wow! Suddenly

Georgia became even more interesting and desirable. He would have to work on this...

Georgia stopped her dancing and walked out to the terrace that looked towards Casa Dura. The knowledge that Peter had commissioned the painting was bewildering. Where did it fit in to everything else that had been happening? How could she live so close to him and know so little about him? What did it mean about his feelings towards her? Why, whenever she made up her mind about him, did he do something that knocked her off balance again? Why did it always have to feel like she was standing on shifting sand?

Peter, Peter, she wept, everything's ruined - everything! And now it felt like there really was no turning back. Only seven years, she thought. It's nothing! And it was supposed to last forever. They were going to show the world what love meant - at least, that had been her plan. Now, the vow had been broken on both sides, and the marriage lay around them in scattered shards, and painfully she wondered whether Peter had ever loved her at all, the reality of her. A painting, something he could own and enjoy and display - maybe he would find that more satisfactory.

She had long felt herself to be a disappointment to him. Her mind went back to a conversation she had overheard, the end of a conversation. Peter and Carl were talking out on the terrace over a few beers and a game of chess. Carl was saying, '...ah, so that's the story. And she's such a lovely, lovely girl. Beautiful little Georgia.' And then, after a pause, 'Is that why you married her, Peter? Because she's so pretty?' Another pause, and then she heard Peter say, ' Yeah, I suppose it was...'

That was the first time it had occurred to her that Peter was not in love with her. Even then she had thought, but he will love me, it will still work, I can make it work. But that was another lifetime. Somewhere amidst the catastrophic events of the last few days they had passed beyond what people called the point of no return. This was the end, and beside this, everything else paled into insignificance. Whether he loved her or not, Peter had been her life. Without Peter, without Casa Dura, she was alone. He had become everything, and everyone she knew was connected to him. She would have to start again. She thought of Tamsin, also starting again. But Tamsin had her family, she had Poppy, she had her work. And me, what have I got? No-one, no-one except Matt...

And this was the worst thought of all. No, I haven't got him! It was all some kind of day dream. I don't know him, I don't know who he is, he's just some guy, some guy I slept with and then threw out of my car!

And then, clear as crystal, she saw his face, horrified, as she drove off. But it was all his fault, she thought, how could he have said those things? It was his fault, but now that was her one particle of happiness gone; the one bit of hope that had appeared, miraculously, on the horizon. And it hurt so much, to even think about him, to remember back to the cove that morning, the comfort of being with him. Her heart felt as if it was being ripped to shreds. Had she lost Matt? Peter, for sure, was lost to her. The intensity of inner confusion felt as though it might consume her, she could not think, could not separate it all out.

The sound of footsteps at the front of the house jolted her out of her distress. She turned to see Gavin walking towards her. Gavin! That was good. Gavin was a known quantity. He had been part of her life for as long as Peter, he knew them both. She thanked God it was Gavin and no-one else.

'Georgia, Georgia,' he said, his voice filled with concern. 'What's the matter, what's happened, Georgia?'

But her face was covered in tears, and she could not speak. She tried, but all that came out was sobs. Anton had followed her out. He tried to put an arm round her, but she did not want to be soothed or comforted anymore. She was beyond being soothed. It was nice of him, but she wasn't a fractious child to be patted and kissed better. She had to start looking after her own adult self.

Gavin looked at Anton questioningly.

'We had a heavy morning,' Anton told him. 'They found evidence that led them to Randall. Seemed to have started with a bizarre encounter between Dita and Tamsin, but that's a whole other story. They also discovered that Peter had been with Isabel. Georgia just found that out. So it's been kinda rough.'

'I know about Randall. I've just come from the hospital,' Gavin said. 'That was a bit of a shock, too, cops marching all over the place, and then to find that he'd -'

Georgia looked up, her face still stained with tears.

'He'd what?' she asked.

Anton went into the house and brought out some tissues for her, and she wiped her face with them.

'Didn't they tell you?' Gavin asked her.

Georgia looked at Anton.

'It just felt like too much to lay on you, Georgia, after all the other stuff. We weren't trying to keep anything from you.'

'So...'

'Randall's dead,' he said bluntly.

'What happened was, the hospital had discharged him,' Gavin said, filling in the details. 'The Guardia were about to cart him off to jail, either that or the manacomio. But as the nurses were getting him out of bed, he made a run for it and the cops opened fire. They aimed for his legs, but he was pretty weak. Apparently it was very quick. His heart gave out. I suppose after the drowning and the drugs and everything...' He paused for a moment. 'I was thinking,' he said, 'it sounds hard, but it was probably for the best.'

Anton nodded in agreement. 'There was no way a guy like Randall was going to survive a Spanish gaol or the crazy asylum. No way.'

Gavin continued the story.

'They had a lawyer there from the American consulate. I had a word with him. He was saying, whatever anyone tried to do, there's no quick route to extradition. The process can only be put in motion after the trial, and that can take months. A lot of months. He'd explained that to Randall.'

'Randall knew it was time to go, Georgia' Anton said, gently. 'His time was up.'

Georgia replied, 'I'm glad he's dead.'

The two men looked at her.

'Peter said he was harmless, but I always felt there was something badly wrong with him. He should have had some proper treatment when he got back from Vietnam. Maybe he wasn't right even before he went, who knows? If he really was the one who killed Isabel, then it's better he's dead.'

'He was the one,' Anton assured her. 'There was stuff only the person who did it could have known. Randall did a lot of talking last night. And he grassed up Malek big time -'

'And Peter,' Georgia interrupted.

Anton and Gavin said nothing.

'Oh,' she said. 'You already knew about Peter.'

'Malek...' Gavin started to say.

Georgia walked to the doorway. 'What time is it?' she asked.

'Coming up for half-two,' Gavin told her.

'Is it all right if I go and have a wash?' she asked Anton.

'Help yourself, sweetheart,' he replied.

Upstairs, Georgia washed quickly, put on some make-up, and brushed her hair. No time to hang around here, she told herself. People to meet. Things to resolve. She folded Anton's blanket and after leaving it down on the sofa, she went back out to the terrace.

*

Gavin and Anton saw Georgia to the car, having failed to dissuade her from driving to Palma.

Walking back to the house, Gavin asked Anton, 'Have you got a light?'

Anton had a pack of Ducados and a book of matches in his hand. He handed them to Gavin. Gavin gave him back the cigarettes. He took Peter's letter, still in the sealed envelope, from his pocket.

'What's that you've got there?' Anton asked.

'Something that's just become obsolete,' he said, and striking a match, he set light to the unopened envelope and let it burn.

CHAPTER TWENTY-ONE

Matt sat alone at a table in a busy waterfront café, slowly eating his way through a plate of the speciality of the day: roast chicken and chips. He was starving and the food tasted good. It occurred to him, as he ate, that nothing, bar illness, had ever caused him to lose either his appetite or a night's sleep.

After the chicken, he ordered a postre of strawberries and ice-cream, and when he had finished it, he leaned back in his chair and took a swig of mineral water from the bottle.

Phil and Andy had done everything in their limited power to persuade him onto the coach. He smiled to himself as he recalled their baffled expressions when he told them he was not going to board it with them.

'But what if you miss the flight?' they had asked.

'There'll be other flights...'

'But - but, what're you gonna do? Where'll you stay?'

'I'll be all right. It's just there's something I've got to deal with. You have a good journey. See you back in London.'

And they were gone, their uncomprehending, slightly anxious faces pressed to the window of the departing coach.

Matt arranged with the hotel manager to leave his suitcase for a short while, and then set off, intending to take a therapeutic walk around the harbour. Looking back, he was aghast at how stupid he had been. He shouldn't have mentioned Isabel, shouldn't have let himself be drawn by Georgia into saying things that weren't right for that moment, for any moment. It was crazy. The question now, was how to repair the damage. Obviously, he had to see her, to talk to her. But would she see him? Yes, he thought, of course she would. She had to. Unless he had hallucinated the previous twenty-four hours, he knew that Georgia's feelings for him were as intense as his feelings for her, incredible as it might seem. He was at a loss to know what it was she saw in him. But the fact that she did see something had transformed the way he saw himself; in fact, the way he saw his whole life. Something had happened, and now there was no turning back.

Matt paid his bill and left the crowded restaurant. He strolled along the quays, surprised to find himself feeling quite sanguine about his future. How could this be? Thinking about it, it seemed to Matt that meeting Georgia had been like coming face to face with the reality of his life for the first time. Hitherto, he had lived a shadow existence; insubstantial and inconsequential in virtually every aspect. He thought about it all: his current occupation working for a local newspaper as a reporter and photographer was boring beyond belief. Trying to break into the music scene, playing little gigs with musicians who weren't really up to it; nothing was happening, nothing had happened for him, and he had lowered his expectations accordingly. He did not know who or what to blame, his environment or his own apathy. He could blame his schooling: it had been useless, leaving him unqualified and unprepared for either work or life in general. Although, something he remembered from an English lesson long ago came back to him, and it seemed to sum up his life. It was a line from a poem: *We had the experience, but missed the meaning.* He couldn't remember the rest of the poem, or the name of the poet, but that line said it all.

Not now, though. Now, now there was Georgia, and

everything had changed. Life was bursting with meaning! He wasn't afraid anymore. He wasn't afraid to face the future, but at the same time, paradoxically, he was scared to death. He wondered if he might, unwittingly, have stumbled on the meaning of courage.

Without consciously intending to, Matt realised that he had wandered onto the path that led to Esteban's bar. He was suddenly filled with an urge to revisit the place where he and Georgia had first sat and talked together, before the nightmare sequence of events following the murder had shaken them like a series of earth tremors, until it felt as if everywhere they walked cracks might open up in the ground and buildings topple and everything be swallowed up.

Matt went and sat on the same rock he and Georgia had sat upon, and he remembered how carefree she had looked, sitting there in her straw hat with her feet dangling in the water. Even then he had longed to reach out and touch her, hold her, kiss her. He exhaled deeply and, looking down, became distracted by the scuttling movements of a small nacreous creature. He became so absorbed in watching its funny sideways scampering, he failed to notice the woman who came and sat, silent, ghost-like, nearby. Until she spoke.

'You are English?' she asked in a strong Spanish accent.

Matt looked up, startled.

She was an attractive woman with thick, shoulder-length, auburn hair, held back from her face with combs; and she wore a short cotton dress with a floral pattern, which showed off her firm, almost athletic figure. Her skin was lightly tanned, and she looked to be in her early thirties. Matt instinctively moved away as he turned to answer her. Something about her made him intensely uncomfortable.

'Yes,' he answered. 'From London.'

'Did you want a drink from the bar?' she asked.

'No,' he replied. 'No thanks. I just came to sit by the

sea for a while.'

'Ah,' she said. 'It's a beautiful place, isn't it? So peaceful, so far from the crowds of the Puerto. Are you staying there?'

'Yes,' Matt answered.

'In one of the hotels?'

'Yes.'

'So you are on holiday?'

'Yes...'

'I live here,' the woman continued.

'Here?' he asked.

'Right here,' she said, turning towards the bar. 'That is my house - next to the bar.'

'You live there?' Matt wondered what this could mean. Who was she?

'I lived here with my daughter,' said the woman. 'My daughter, Isabel. But we have suffered a great tragedy. A great tragedy...' Her voice began to break.

Matt did not know what to do. He was desperate to escape. 'I'm sorry,' he said weakly.

'Maybe you saw the newspapers?' she asked him. 'It was the main story - on the television, too. You see, my daughter, my beautiful daughter, she is dead - murdered! Only two days ago - you didn't hear about it?'

'I - I heard something. It happened in another village?'

'Santa Marta,' she replied quickly. 'There are some evil people in that place. They live scandalous lives, people who have no respect, no decency. My daughter was murdered by a man who violated her, who degraded her. She was bound so that she could not resist and she was naked, completely naked! And then, then,' Dita's voice was now wracked with sobs, but still she continued, '- he killed her! He took a knife, while she was tied, helpless, and he stabbed her, and left her cut and bleeding, to die...'

Matt watched, as if turned to stone, as she wept. Suddenly she threw back her head and let out an unearthly wail.

'Oh God, how could you let this happen? Why did you

let this happen?' Dita cried out her pain, her hands clutched to her breast.

Matt was terribly disturbed. He could not leave her, but he was overwhelmed by her distress and he had no idea how to comfort her. Then he remembered that he had a handkerchief in his pocket, and he took it out and handed it to her.

'Please,' he said, 'take this.'

Dita shook open the handkerchief and held it over her face as she wept.

'Can I walk you to your house?' Matt asked.

Slowly, Dita wiped her face and blew her nose noisily. She rose from her sitting position, and as she did, Matt got up too.

'Yes,' she said. 'Come with me. I will give you a clean handkerchief. And I want to show you something.'

Matt followed her reluctantly to the bungalow. Dita opened the door, and invited him to enter.

'Wait,' she said, leaving him in the small entrada.

Matt looked around. He saw a heavy mahogany sideboard, covered in old family portraits in large, ornate frames. Against the opposite wall there were two high-backed chairs, and between them a table on which stood an alabaster vase filled with red and white carnations. In a niche in the wall reposed a statue of Santa Catalina, the local saint, gaudily coloured with green and white paint. The entrada smelt of cool stone and flowers and a hint of perfumed Spanish soap.

Dita returned with the clean handkerchief.

'Here,' she said, passing it to Matt. 'Take it.'

'Thanks – there was no need, really -'

'Would you like a drink? A coñac?'

Matt, not usually a great drinker, decided that he needed one quite badly.

'Coñac would be good,' he replied.

Once again, Dita left him alone in the entrada. He waited with anticipation, but he no longer felt so nervous.

The woman, as he assessed it, was wracked with grief, but not mad, not dangerous. When she had cried out, he had been astonished to find in himself a strong desire to cry out with her. Why, he did not know, but that had been his reaction.

Dita came back and handed him a glass. She filled it generously. Matt was relieved to see that she herself was not taking a drink. She opened a door that led off from the entrada.

'This is my daughter's room,' she said. 'I want to show it to you.'

Matt hesitated for a moment, and then walked in after her.

This was a room, he thought, whose occupant would never return. And yet, it was filled with her presence. A typical teenager's room, it was a bit messy, one drawer half-open, the clothes spilling out. The dressing table was covered with jars of make-up, a jewellery box, and an ashtray filled with lipstick-stained cigarette butts. The bed had been made and was covered in a flowery bedspread. The wall was plastered with posters of pop stars and a pile of magazines lay upon the floor.

Dita leaned over the bed and took a box from the window sill. The shutters were closed, and the light in the room was dim. A rag doll lay upon the pillow.

She sat down on the bed, and motioned to Matt to sit beside her. The box had a little drawer, which Dita opened. Inside, it was divided with index cards, marked with numbers from naught to sixteen. It was filled with photographs. Dita removed some randomly, and showed them to Matt. Photographs of a plump baby dressed in lacy bibs and bonnets, the fat little feet crammed into patent leather shoes. A sturdy toddler, pushing a toy cart; a snaggle-toothed schoolgirl in spectacles, sitting at a desk, ink on her fingers.

And then, Isabel, shortly before her death, sitting on the rocks where he and Georgia had sat, her long hair blown about by the breeze, her head to one side, smiling for the camera. She looked cheerful, ordinary, chaste.

Matt was unable to speak. In a moment of stunning clarity, he understood Georgia's horror and outrage. He had unwittingly identified himself with the crime that had been committed against this young girl, and he felt a dreadful sense of revulsion and shame. He turned to Dita and shook his head.

'I'm sorry, I'm so sorry,' was all he could say.

Dita got up from the bed.

'You are a young man,' she said. 'Please tell me. How could they let her die like this? Was she an animal, to be used and slaughtered? Would they let this happen to one of their own children?'

Matt shook his head again.

'I don't know,' he said. 'I don't know how such a thing can happen.'

Together they walked to the door. Matt took one more look around the room, and then they left.

Outside, Dita said, 'I wanted you to see who she was, so that someone would know that, after all, she was just a girl. A little head-strong, yes, but with her whole life in front of her. That's all.'

'I understand,' Matt said, handing her the empty brandy glass. 'Good-bye, Dita.'

'Adios - Matt,' she replied.

It was not until much later on that it occurred to either of them that, without introductions, they had known each other's names.

CHAPTER TWENTY-TWO

The airport was thronging with high-season tourists, the school holiday crowd, out in full force. Georgia picked her way past families of noisy children with mountains of hand-luggage, through the main reception area, until she reached the departure lounge and the small VIP section. Through the glass door she saw Peter, sitting by himself in an armchair, looking sternly at his watch.

'Sorry I'm late,' she said, installing herself in a chair opposite him. 'There was some kind of hold up on the road out of Santa Marta. The Guardia were blocking the way down to the Cala. You can imagine the tailback it caused on that stretch of road...'

'Blocking off the road to the Cala?' Peter asked. 'Any idea why?'

'I've got so used to Guardia action everywhere I look, I didn't even think about it. Something to do with their investigations at Malek's place. I suppose...'

'Well, yeah, of course that.'

Peter's face was dark and stormy. Georgia waited for a reaction, thinking he looked as if he might erupt at any moment. But then, after a moment or two, he seemed to relax. He took off his glasses and examined them for specks of dust.

'Got a hanky?' he asked her.

Georgia looked in her basket and produced a couple of

the tissues Anton had given her.

'That's the best I can do,' she said, handing them to him.

He breathed on the lenses and then rubbed at them. He held the smart, tortoise-shell framed spectacles up to the light and, satisfied, he put them back on.

Georgia waited.

'Sorry for dragging you all the way out here,' he said at last. 'Was it all right, the journey? Apart from the hold-up at the Cala?'

Georgia felt completely exasperated. She was tired, she hadn't wanted to come. And most of all, she was concerned about Matt. She did not want him to go back to London without seeing him again. She did not want him to go away at all. Inside, she felt a frantic need to find him, to explain how she felt, to make him tell her how he felt. She needed him close to her and her need was so urgent and so strong, it made it almost impossible for her to think rationally. And it rendered everything else irrelevant.

'It doesn't matter,' she answered tetchily. 'What do you want to talk about?'

'It's fairly obvious, isn't it?' he snapped back, picking up on her impatience. 'If we're splitting up, which is what it looks like, don't you think there are one or two things we should discuss?'

'What, like practicalities, you mean?' she asked hopefully.

'Among other things...'

'Peter,' Georgia answered in a fierce nervous whisper, 'this isn't the time or the place to go into why we're breaking up. We can't discuss that now.'

'Full stop?'

Georgia held her hands over her face for a moment. Then she looked up with a desperate expression.

'All the talking we've done,' she said. 'Where's it got us? You make accusations, I get defensive. I tell you how I feel, you pick holes in every sentence. We shout, I get upset, end of discussion. What's the point?'

Georgia was aware that she was raising her voice and unable to control the sharp, angry tone. 'It's over!' she went on without wanting to. 'Why not just accept it, and try to get through this final stage with a little dignity? It'd be a new experience for both of us.'

Peter's eyes narrowed. 'God, you're a bitch, Georgia.' He spat the words at her. 'I'd forgotten what a bloody bitch you can be -'

Georgia was on her feet. 'What I am,' she said, her voice suddenly calmer and quieter, 'is an idiot to have come here. Goodbye, Peter.'

Peter jumped up from his chair. 'No, wait...' he said. 'Forget everything. Let's start again. For God's sake, Georgia, we haven't got much time left.'

Georgia hesitated for a moment, and then, reluctantly, sat back down again.

'There's really no chance of patching things up?' he asked, eyeing her with a quizzical expression.

She just looked at him in amazement.

'All right,' he relented. 'So what do you want to do? I don't imagine you want to stick around in Santa Marta?'

'I thought I'd go back to London.' Georgia bit her lip. 'I just have to...to get my head together. I need some time to get over all this,' she said.

He looked at her over the top of his glasses. God, he looks so hateful, sitting there like that, she thought. He looks like a really nasty piece of work. She thought about how hard she had tried to understand him, to get beneath his skin, to know the real Peter. It had been to no avail: she knew him no better now than when they had first met. Perhaps less well.

What was it Tamsin had said the other day? "Peter always plays his cards close to his chest..." That's about right, she thought, angrily. The nights I've spent, hundreds of nights, listening to his tortured ramblings about his miserable schooldays, his cold, authoritarian father, Cristiane's unreasonableness, Gavin's meanness. And poor Peter, the personification of honour, decency, sensitivity, mistreated and deceived on all sides.

At that moment, she had no sympathy for him. All she could see was his selfishness, his ruthlessness, his talent for manipulating the truth and blaming everyone else for his own shortcomings and misfortunes. Projection: wasn't that what the psychoanalysts called it? Throwing your own faults and weaknesses out onto everyone else? Georgia was in no mood to make allowances: her judgement was harsh and one-sided; she knew it and did not care. He had hurt her too much, and she had no desire to show him any leniency.

Something else came back to her, a joke Tamsin had once made about him. "The thing about our Peter," she had said, "is he could hide behind a blooming cork-screw." Peter himself had laughed as much as anyone else. But it was a hard, bitter laugh.

'Peter,' Georgia said, 'I don't like the way you're looking at me. And I'm desperately tired, so why don't we get this over with? Just tell me what it is you need me to do.'

'Well, how kind of you,' he said with mock politeness. 'It's all perfectly straightforward, really, isn't it?'

'I didn't say that...'

He stared at her, a hard look in his eyes.

'Stop looking at me like that!' she said.

He dropped his voice. It became low and hostile.

'I've had an offer on the house,' he said.

'On Casa Dura?'

'It's that German music baron, the guy who owns Steve Southern's record company. He wants to turn it into some kind of super-luxury hotel-come-studio facility for his top artists to use.'

Georgia was completely taken aback. It was the last thing she expected. But then little thoughts flashed through her mind. Carl Frankel: the times they are a-changin', Georgia, even for Casa Dura. And then the Vogue spread, of course! That was the reason for it: to show off the house, a great big advertisement. Peter never did anything without a motive. That's why he had put up with all the hassle, with having Cristiane around. I should have known, she thought. But still, she could hardly believe he really meant it.

'You'd sell Casa Dura?' she said.

'Sure I would. If I'm going to be solo, I'd be better off based in California. He's offered me a lot of money. Carl Frankel's been hired to do the re-build. Yes, I'm selling. The way I feel right now, I never want to set foot in the place again.'

'I'm shocked,' was all she could think of to say.

'Are you?' he asked.

Georgia saw in his expression some new grievance that put her on guard.

'Of course I am,' she said coolly. 'I know you talked about letting it out, but you've never mentioned the possibility of selling up. Quite the reverse.'

'Ah, but that was when I thought it was my home, where I lived with my wife. I feel differently now that I know it's the place my wife takes her lovers, the moment my back's turned.'

'What are you talking about?' she said quietly.

Now Peter's look was triumphant.

'Oh, come on, Georgia. I know all about your little affair. You haven't exactly made any effort to keep it to secret, have you? It seems it's common knowledge. Amazing how these situations always descend into cliché - the husband being the last to know, that sort of thing.'

Georgia said nothing. It seemed the only option open to her.

'Is it serious?' he asked.

'I don't know. Maybe,' she replied cautiously.

'And how long's it been going on?'

'I met him three days ago,' she said quietly.

'And you call that serious?' he snorted.

'I said maybe.'

'No wonder you were so determined to stay behind!'

'I don't want to discuss it. Unless you feel like talking about Isabel?'

He glared at her. An announcement was made over the Tannoy, and a stewardess approached them.

'Your flight is waiting to depart, Senor Gael,' she said with a brilliant smile.

Peter got to his feet. He took an envelope from inside his jacket and gave it to Georgia.

'I'm meeting Jonathan in Madrid, and then we're flying on to LA. When you leave for London, give the keys to Carl, will you?' He pointed to the envelope. 'That's a cheque. Should keep you afloat until I manage to free up a bit of capital. I suppose we'll have to work out some sort of a settlement via the lawyers?'

'It's what usually happens,' she answered unhappily.

They stood, each trying to think whether there was some last-minute thing still to be said.

'Well,' Peter said, 'It looks like I'm going to miss the full dénoument, so far as the murder's concerned.'

It was a stupid thing to say, and he regretted it immediately. For her part, Georgia decided to let it pass, pointedly so.

The stewardess was hovering anxiously.

'Goodbye then, Georgia,' Peter said. He seemed reluctant to go.

'Have a good journey,' she replied. 'I hope it goes well for you - the film and everything.'

Peter picked up his bag.

'Thanks,' he said. The stewardess started walking towards the departure gate. Peter made a move in the same direction, but then turned back to Georgia.

'Georgia!' he called. 'One last thing: just remember, it's you who's opting out of this marriage, not me. You're the one who's breaking the contract -'

Georgia had just about kept her cool so far and, even worn down by his ploys as she was, she was determined not to lose it now, no matter what the provocation.

'What contract's that, exactly?' she asked.

'Our marriage contract,' he replied.

'There's no such thing as a marriage contract,' she shot back. 'It's not like one of your deals where one person stitches the other person up. It's a promise between a man and a woman to love and honour one another. For a whole catalogue of reasons, I haven't been able to keep that promise, and nor have you. So just stop pointing fingers! You're not going to dump the whole blame for this on me, no matter how much you'd like to.'

Peter was about to make a biting retort, but the stewardess called to him again, plaintively.

'Senor Gael, please, I must ask you to hurry!'

Georgia remained resolutely silent as he turned on his heel and overtook the stewardess, barging angrily though the departure gate in front of her.

*

When Peter had gone, she noticed a large crowd spilling out of another part of the building onto the tarmac. Over the Tannoy came a voice announcing the departure of the 17.25 flight to London. Georgia walked up to the window. Peter's plane was already moving along the runway; the passengers returning to London were starting to board theirs. Georgia searched the crowd avidly, desperate for a glimpse of Matt. But she could not see him. She wondered if it would be possible to get a message to him at this stage, or if it was too late. Why wasn't he there? Had he already boarded? She approached a steward, walking past her with a tray of champagne. He offered her a glass.

'No thank you,' she said. 'I want to know if it's possible to get a message to a passenger on the flight that's just about to leave for London. Can you help me?'

'I'm sorry, Senora,' replied the man. 'You will have to ask at the desk that deals with that airline.'

Georgia did not stop to thank him. She rushed through the reception area to the airline desks. Damn! It must be a charter flight, she thought, and she had not looked to see the name of the tour company.

She went up to the enquiry desk. There was a queue of several people. She waited for a couple of minutes and then went to the front. A tall, middle-aged woman standing close by, clearly English by her dress and manner, looked at Georgia disapprovingly. Georgia looked back, and there was a brief moment of recognition, but then it passed and she turned her attention back to the matter in hand.

'Excuse me,' she said to the stewardess who was busy looking something up in a timetable.

'I am already dealing with someone,' said the stewardess. 'Please wait your turn.'

'I'm sorry,' said Georgia, 'but this is urgent! I have to get a message to someone on board the flight for London. I just want to know the name of the charter company so that I can get the right desk.'

'You will have to wait. I'll try to find out.'

'But it's due to take off,' said Georgia. 'There's no time!'

Georgia could see that the stewardess, annoyed at being interrupted, was not about to put herself out.

'OK, don't bother,' she said. 'I'll find out for myself.'

Georgia turned away from the desk. There seemed to be an endless number of desks for charter companies, and all of them besieged by lines of tourists. Georgia was in despair. She knew nobody would help her. Looking round, she noticed through the window the steps being rolled away from the plane that very shortly would take Matt back to London. It was too late! She had wasted so much time, first with Anton, and now Peter. And the one thing that mattered, she had left until it was too late.

In the midst of the sea of people milling around her, all intent on getting to their destinations, Georgia felt lost and forlorn. Everyone was on their way somewhere - except her. The thought of returning alone to Casa Dura was unbearable. She stood still for a moment, thinking that Matt had been here, in this place where she now stood, not long before, and that this was as close to him as she could get until such time as she herself was back in London. The muscles in Georgia's throat ached at the realisation that it might be some time before she was with him again. All she could do now was wait for him to contact her. She did not even know his surname!

Suddenly, she could not stand to be in the airport a moment longer. She pushed her way to the exit, and the stifling heat of the day outside the air-conditioned building hit her like the heat from an open oven. She rushed blindly towards her car, gleaming white in the sunlight, not far from the exit, and started searching in her basket for her keys.

'Georgia.'

She turned quickly, not daring to believe her ears, and there was Matt, walking quickly towards her.

'Matt!' she cried.

They looked at one another, and then she threw her arms around him, and he held her tightly to him. They stood like that, breathing fast, their hearts pounding against each other.

Georgia buried her head in Matt's neck, and she was soothed and uplifted at the same time by the now familiar scent of his skin. 'Thank you, thank you, God!' she prayed silently.

Matt held her away from him so that he could look at her. He searched her face for some sign of what he should say, but he quickly saw that there was no need for words at all. In his face, Georgia saw happiness, relief, and something else, something indefinable. She smiled at him, and her face was radiant, bathed in light.

CHAPTER TWENTY-THREE

Driving back, it felt like flying. Through the city they sped, up to the coast road that winds its broad, handsome way through endless olive groves, sea on one side, mountains on the other, soaring up to the heights of Santa Marta, where they arrived in time for a sunset that flooded the sky with red and gold and bathed the whole village in a wash of burnished pink.

Georgia pulled up in the main drag, opposite the café.

'Where are your things?' she asked Matt.

'Back at the hotel.'

Georgia took her hands from the steering wheel and pushed her hair back from her face. Driving she had felt exhilarated, alert, clear-headed. Now she was disorientated, and struggled to follow what he was saying. A dull melancholy pervaded her senses. She shook her hair, in an attempt to shake off the sadness. It's this place, she thought, this place and...and everything. She could not bear, even in her smallest thoughts, to get too specific about recent events. Certainly not those concerning Peter; definitely not Isabel. Quiet, she told her thoughts, but too late.

Matt was talking, and she had to make herself listen.

'I didn't get on the coach to the airport. I had to see you again. So after the rest of them left, I just wandered round the Puerto for a while, trying to figure it all out. Then something strange happened.'

'Oh?'

'I found myself up at Esteban's bar. I was sitting there, out on the rocks, when this woman appeared. She came and sat next to me.'

'What did she want?'

'To talk. About her daughter...'

Georgia felt the blood drain from her face.

'Dita...' she said.

He nodded.

'We sat on the rocks. She talked about the murder. And while she was talking and crying, something happened to me. I realised why you were so angry with me. I couldn't believe it - that I'd been so unthinking, so stupid. I felt ashamed.'

Georgia reached out for his hand, and waited for him to continue.

'She said she wanted to show me something up at her house. I didn't want to go, but I was so sorry for her, Georgia. I've never seen anyone suffering like that...'

Georgia herself felt an unbearable sense of grief. For Dita, and for herself. Isabel, so young, still a girl. And she thought of her own lost baby, not seen, un-named, but real all the same; the sadness of it, that hardly ever left her. Where were they now? Dita's daughter, her own unborn child? Could they sense, or see, the impact their short lives, their deaths, were having? May they rest in peace, the prayer said. But how could they rest, if all those they had left behind were in turmoil? It's got to start with us, she thought. We have to be at peace with ourselves. I have to let the baby go. I have to find a way.

Her mind went back to the awful moment when Peter told her that Isabel had been murdered. The disbelief. And, later, the feeling that no-one else cared, that this particular life had been worth less than other lives. She remembered leaning against the olive tree as dawn was breaking, praying for Isabel before she went to bed. Since then her emotions had flown about with each new revelation.

Up to that moment, loathing had been uppermost, but, with a lump in her throat, she dreaded facing up to her true feelings.

Swallowing hard, she asked, 'What happened then?'

'She gave me a drink,' he said. 'Then we went into Isabel's room. She showed me photos of her, when she was a kid. She just looked so normal. A normal kid. That was what Dita wanted me - wanted someone - to see. Then I left.'

Georgia took a tissue from her basket and held it to her eyes.

'She said, Goodbye, Matt.'

Georgia looked at him questioningly.

'I hadn't told her my name. I'm positive of it. How did she know my name?

Georgia shook her head. Her mind was going blurry again. Then she asked him, 'So, how did you get to the airport?'

'I knew you were meeting Peter there at four, so I hitched a ride with another coach from one of the other hotels at the Puerto and just hoped I'd be able to find you.'

'I need some coffee and something to eat,' she said at last. 'Shall we go over to the café?'

The sky had darkened while they were sitting in the car, and as they got out Georgia noticed that for the first time in what seemed like weeks and weeks, it was clouding over. She felt a few, light drops of rain on her bare arms and shoulders, and as they sat themselves at a table, the rain pitter-pattered steadily on the palm-covered roof. Within seconds the immense figure of Carmen, the wife of Pepe, the bar owner, appeared beside them.

'Do you know who is here?' she whispered to Georgia. 'Dita and Esteban! Esteban was released an hour ago. Dita thought it would be good for him to come and see his friend, Pepe. They are eating inside. What a tragedy! Their only child! A tragedy!'

Matt and Georgia looked towards the dark interior of the café.

'And you, you have had your own troubles, Guapa?' she asked Georgia.

'It's been a strange time,' Georgia replied.

'Indeed!' Carmen agreed. 'And it's not finished yet...'

She took their order and glided back inside, leaving Matt and Georgia to muse over this latest piece of news and Carmen's ominous prediction.

'Georgia?'

She had been gazing out at the street, unusually quiet for that time of the evening, her thoughts far away.

'Yes?'

'There's something I want to tell you.' He hesitated.

'I'm listening,' she said

'What I said in the car. At the Puerto?'

Georgia felt her heart sink.

'After you'd gone, I realised what it must have sounded like to you. I want to explain, but it's difficult. Anyway, I'll try.' He took a deep breath.

'Before last night, I'd never used the expression, 'making love'. Because it had never applied. Last night, with you, I learnt what it meant.'

Georgia looked down and said nothing. Matt leaned forward and lifted her chin, forcing her to look into his eyes. She saw in them a nakedness, an awkward vulnerability, the sincerity of what he was trying to tell her. She nodded for him to go on.

'The moment we met, Georgia, everything changed. I changed. What I did before doesn't count now. It was like the kind of life you lead in a weird dream, a series of senseless, unconnected events. Faceless people. Nowhere places. And all of it riddled with a vague sense of unease and inadequacy.'

'But, Matt,' she exclaimed, 'that's like writing off your whole life!'

'There isn't anything to write off. Compared to the last

three days, the previous twenty-six years had no reality. Just a waiting time, that's all it was. Waiting for now. I feel like I've started to think, Georgia, to make decisions, to realise I have choices. I never did that before. I just let things happen, went with the flow. I knew there had to be more, but I didn't let myself dwell on what that might be because I couldn't see a way out. And there was never anyone to talk to about it. I've talked more to you in the last couple of days than to anyone else the rest of my life put together.'

'Wasn't there anyone you were close to?'

'Not really. Friends, my parents, girls, they all seemed to have their own ideas about who I was and what I should be doing. I just went along with it.'

'But what about you? What did you want?'

'Pass. I think I'd given up hoping for any kind of satisfactory future.'

Georgia looked appalled. 'At twenty-six? You'd given up?'

'Georgia, it was a different world - believe me! Jobs, friends - I just hung onto what I had. Even when I knew it wasn't right. There didn't seem to be an alternative.' He paused to consider it all. 'Music. That got me through. And if I'm honest, that's what I dreamed of doing. But I didn't believe I could ever make it work for me, not really.'

'And now?'

'Now? Like I said, now everything's different.' The look in his face was serious, focussed. 'Now I know what I want.'

Georgia was about to venture a response when Carmen arrived with their order. She deftly unloaded a tray of food and drink onto the table in front of them.

'Bocadillos,' she announced, producing a basket of crusty rolls filled with slivers of Serrano ham and tortilla. She gave Matt a bottle of coke and a glass filled with ice, and Georgia a cup of steaming coffee and a jug of milk.

'Café con leche,' she said, pouring the milk into the cup.

'Gracias, Carmen,' Georgia replied.

Carmen leaned down and spoke in a hushed tone.

'Esteban is feeling better,' she said. 'He has eaten and now he's watching football on the television.'

'That's good,' said Matt and Georgia in unison, their mouths full.

Carmen laughed at them. She ruffled Matt's hair and winked knowingly at Georgia. 'Nice!' she said.

As they ate, the café started to fill up. Matt recognised some of the faces from the night before. There was a muted buzz in the air, and the conversations around him were drowned out by the slow, steady clatter of the rain on the palm-covered roof overhead. He noticed that Georgia seemed detached from the in-flux of people around her, and that she was consuming her sandwich with single-minded determination. He found the way she was eating endearing, like a child who has been told to finish off its food, and then struggles diligently to do so.

'You don't have to eat it if you don't want to,' he said gently. Her face was drawn and the sheen had gone from her cheeks. But she just shook her head and went on eating. After finishing the last mouthful, she wiped a few crumbs away from the corner of her mouth.

'It's the only thing I've eaten all day,' she said. 'I was starving.'

'It looked like it,' he replied.

He noticed that the muscles in his own face were tense, and his back and shoulders felt almost rigid. There was something in the air, in the atmosphere, a sense of anticipation. There was nothing left of the party mood of the previous night, and the summer heat was cooling in the soft grey rain. People were talking, but their talk was subdued, private. He noticed the surreptitious glances, the guarded looks, as Carmen, large and majestic, moved gracefully between the tables bearing her secrets as surely as her trays of drinks and snacks. In the middle of his surveillance of the scene around him, Gavin Johnston and James Parker arrived at the table.

'Good evening, Georgia, my dear. Good evening Matthew,' said James, cordially.

'Hi,' said Georgia, 'come and sit down.'

'Heard the latest?' asked Gavin. He and James had been drinking back at his house, and his cheeks were slightly flushed, his eyes sparkling.

'Do we really want to know?' asked Georgia.

'I'll tell them,' said James, equally sparky. 'Basically, my friends, you know that young Randall, before his unfortunate demise, dished the dirt on Tom Malek? Well, I heard from a source close to the Guardia that he told them in his final statement that Malek had been involved in bringing consignments of dope and acid onto the island and running a little sideline in porno flicks.'

'So what's new?' asked Georgia. 'Anyone could have guessed that.'

'What's new, my dear,' said James, 'is that it never previously came to the attention of our friends and protectors, the Guardia Civil. And, incidentally, Georgia, this is not just a little amateur dabbling. This is heavy shit. Apparently he has some whole kind of warehouse operation out in the wilds of Kent. Kent, for fuck's sake!'

Georgia became interested.

'I noticed the road to the Cala was blocked off - is that connected?'

James nodded. 'Sure is. They're down at Malek's place searching every last goddam' centimetre of the joint. Randall told them where they could find Malek's stash and where the fruits of his photographic ventures were kept. But they'll be hunting for any other hidey holes Randall might not have known about. They've got the dogs down there, for Christ's sake!'

Georgia just listened, integrating James' story. Putting the pieces together with what she already knew.

'Randall said the acid he was on last night was supplied by Malek,' James continued. 'And it was bad, man, spiked.

Said the second it kicked in, he knew'.

Then Gavin leaned forward, pressing the point home in case either Georgia or Matt had not got the full meaning. 'Implying,' he said, 'that Malek had deliberately tried to snuff him out.'

'Has Malek been arrested?' Matt asked.

'Too fuckin' right!' James roared back. 'They threw the book at him, man!' He started counting off the accusations on his fingers. 'Attempted murder; possession of illegal substances; trafficking in illegal substances; importing illegal substances; importing and exporting obscene material -'

'You name it, basically,' interrupted Gavin.

'At the end of all this,' James jumped back in, 'they're gonna stick that boy in the slammer and throw away the key...'

'God, I hope you're right,' said Georgia. 'Maybe there is such a thing as justice.'

'Going somewhere, Georgia?' James asked.

'Just up to see Tamsin,' she replied, picking up her basket and pushing her chair back from the table.

Matt started to get up, too.

'No,' she told him. 'I want to go on my own. Will you wait here for me? I'll be about half an hour.'

'Fine, I'll have another Coke,' he said, raising his empty bottle.

'Coke?' echoed James. 'Hey, Matt, you want to watch yourself - that stuff corrodes the arteries...'

Georgia left them to their bantering. The rain had stopped and now the night was humid, the air heavy with the scent of flowers and damp earth. Georgia stopped briefly on the road up to the casita to break off a sprig of honeysuckle. She crushed the yellow and white petals between her fingers and inhaled the sweet perfume.

CHAPTER TWENTY-FOUR

'It's getting dark,' said Tamsin. 'Shall I light some candles?'

'Good idea,' replied Georgia, as she held Poppy on her lap. Poppy was not responding to Georgia's attempts to cheer her up, and Georgia had resorted to jiggling her up and down, hoping to delay the inevitable wails.

'Poor Poppy,' she exclaimed, 'we're not very happy today, are we?'

'No, we aren't,' Tamsin answered, blowing out the taper. She had lit candles and tea-lights on the mantelpiece and in sconces in the walls, and all at once the room was bathed in their soft warm light, and the baby, her attention captured by a flickering yellow candle flame, was soothed by the change in ambience.

'She's tired,' said Tamsin, taking the baby from Georgia and putting her to her breast. Poppy began to feed at once, and within seconds, her little eyes were closing.

'Bad night?' asked Georgia, sipping at a large earthenware cup filled with one of Tamsin's herbal concoctions, the liquid swamped with fresh greenery.

'You could say that,' Tamsin answered flatly. 'I had a miscarriage.'

Georgia winced. 'Oh no!' she said. 'How awful for you...'

Tamsin kept her eyes fixed on Poppy's face. 'Did you

hear about my encounter with Dita last night?' she asked.

'Vaguely. I heard something.'

'It was when I was in the car with her, it started. I practically had to crawl back into the house on my hands and knees. After that - well, you know how it goes. It hurts a lot, you bleed a lot, and then, a few hours later, it's all over.'

'How are you feeling now?'

'I can't lie: right now I just feel a great sense of relief. It was all such a mess. I feel as if I've been given a reprieve, even if I don't deserve it.' She paused to detach the now soundly sleeping baby from her breast. 'I'm sure I should feel guilty not to be sad, but no. Just relief.'

'No need to feel guilty,' Georgia said. 'Nature took care of you.'

'Thank God someone did,' replied Tamsin. 'I was at my wits end.'

There was nothing more to say on the subject, and it felt right to offer a moment's silence in recognition of the frail life that had existed so briefly, barely noticed. Just a wisp of a touch, was how Tamsin had thought of it, like the brush of a butterfly's wing...

'She's fast asleep,' said Georgia eventually, looking down at Poppy.

'Yes. I'm going to put her in her cot. Back in a minute.'

Georgia was left gazing into the candlelight, recalling her breakfast with Tamsin only two days earlier. It seemed like light years separated them from that morning, before the horror of the murder and its apparently endless repercussions had been unleashed. When Tamsin came back into the room, Georgia thought that she too must have been remembering that morning, because in her hands she held the box of Tarot cards that they had used to look, with such uncanny accuracy as it turned out, into Georgia's future.

'I feel bad about the things I kept back from you, Georgia,' Tamsin suddenly announced. 'It was like I was caught in this quagmire and I couldn't pull myself out.'

'Honestly, you don't have to explain,' Georgia interrupted. She had come armed with questions, seeking answers, but with the news of the miscarriage, she had lost all interest. None of it seemed important any longer.

'The baby,' Tamsin interrupted. 'It was Tom Malek's'.

Georgia was stunned. She could hardly believe Tamsin had said it, but on the other hand, it made sense. No wonder Tamsin was so reluctant to reveal the father's name. Malek!

Tamsin looked down at the box in her hands. 'It wasn't a major thing,' she went on. 'I want you to know that. In fact, I loathe him as much as you do.' She paused for a moment, but since Georgia made no comment, she went on. 'We were at dinner at Ava's one night. Usual kind of evening, with the wine flowing, you know? I don't actually drink much since I had Poppy. Can't handle it – a couple of glasses is enough to finish me off. But I hadn't discovered that yet. Malek insisted on taking me and Poppy home, and seeing us in. He was being so nice, I suddenly thought, why don't I like him? I thought maybe I'd got him all wrong. Anyway, he hung around while I put Poppy to bed. We sat up, talked, played some music. He rolled a joint... I just let it happen,' she said gloomily. 'It was ridiculous, ridiculous...'

'Was that when he told you about Peter and Isabel?' Georgia asked bluntly.

The question had come without warning or preamble, and Tamsin faltered. 'Er - no,' she said. 'He came back the next day. To gloat, I suppose. I think he may even have quite liked the idea of an interesting little romance between us, but I gave him the cold shoulder. That was when he told me. Actually, I didn't believe him. You know how he likes to stir it? It sounded so preposterous. I thought he must be making it up, telling me in order for it to get back to you. There was no way of checking it out, short of asking Peter outright, and obviously I wasn't about to do that.'

'I see,' said Georgia. Suddenly, she just wanted it to

end. She found she did not want to know any more. What good would it do? It had happened. The details were immaterial.

'Why've you brought the cards in?' she asked, to change the subject.

'Ah, the cards!' said Tamsin. 'Remember the last reading I did for you?'

'The Full Moon – how could I forget? And the Tower, and the weeping woman...' Georgia shuddered.

'Close, wasn't it? I've been thinking about it a lot. At the time we did the reading, the murder had already happened, of course. But all that other stuff... It's a bit scary, really. You know, when my mother found out I was learning to read the cards - oh, years ago - she didn't like it at all. She warned me off it, said it was playing around with the occult. "Never meddle with the dark arts, darling!"' Tamsin mimicked.

Georgia laughed. 'Isn't she supposed to be arriving any minute?' she asked.

'She's here. She arrived a couple of hours ago. She's just having a rest after her journey.'

As if on cue, a tall woman, barefooted and dressed in a long green striped robe, appeared on the stairs. The woman from the airport! Georgia knew she had seen her before.

'Mummy, you remember Georgia, don't you?' said Tamsin.

'Georgia, how nice to meet you properly at last,' she said. 'We only had time for a brief hello at Tamsin's wedding, but I've heard so much about you since then, I feel I know you and your husband quite well. Do call me Judith.'

'Hello, Judith,' replied Georgia, smiling politely.

She wondered whether to mention the airport, but Judith had wafted past her into the kitchen. Her greeting had sounded more like a dismissal and she clearly had no recollection of ever having seen Georgia before.

'Now Mum's arrived, I'm going to start packing up and getting ready to go,' said Tamsin. 'We reckon we'll be ready to roll out of town early next week. Mummy's marvellous at getting everything organised,'

I bet she is, thought Georgia, deeply intimidated by the glacial Judith.

'What about you? What are your plans?' Tamsin asked.

'Same as you, really. I have to close the house up, that's all. Not even a major close up. Peter's getting rid of it, you know. Carl's going to be handling it all. Apparently it's been in the offing for a while. Remember the Vogue spread? I told you he had an ulterior motive...'

'I can't believe it!' Tamsin exclaimed

Georgia eyed her uncertainly.

'No, Georgia, honestly, *that* I knew nothing about. I'm really shocked.'

'I only found out a couple of hours ago myself,' Georgia replied. 'I'm still reeling.'

Judith reappeared from the kitchen bearing what looked like an enormous gin and tonic.

'I'm going back upstairs,' she informed them. 'I'll leave you two girls to yourselves.'

They watched her ascend and disappear into her room.

'Anyway,' said Tamsin. 'To get back to the cards.'

'Tamsin,' Georgia started, nervously. 'I don't really -'

'It's okay - I'm not planning to do another reading. That's what I wanted to tell you. I'm going to leave the cards behind when I go. I just wondered if - since yours was the last reading – you'd like to have them?'

'Me?' Georgia asked, horrified. 'No, I don't want them,' she said.

Tamsin looked down at the cards in their purple cloth.

'Well,' she said, 'I'll just leave them here, in that case. For whoever finds them...'

She put the cards into a linen chest on the floor behind her, and rubbed her hands together briskly.

'There,' said Tamsin. 'No more cards. Closure.'

Georgia nodded. But inside she felt it was only a gesture. A move in the right direction, but they would be fooling themselves if they thought they would be free of all that had happened so easily. She herself, she knew, was going to have to live with it, process it all, for quite a while to come. And something told her it wasn't over yet.

'So,' asked Tamsin at last. 'What's going to happen with you and your new man?'

'Nothing certain. He was supposed to go back to London today, but what with everything, he's stayed on.'

'I must say, he's quite dishy...'

Georgia laughed.

'Not a bit like Peter,' Tamsin commented.

'No, he's not like Peter.'

'I know - why don't we meet up tomorrow?' Tamsin suggested eagerly. 'We could go down and swim in the lagoon. Have a picnic in the pines -'

Georgia thought for a moment.

'I wouldn't advise swimming,' she said. 'Not just yet.'

The comment brought Tamsin up sharply. For a moment she felt a dark mist wafting round her. She took a large sip from her cup, and felt slightly better.

Georgia drained her cup, too, and got up.

'Fact is,' she said, 'the only thing I really want to do is sleep. Just sleep and sleep and sleep for a long, long time.'

Tamsin got up too. 'We have been in the wars, haven't we?' she said.

'At least we're still alive to tell the tale,' Georgia replied.

Tamsin walked with her to the door. Outside, they both instinctively looked up at the sky. It was shrouded and dark: no moon, no stars.

'When the cloud comes down the mountain like that,' said Tamsin, 'it just sits there, doesn't it? It feels like you may never see the sun again.'

She watched as Georgia waved and closed the gate behind her. Back inside the casita, she surrendered to exhaustion. She blew out the candles and, without bothering to undress, fell onto her bed and slept.

CHAPTER TWENTY-FIVE

Matt looked down at his watch, and saw that it was nearly an hour since Georgia had left; an hour he had spent engrossed in conversation about Santa Marta and its inhabitants with James and Gavin. It had amused Matt to listen to the easy repartee between the two men. James and Gavin were old friends, well-acquainted with one another's foibles. As they teased and taunted one another, people stopped by at the table to have a few words, everyone eager to know the latest news, interrupting James' and Gavin's anecdotes and stories from summers past and bringing them back to the current drama that was still unfolding before them. Matt started to worry about Georgia's absence.

'Sure, this is an extreme event, without any question. This is certainly serious shit,' James was saying. 'But don't let anyone tell you Santa Marta isn't one tough town. Survival of the fittest, that's Saint M.'

'I got that, right away,' ventured Matt. 'I mean, it's fantastic, but it's wild.' He pondered for a moment, and then added, 'Anywhere this beautiful, it's got to have a dark side.'

'That's right, most perceptive of you. What you see in the landscape is mirrored in the people who live here,' Gavin agreed. 'We're all infected by it to some extent. Some of us are a bit older and wiser, but it isn't unknown for people to lose it big time in Santa Marta.'

'Winter's better, I always maintain,' said James. 'Summer, you get the happy people, the ones who are here for a good time. On the surface it's all, well isn't this nice! And la di dah di dah! Just don't get broke or sick or in any other kind of trouble. Wintertime, it's more sincere. This shit that's just happened? Could only happen in August. Every year I tell myself, no more summers here for Mrs Parker's boy. One day I'll take my own advice and save myself a whole passel of trouble...'

Matt was facing away from the steps leading up into the café. Thinking of Georgia again, he turned round in his chair to see if there was any sign of her and, just at that moment, she appeared.

'Hi!' she said.

'Hi!' he replied, relieved.

She plonked herself down in the seat beside him.

'How was Tamsin?' he asked.

'Fine.' Georgia noticed James looking inquisitively at her, and chose her words carefully. 'She was telling me all about her strange adventure with Dita last night-'

'So is she -' Matt started to say.

Georgia flashed him a warning look.

'I mean,' he said, doing a quick re-think, 'was that why she didn't make it to the sheep-roast?'

'Yes,' Georgia replied, abruptly.

She had been sitting back in her chair, but she straightened up sharply as a pair of large, masculine hands gave her shoulders a slow squeeze from behind.

'Boy, you're tense, Georgia! Like a massage?'

Georgia pulled away from the squeezing hands and turned to see Tom Malek standing behind her.

Gavin, walking back to the table with a fresh round of drinks, saw Malek and stared.

'Hey, Tom,' he said. 'Didn't expect to see you here tonight...'

'Ever heard of lawyers? Or bail?' Malek shot back at him. 'I'm a free man, Johnston - and that's how I'm planning to stay. Those bastards aren't gonna pin a thing on me. Just had to come by and let you guys know the good news. Didn't want Georgia fretting...' he said with a wink and a conspiratorial grin.

Georgia was about to make a biting retort when a frisson ran through the café. The chattering ceased and she saw that Esteban and Dita were standing in the doorway of the bar. As Georgia watched, Esteban's facial expression changed. His sallow complexion paled and his jaw began to tremble. Dita had been holding his arm, but now he shrugged her aside and came staggering at a reckless pace towards the table where Georgia and Matt sat.

Suddenly, the air was throbbing with adrenalin. Georgia, on the verge of panic, turned and saw Malek twist around, trying to get to the steps. But, in the crowded café, a party had seated themselves at the table immediately behind, and he was completely wedged in. With only seconds in hand, Matt was on his feet. He pulled Georgia out of her chair, holding her towards him, their backs against the railings.

Everything seemed to happen at breakneck speed. In one clumsy leap, Esteban was upon Malek, driving his clenched fist into Malek's face and, at the same time, dragging him to the ground. Malek held up his arms to shield himself from the blows, but Esteban had hooked his free arm around Malek's neck in a vice-like hold. Then Malek was down, and Esteban fell on top of him, shouting, punching, thumping, crying, while Malek writhed and struggled furiously to fend him off.

'Para mi hija!' Esteban croaked as his stranglehold tightened and the punches continued to fly into Malek's prone torso. 'For my daughter, my daughter!' Esteban's choking cries rang out.

Georgia and Matt stood back from the flailing, fighting bodies as best they could, until Pepé deemed the moment right for intervention. He and Carmen came forward with Dita and, braving the fray, they reached down with shouting pleas to wrest Esteban away from Malek, who had rolled himself into a ball. But as they hauled Esteban up, he kicked out violently at Malek's face and ribs and groin. Malek let out a moan of pain, but then, apart from the sound of his intermittent groans, and Esteban's laboured panting for breath, a strange silence descended around them. The hush lasted for a long, highly-charged moment, and then a voice shouted out:

'Bravo! Bravo, Esteban!'

Georgia looked around to see who had shouted, and the cry came again, this time accompanied by a ragged but fervent chorus,

'Bravo! Bravo! Bravo!'

As the cheers died out, there came the awareness of the sound of sirens and cars breaking sharply down in the street. The car doors were flung open and four or five police officers raced up the steps. Esteban straightened himself as best he could, and Dita brushed at his shirt front. Quickly, Pepé walked them down the steps, past the officers, to their own car.

The officers went briskly to where Malek was pulling himself up from the ground. With a notable lack of respect, they asked him what had happened. He told them it was nothing, nothing, but not completely satisfied with this statement, they walked him down to one of the waiting cars. With Malek slumped in the back seat, they piled in themselves and, without another word to anyone, drove off at speed.

Gavin, who had been holding the drinks he had bought for himself and James and Matt, put them down on the table. James picked up his beer and downed half of it straight off.

'You need a drink, too,' Gavin said to Georgia. 'What can I get you?'

Georgia was trying to avoid looking at the ground where Malek had fallen. It was streaked with blood, and the chairs she and Matt had been sitting on now lay on the floor in a mangled heap.

'Nothing for me. I'm fine,' she said. 'Anyway, we have to go.'

Gavin stooped down and helped Matt pick up the chairs.

'He took a bit of a pasting,' Matt said.

'Ah, he had it coming,' replied James, draining his glass.

Matt straightened up the last of the chairs. He noticed his hands were shaking.

'Only him?' he asked, swallowing to keep the emotion, the anger, from his voice.

'What're you saying, my friend?' James came back, sharply.

'Just that it seems like everyone knew what was going on, but no-one said anything. No-one did anything about it. Now a girl's dead, Malek's been thrashed and carted off, and what? Everything goes back to normal? It just seems like, maybe he's not the only one who had it coming. That's all.'

James gave him a hard look.

'Well how about that?' he replied. 'So we're none of us perfect.' And with the glint still in his eye, he leaned forward and added, 'Not even you, my man, not even you.'

CHAPTER TWENTY-SIX

'Georgia,' said Matt, 'I'm sorry, but that's not a mouse or a creaky floorboard. That was definitely a door closing.'

'Probably the breeze. Antonia may have left a window open upstairs. I'll go and have a look. I want to get a shawl, anyway.'

They were sitting in the kitchen at Casa Dura, drinking tea and talking quietly about the day's events. As they chatted, Matt picked out chords on Georgia's guitar. We're acting like a couple already, Georgia was thinking, and I haven't even had time to stop being a couple with Peter. It was odd, but nice all the same. She liked Matt's presence. He had a good vibe, it made her feel safe.

She ran lightly up the stairs, and grabbed a shawl from the back of her bedroom chair. The window was closed, no door-slamming breeze blowing in there. She looked in at the bathroom and the smaller guest room, but the windows were all shut. That left the big spare room, but no-one ever went in there. I suppose, she thought, the latch could have slipped or something. She pushed the door open, and looking in, she froze.

Sitting on the floor, his back to the wall, Luc was surrounded by the remnants of a loaf of bread, an almost empty bottle of wine, bits of cut up sheet, and the big bread knife that Antonia had been searching for that morning.

He looked up at her, his eyes dark-ringed and bloodshot.

'Luc,' she said, trying to sound calm. 'What are you doing here?' She noticed plaited strips of torn sheet lying coiled on the floor. It all looked deeply ominous.

'I was making a rope,' he said, with a slight slur.

Georgia looked at the knife, and felt her heart begin to pound. No, she thought, don't jump to conclusions; there's an explanation, there must be an explanation.

'What for?' she asked. She noticed he was trembling. 'Are you frightened of something, Luc? What's the matter?'

He tried to formulate an answer. It was all getting a bit weird inside his head. There had been a plan, something he had to do. What was it? Oh, yeah. He had to weigh up the consequences. But the consequences of what? And in any case, he was sick of being alone in that room, sick of being hungry and scared, he needed someone to talk to. He made up his mind: he'd talk to Georgia. It'd probably be all right. He'd take the chance.

'I know what happened,' he said, his voice a bit faint and strung out. 'I know who killed Isabel.'

Georgia just looked at him and waited.

'I was there,' he said. 'I saw it happen. And then I ran away. But he knows I saw, he knows, and if he finds me -'

Georgia could hear the panic rising in his voice, and realised that Luc probably had no idea what had happened that morning.

'Do you mean -' she started to say.

'Randall,' he blurted out. 'It was Randall.'

'So what's the rope for?'

'Don't touch my rope! It's mine - it's -'

'I'm not touching it, Luc. I was just asking, what's it for?'

'It was in case he found me, and I needed to escape, to get out of the window. But it's not very good, is it? I've never tried making a rope before.'

Georgia went over to where he was sitting and knelt down beside him.

'It's OK Luc,' she said. 'The police know it was Randall. There's nothing to be afraid of.' And she added, cautiously, 'Randall's been dealt with. You won't be seeing him again.'

'Randall? Are you sure about that?'

Georgia nodded.

'Absolutely,' she said, and then asked, 'is that why you ran off from the house this morning?'

Luc was rubbing his arms compulsively. He reeked of alcohol and stale sweat and dirty clothing; the smell was disgusting, and Georgia had to resist covering her face with her hand.

'Yes,' he said. 'Sorry, I nicked this knife and some food and wine. Oh, and Antonia's key. I thought I could lie low until they worked out it was him - I mean, I reckoned he probably left some kind of evidence -'

'Well anyway, they got him,' said Georgia.

Luc hung his head. Georgia could not see, but suspected he was crying.

'Isabel,' he said. 'She wasn't as bad as she seemed. She just got caught up in that - that whole web. I liked her. I was trying to get her to think about coming to France. You didn't know her, did you? Not really. But she was actually very bright. Really bright...'

He sniffed, and wiped his nose with the back of his hand.

Georgia waited; listening, thinking, forcing herself to be calm.

'I've applied to the Sorbonne,' he said. 'I come into a bit of money when I turn eighteen next month. I need to get away from this, from Santa Marta, from London, all of it. Mum doesn't want me to go to Paris. She wants me to go to Oxford, like Peter. But she can't stop me. I'll be able to pay for it myself.'

'What subject are you going for?' Georgia asked, trying to sound normal.

'History of Art,' he replied.

'What a co-incidence,' said Georgia. 'I was at the Sorbonne -'

'Were you?' he asked. 'I didn't know. Anyway, I thought, once I was installed, Isabel could come over and stay, have a look at it, see something of the world outside of this place. People get into such a rut here. It's like they think it's the centre of the universe or something, like nowhere else exists.' He shook his head. 'I can't believe it. I can't believe she's dead.'

Georgia thought she had better take it very slowly.

'You know,' she said, 'a lot's happened while you've been hiding yourself away up here. Why don't you come downstairs and we can be bit more comfortable? You must be feeling pretty shaken up...'

Luc was literally shaking, and Georgia suddenly felt that the conversation was not going quite as well as she had hoped. He put his right hand down to the floor and felt for the knife. Finding it, he covered it with his hand.

'I don't want to go downstairs,' he said. 'I want to stay here. Stay with me. Stay and tell me about the Sorbonne.'

All I have to do, she thought, is make it to the door. How long could that take? If I can just make him relax a bit, I could do it. And then she thought, Matt, why haven't you come to look for me? You must know it doesn't take this long to get a shawl. Put the bloody guitar down and come and save me from this little nutcase! God, she thought, is there never going to be any let up?

'I was eighteen,' she started, easing herself into a less awkward position and at the same time moving away from Luc, very slightly, so that he would not notice, 'and it was the first time I'd been abroad on my own...'

Suddenly she heard voices in the entrada. Please, she thought, for God's sake, please get up here!

Luc heard as well, and grabbing his half-made rope, ran to the window.

'No, Luc!' Georgia shouted. 'Don't be an idiot!'

'Who is it? Who's down there? They've come for me haven't they?' he shouted back.

Georgia heard feet on the stairs and the door flew open. Matt rushed forward and pulled her out onto the landing, and several police officers, including the two she had seen that morning, took the short cut to the window, jumping over the dust-sheeted bed. One officer grabbed Luc round the waist and heaved him down into the room from the window recess, which he had climbed up onto with lightning speed, ready to jump to the stony ground beneath.

'No!' he was shouting. 'I didn't do it! It wasn't me!'

Below, a car drew up. As Matt and Georgia made their way back down to the entrada, Cristiane burst into the house, frantic.

'Is he here, is he here, Georgia?' she shouted from the foot of the stairs.

Georgia turned and pointed towards the room upstairs. She stood with Matt and watched as Cristiane ran like a fury at the officers who were now grasping Luc, one on either side of him.

And suddenly it was all so clear: the realisation dawned as she saw Cristiane thrust herself between the officers to get to her son. That was it, she thought. How stupid, how stupid of me. Of course, it was all for Luc. She wanted to make sure he didn't lose that vital contact, that relationship she knew was so important to him. It wasn't about Peter at all. All that time, Cristiane had been trying to make up to Luc for the father who had gone. She remembered Peter telling her that Frank Ewald had left Cristiane practically penniless: a small house with a big mortgage, and a few hundred in trust for Luc when he came of age. She must have struggled, Georgia thought, it must have been hard providing for Luc, bringing him up on her own. Then she saw Luc's face as Cristiane went flying up the stairs towards him, and heard him yelling, Mum, Mum! Don't let them take me! I didn't do anything! It wasn't me! Don't let them take me, Mum!

After that, all Georgia could recall was a chaotic amount of noise as somehow the officers got Luc past Cristiane, down the stairs, and bent him into the back of their car. Cristiane, right behind them, jumped into her old Citroen, ready to drive to wherever it was Luc was being taken. I missed it, Georgia thought, I'd been so distracted by all the other things about her that annoyed me. But it's so obvious; Luc's all that's ever mattered to her. The rest was just Cristiane's way of getting by.

And then they were gone, and it was quiet again, and Matt said, 'Georgia, we've got to get out of here.'

'I know,' she had answered. 'I couldn't sleep in this house tonight.'

'Right,' he said. 'Chuck a few things into a bag and we'll go and stay at my hotel in the Puerto. It's not five star, but it'll do for tonight. We can shower and sleep and tomorrow we'll work out what to do next. Come on, Georgia, I'll help you.'

'I want to,' she said, 'but I don't think I've got the strength to do any more driving.'

'I'll drive,' he said. 'Come on, love, let's get your stuff.'

* * *

How many hours have I spent in this car today, she wondered, as the lights of the Puerto came into view? Hours and hours, backwards and forwards, no wonder I feel dizzy.

But then, at last, the day was over. They had showered together, Matt not wanting to leave her alone for an instant, and then he had wrapped her in towels and rubbed her hair, and when she was all dry, he tucked her up in bed.

'Matt,' she said drowsily, 'what'll happen tomorrow?'

'Tomorrow we'll sort a few things out. That's all.'

'Do you have to be back at work or anything like that?'

'Don't worry about it. I'll ring them. How soon do you think you could be ready to leave?'

'Soon - if I just take the essentials and get Antonia to

pack up the rest of my stuff and have it sent on.'

'Fine,' he said. 'In that case, all you have to do now is close your eyes.'

He kissed each eyelid, and put his head down on the pillow next to her.

'Are you all right?' he said softly.

He must have asked a dozen times since we left Casa Dura, she thought.

'Yes, honestly. I'm fine.'

But was she? Am I all right? she asked herself. Or is it all going to suddenly hit me like a ton of bricks?

'You can't really be all right,' he had said earlier. 'You're probably traumatised, and you just don't know it yet.'

'No,' she had insisted. 'I'm not. I really am OK. I'm OK because of you. Because you rescued me, you saved me.'

And that had been her undoing, that was the moment when it had all surfaced, and she just thanked God that it happened when they were in the shower, and the emotion was hidden under the thrust of the water, gushing over them.

'You're my hero,' she told him, later, smiling, but meaning it in a way she knew he would never be able to fully understand, and that she would never be fully able to explain.

She had been so exhausted then, but now, here she was, wide awake. She supposed it must be the adrenaline, still coursing through her blood stream. And, oddly, she did not mind. She liked being in the anonymous hotel room. It was quite a sweet room, she thought, modest and unpretentious. The bed with its thick, deep mattress was much nicer to lie in than her big four-poster at Casa Dura, which was ornate and old but hard, not really comfortable. The orange and white striped curtains at the window blocked out the sky, so that she felt shielded, sheltered; protected from the dark. Here, there were no ghosts of lecherous Counts or their sad young mistresses; no creaking beams or mice or deranged public school boys; no stifling scent wafting in on the warm night air.

Finally sleep came to her as dawn broke to the din of the basura lorry doing its rounds in the street below, collecting the rubbish with a series of clanks and thumps as bins were picked up, emptied, and thrown down again. It was a good kind of noise, she decided. A normal, everyday noise; workmanlike, purposeful and devoid of any sinister undertone.

CHAPTER TWENTY-SEVEN

In Santa Marta, the rain had cleared the air, so that the atmosphere in the village became lighter, refreshed. The heat wave had passed, and the blue of the sky was more limpid, more true, and lovelier for the gigantic puffs of brilliant white cloud that sailed gracefully across it. The fincas in the huerta were yielding up their bounty; green netting was stretched out along the terraces, underneath the apricot, fig and almond trees, and the farmers brought ladders and poles for gathering the fruit. Their wives came along with the sacks and trays in which the ample pickings would be collected. The time of harvest had begun.

In the days that followed, the summer visitors began their own preparations for the *grand départ*. Houses were cleaned from top to bottom, windows thrown open, and a troop of local women swathed in overalls and armed with brushes and brooms and bottles of bleach took up occupation. The wash-house in the lower part of the village became a constant hive of activity, the washer-women noisily up to their elbows in suds. The village taxi was fully booked, shuttling back and forth to the airport, and roof-racks were loaded up for those who were doing the journey to Paris or London by car. There was a different kind of energy in the town, a different dynamic, and an almost tangible sense of relief that the weeks and months of extended leisure were over, to be replaced by a return to structure and order, schedules and timetables. Back to work, to civilisation, and home! Gertrude Stein had got it exactly right: there's only so much paradise a normal person can stand.

Tamsin and her mother were among the first to go. The formidable Judith did not waste any time; three decades of experience as a diplomatic wife had honed her organisational skills to an impressive level. A lorry from Pickfords duly appeared, and the contents of the casita were systematically removed under her expert supervision. Tamsin, she had sent to bed, so that she would be rested and in good shape for the journey back to the family home in Sussex, and little Poppy was placed in the full-time care of the excellent Ana, with a strict routine of four-hourly bottle-feeds and regular naps, on which the baby gurglingly thrived.

Down in the old part of the city, Cristiane's gallery was open for business with Anton temporarily in charge. Cristiane herself was otherwise occupied. The Guardia had finally managed, not without difficulty, to extricate a statement of sorts from Luc, soon after which his descent into psychosis reached its nadir, and he was transported by special ambulance to a private clinic just outside the city. Frail and heavily medicated, he was allowed no visitors apart from his mother, who spent much of each day at his bedside. But he received a telegram from Peter in Los Angeles, and an open invitation to visit the set in New Mexico as soon as he was up to it. There could even be a job for him as a runner, Peter promised, when he was well enough. Luc read the telegram many times, until the thin, crackly paper became soft and crumpled and the letters faded to the point of illegibility. But by then it did not matter; he knew the message off by heart.

Eventually the day came when it was Georgia's turn to take her leave. Alone, she wandered through the old house, room by room, touching a finger to a wall or a piece of furniture that had been part of her life during the seven years since she had arrived there as Peter's bride. So this is it, she thought, the final goodbye. The Santa Marta years were over for Georgia, and what awaited her was a mystery, as fathomless as her future at Casa Dura had once been. Antonia cried terribly, but Georgia was dry-eyed, her crying all done, as she and Matt climbed into the back of a taxi. Her last view of the house, as the sun was setting, covering it in a gentle sheen, was with Antonia in the great arched doorway, waving a handkerchief until they were out of sight.

Twilight had fallen by the time the taxi reached the main drag, just in time to see the tail end of a small procession wending its way up to the church at the top of the hill. At its head, the men of the village were taking it in turns to bear a slender whitewood coffin and its occupant on the steep upward path to its final resting place.

Immediately behind the pallbearers, Dita, heavily veiled, walked arm in arm with Esteban. Inside the open casket lay the body of their daughter, robed in white and scattered with rose petals, her long hair wreathed in laurel and jasmine and sweet thyme, rosary beads entwined in her pale fingers.

In the cobbled plaza in front of the church, a small congregation awaited their arrival, many holding lighted candles in the dusk. At a discrete distance stood a modestly-dressed, middle-aged couple, quiet and unobtrusive, uninvited but needing to be there, to add their prayers to those of the other mourners. They would be returning home the following day, to a small town in Kansas, taking with them the body of their own child, their boy. There, he would be buried in the little cemetery behind the church where he had once worshiped with his family, back in the days before he had been called away to fight in a war that raged incomprehensibly, somewhere in a far off land.

*

And then the summer was ended. Santa Marta was left to her own, the ones who were able to endure both the pleasure and the pain of living so close to heaven; who understood that beauty comes at a price, and the price must always be paid.

Lightning Source UK Ltd.
Milton Keynes UK
UKOW040607121212

203547UK00001B/9/P

9 781930 067967